Nerrisa's Abrauxian Protector

Nerrisa's Abrauxian Protector
Book Three of the Abrauxian Brides Series
Lisa Clute

NIGHT QUILL PRESS LLC

Copyright © 2025 by Lisa Clute

All rights reserved.

No part of this publication may be reproduced, distributed, or transmitted in any form or by any means, including photocopying, recording, or other electronic or mechanical methods, without the prior written permission of the publisher, except as permitted by U.S. copyright law.

The story, all names, characters, and incidents portrayed in this production are fictitious. No identification with actual persons (living or deceased), places, buildings, and products is intended or should be inferred.

Book Cover by Dhananj@bookcover4you.com

Visit Lisa Clute's website at: www.liscluteauthor.com
Published by Night Quill Press LLC
USA

Dedication

For every woman who's ever had to fight twice
as hard to be heard, who's been underestimated,
overlooked, or told to stay grounded.

This is for you.

May you always find your wings.
May you always remember how to fly.

Content Warning

This book is for readers 18 years and older. It contains themes and scenes that may be triggering for some readers, including:
- Alien kidnappings

- On-page violence and battle scenes

- On-page intimacy

- Injuries and torture

- On the job sexual harassment

- Cursing

- Death (limited to antagonistic and peripheral characters)

Contents

Series Recap   1
In case you missed it!

Prologue - Nerrisa   6
Unfortunate Decisions

1. Chapter 1 - Nerrisa   12
   Welcome to the Cage

2. Chapter 2 - Nerrisa   37
   Then the Ceiling Falls

3. Chapter 3 - Frakyss   58
   Chasing the Flame

4. Chapter 4 - Nerrisa   70
   The Pilot and the Sprout

5. Chapter 5 - Frakyss   86
   Close Enough to Burn

6. Chapter 6 - Nerrisa　　　　　　　91
   No Longer Grounded

7. Chapter 7 - Frakyss　　　　　　　99
   Wings He Gave Her

8. Chapter 8 - Nerrisa　　　　　　　105
   Roots and Wings

9. Chapter 9 - Frakyss　　　　　　　113
   The Royal Wedding

10. Chapter 10 - Nerrisa　　　　　　125
    The Hidden Ones

11. Chapter 11 - Frakyss　　　　　　134
    A New Chapter

12. Chapter 12 - Nerrisa　　　　　　143
    The One I Didn't Miss

13. Chapter 13 - Frakyss　　　　　　156
    Celebrations and Shadows

14. Chapter 14 - Nerrisa　　　　　　171
    Crowns and Cracks

15. Chapter 15 - Frakyss　　　　　　195
    Gifts We Hide, Truths We Share

16.	Chapter 16 - Nerrisa The Genomia Connection	211
17.	Chapter 17 - Frakyss He Who Lit My Eyes Red	232
18.	Chapter 18 - Nerrisa Hunted by Angels	255
19.	Chapter 19 - Frakyss Lunarite and Life Force	278
20.	Chapter 20 - Nerrisa The Aetherian Enigma	288
21.	Chapter 21 - Frakyss Pulse of Aether	300
22.	Chapter 22 - Nerrisa Welcome to the Family	307
23.	Chapter 23 - Frakyss Wraith Season Whiteout	318
24.	Chapter 24 - Nerrisa Stasis Pod Squad	325
25.	Chapter 25 - Frakyss The Keeper's Library	337

26. Chapter 26 - Nerrisa 354
    Power and Pancakes

27. Chapter 27 - Frakyss 360
    Freighters, Family, and Freedom

28. Chapter 28 - Nerrisa 367
    The Blooming Season

29. Chapter 29 - Frakyss 382
    Trips and Troqels

30. Chapter 30 - Nerrisa 391
    Cargo of Souls

31. Chapter 31 - Frakyss 398
    In the House of My Father

32. Chapter 32 - Frakyss 413
    The Secret Cove

33. Chapter 33 - Nerrisa 426
    For Future Reference

34. Chapter 34 - Frakyss 434
    With This Ring, I Thee Wed

35. Chapter 35 - Nerrisa 441
    Always and Forever

36. Chapter 36 - Frakyss Stalking a Monster	448
Epilogue - Nerrisa The Spark of Something Greater	453
Outtakes	457
Also by Lisa Clute	467
About the Author	470

Series Recap

In case you missed it!

In *Book One, Astrid's Abrauxian King*, Astrid Akselsen, a compassionate child psychologist and steady voice of reason, only wanted a peaceful yacht vacation with her twelve best friends. Instead, she wakes up in a massive hangar on a distant planet, surrounded by towering horned males with no concept of personal space and one determined alien king.

King Jakvar of Abrauxia calmly informs her that she and her friends have been brought across the universe to save his species from extinction. A plague wiped out the Abrauxian females, and fate, along with science, has marked Earth women as their last hope.

Astrid is stunned. Becoming someone's genetically matched queen was never part of her five-year plan. Jakvar may be noble and respectful, but Astrid refuses to be treated like a prize. She wants to protect her friends and find a way home.

Life on Abrauxia proves far more dangerous than royal ceremonies and awkward conversations. A bombing nearly kills her. A fanatical elder targets her and the King. When a deadly threat descends from the stars, Astrid must choose not survival, but leadership.

With every challenge, she draws strength from a legacy hidden deep in her blood. It is a power she has never spoken of, even to Jakvar, and it could change everything.

Through it all, Jakvar remains constant. Loyal. Protective. Vulnerable beneath the weight of his crown. In him, Astrid finds not captivity, but partnership, built on trust and choice.

She did not seek power. She was taken. But when a broken world cried out, Astrid answered. Not as a symbol, but as a force. A queen by her own making. A leader of land and sea. A mother to children who are half Abrauxian, half something far older, and entirely extraordinary.

She stayed to shape a legacy that will change worlds.

NERRISA'S ABRAUXIAN PROTECTOR

In *Book Two, Naia's Abrauxian General,* Amoranaia Kalakaua, a skilled locksmith, hacker, and fiercely independent island girl, is only looking for a break. A sun-drenched yacht vacation with her best friends sounds perfect. Instead, she is abducted across the stars, thrust into an impossible fated match, and forced to face one of the most feared warriors in the galaxy.

Naia is genetically matched by the ancient Ulae'Zep to Supreme General Grizlor, a battle-scarred commander who sees her as too small, too young, and too fragile to stand by his side. Every rejection drives Naia closer to the edge.

Brokenhearted and desperate to reclaim control, she plunges into the ocean trench behind the palace and disappears into the abyss. There, she joins forces with the mighty troqel and discovers a hidden enemy facility growing a second plague, one designed to wipe out the last hope for Abrauxia's survival.

Naia hacks the enemy systems, unleashes her dormant Aquar'thyn powers, and freezes the facility. Zaphre Kragmals, the troqel king, destroys it completely. But victory comes at a price. Drained nearly to death, Naia is rushed back to Epree Island with only the slimmest chance of recovery.

While she fights to survive, Grizlor is light-years away, crushing rebellions and uncovering brutal experiments aimed at weaponizing human women. When he returns to Abrauxia, he finds Naia missing and realizes too late what she truly meant to him.

Naia is named a baroness for her bravery and given a breathtaking island home near the palace. But the fight is not over. A second enemy facility threatens everything, and Naia is forced to work alongside the very male who shattered her heart. Across battlefields and starlit oceans, they uncover hidden truths, confront deadly threats, and begin to forge a bond stronger than fate itself.

When the final battle comes, Naia sacrifices herself once more to save Grizlor and their team. In the place beyond death, she learns the truth. She and Grizlor are two halves of a legacy older than any world. He is the power. She is the weapon. Together, they are unstoppable.

Naia returns, reborn with golden light in her eyes and healing power in her hands. She and Grizlor unite in a marriage of fire and ocean, and together they welcome twin daughters destined to change the future of Abrauxia.

Naia never sought greatness. She fought for survival. But when destiny demanded everything, she answered with more.

Prologue - Nerrisa

Unfortunate Decisions

The cockpit vibrates with the roar of the engines as I maneuver the sleek state-of-the-art spacecraft through a series of high-stakes maneuvers, my fingers moving quickly over the controls.

Each twist and turn feels exhilarating and real as the simulator replicates the weightlessness of space, and the rush of g-forces presses me into the seat.

As a young female test pilot, I've faced skepticism and challenges at every turn, but today, with the simulated ascent to Martian orbit under my belt, I feel an electrifying surge of empowerment. The simulation screens erupt with a cascade of green lights, signaling a flawless test run for the Mars Mission.

As I step out of the simulation unit, adrenaline still coursing through my veins, I catch the familiar silhouette of Colonel Harris leaning casually against the wall.

His expression is unreadable, but the predatory glint in his eyes sends a shiver down my spine. I keep my head high and my stride steady, determined not to show any sign of weakness as I walk past him.

"Great job in there, Byrne," he says, his voice smooth, laced with an undertone that makes my skin crawl. As we head down the corridor, he sidles up to me, brushing against my arm in a way that feels invasive. The weight of his presence looms over me, and I quicken my pace.

"Let's celebrate your little victory," he murmurs, suddenly pinning me against the wall with a force that knocks the air from my lungs.

My heart races, not from excitement, but a primal instinct, a fight or flight response that surges through me.

"Listen, Nerrisa," he growls, his fingers digging hard into my upper arms as he leans closer. The rancid stench of old coffee and something sour hits me like a slap. I fight the instinct to jerk away, to scrub his breath off my skin.

"You know how competitive it is for the Mars Mission. You can have all the perfect scores you want, but if you don't play nice, you might as well forget about it."

His threat hangs heavy between us, and my anger boils up, mixing with the fear. This is not how it's supposed to be. I swallow hard, reminding myself of my worth, my skills, and what I've fought through to get here.

"Get your hands off me," I say, keeping my voice steady, but my heart hammers.

His eyes narrow, but I refuse to back down. I won't be intimidated. With that, I jerk away and push past him, the confrontation lighting a fire in me. I adjust my flight suit, the drab desert tan coverall wrapping around me like armor.

Days pass, and I continue to avoid him or at least deflect his advances when I can't. Each time I reject him, his seething frustration becomes more evident. I feel the tension building, the stakes rising with every encounter.

It takes everything I have to manage my growing fear of him and his control over my future.

I don't dare file a report against him. I've seen what happens when a female pilot complains about a commanding officer's advances.

She's the one who always leaves the program for a desk job in Greenland.

Then, the announcement for the Mars Mission comes, and my heart races. I gather with my fellow pilots, all of us eager and nervous. As the names are called, I hold my breath, praying my hard work paid off.

When my name is announced, the thrill of victory courses through my veins.

As I step forward to accept the assignment, I notice Colonel Harris watching from the back, his face a dark mix of fury and surprise.

A few days later, I get the summons I've half expected. My stomach knots the moment I see the message, and the unease only deepens as I make my way to his office.

When I step inside, he is already seated behind his desk, posture rigid, eyes sharp and unreadable. The door clicks shut behind me, sealing us in. I force myself to stand tall even as a bead of cold sweat traces down my spine.

"Nerrisa," he says, his voice low and clipped, "I'm afraid we had to make some adjustments to the Mission roster."

The words hit harder than I expect, sending a jolt of dread through my chest.

My heart sinks. "What do you mean?"

He leans back, a smug expression on his face. "You've been scrubbed from the program. It seems there are concerns about your performance. Some believe you're not ready for the demands of Mars."

I stare at him in disbelief. "You did this because I wouldn't have sex with you. I've earned my place! I've proven myself time and again."

He shrugs, feigning indifference. "It's just business, Nerrisa. You know how competitive it is. Sometimes, unfortunate decisions have to be made."

Anger boils within me. "You used your power to punish me for rejecting you. This isn't right."

He smirks, leaning forward. "You should have considered that before. This is a man's world, and

Chapter 1 - Nerrisa

Welcome to the Cage

I blink against the harsh light flooding the room. Panic surges through me. This isn't my cabin on the mega yacht, *Seaduction*. I'm in a white metallic pod with the sharp scent of antiseptic filling my nostrils.

As I sit up, I'm confronted by a towering figure looming over me, a giant male marked with elaborate tattoos and heavy scars. Huge horns curve from his forehead, and his glowing red eyes slice through my confusion like a heated knife.

"You are mine," he growls, his voice a deep rumble that reverberates through the air. "You are my mate."

"Mate?" I echo, my voice sharp and rising. "I'm not your anything!"

He doesn't answer. Just clamps his massive hands around my arms and jerks me out of the pod you need to play the game to succeed. Go ahead, complain." He leans back, and his chair squeaks.

"You might want to use that month-long leave you're taking to figure out the best way to get back with the program."

As the words leave his mouth, it feels like the floor rips out from under me. Rage surges up, hot and blinding, and I have to turn away before I do something reckless. My fists clench at my sides. I bite down hard on the furious words clawing their way up my throat, knowing one wrong move would only seal my fate.

He sits there, calm and composed, while my dreams crumble into ash at my feet.

I walk out stiffly, every step fueled by a bitter mix of fury and heartbreak. My chest aches with the weight of it, but I refuse to let him see me break. Not here. Not now.

This isn't over. He might have cut me from this mission, but he won't steal my future.

I swear to myself, with every fiber of my being, that I will find another way. I will find another ship, another sky, and no one, not even Colonel Harris, will stand in my way again.

and sets me on my feet like broken tech that needs repairing. He leaves one hand gripping my bicep.

"No. Don't touch me!" I snap, planting my feet. My bare heels skid on the rough concrete floor as I try to twist away.

His grip tightens.

"Let go of me!" I scream, slamming my free hand into his chest, but he's unmoved.

He drags me through the hangar doors and out into a blinding alien landscape. The light is harsh purple. My brain can't catch up to the speed of everything happening. My breath shortens and my skin slickens with sweat.

"Stop it! Let me go!" I fight harder, yanking against his grip. And then I slam the ball of my bare foot into his shin, aiming for bone through the high, black leather boot.

He grunts but doesn't slow. Doesn't speak. Just keeps pulling me down the black marble lane.

A sleek building looms ahead. He drags me through the entrance. Cold air blasts against my skin and the sharp, sterile scent of disinfectant burns my sinuses.

A clinic.

He pulls me into a hallway where another mountain of an alien disappears through a door with Naia on his hip like a toddler.

My heart stutters.

"No. Don't you dare," I growl as the alien leading me yanks me through the same doorway.

The room is cold and far too clean. A metal exam table waits like a trap. He pushes me toward it, and when I resist, he lifts me just enough to plant me on the edge.

I launch off the table and hit the floor in a crouch, adrenaline blasting through me. My bare feet slap the tile as I bolt past the massive alien who brought Naia. He turns, but I'm already in the hall, sprinting toward the exit.

I make it halfway.

A shadow surges behind me.

Then I'm airborne.

He grabs me from behind and tosses me over his shoulder like I weigh nothing. My stomach lurches as the hallway spins. I kick, thrash, land fists on his back, but it's like pounding stone.

"Put me down, you overgrown, horned caveman!" I scream.

He doesn't answer. Doesn't flinch.

He turns calmly and carries me back through the doorway like I'm a stubborn backpack, then drops me unceremoniously onto the floor.

I bounce, catch myself, and scramble upright, chest heaving.

His glowing red eyes are steady and unapologetic when they meet mine.

I glare back, practically vibrating with rage, refusing to blink.

"Stay," he commands, the word sharp and final, and thrusts up a hand to block me as the door slides closed.

I rush it.

The panel seals with a hiss just as I reach it, and I slam full force into the smooth surface. My forehead clips the edge, and my butt hits the floor with a solid *thunk*, and I growl my frustration and anger.

Jumping up, I slam my fists against the panel. It doesn't so much as flicker. No handles. No seams. Just a door pretending to be a wall.

I spin, scanning the room for another way out.

One exam table, white and smooth with long drawers built into its base. A cantilevered desk extends from the far wall, sleek and clearly meant for a technician rather than a patient. There are no other doors and no windows.

Naia sits on the edge of the exam table, thumping her heels against its front. Her eyes are calm. *Too* calm.

"Why are you just sitting there? Aren't you even a little pissed we've been abducted by aliens?"

She blinks at me.

"Is that what this is?"

I throw my arms into the air. "I don't know, Naia. Do you know of any Caribbean resorts where giant gray warriors with horns, prehensile tails, and glowing eyes haul women off in see-through lingerie for nefarious purposes? Because this fashion statement hasn't been relevant since our middle school sleepovers."

A laugh bursts out of her mouth.

"What's so funny?"

"You said 'nefarious,'" she snorts, swiping at her face. "It sounds like we've been captured by a comic book villain. Should I start my dramatic monologue now or wait until after the dissection?"

I roll my eyes. "This isn't a joke, Naia. We need to get out of here before they come back and start slicing us open for their next science experiment."

I spin and aim a savage side kick to the door. The smack echoes, but the door doesn't budge.

"I don't think cutting us up is the plan. Mine called me his mate."

Stopping mid-step, I glare at her. "So did the red-eyed bastard who dragged me in here. Doesn't mean I'm interested in his freaky alien probe. I don't want him. I don't need him."

She laughs. "Mine's kind of hot. In a terrifying monster way."

Hands flying up in exasperation, I snap, "Perfect. You're already developing Stockholm Syndrome and we've been conscious for ten damn minutes. Fine. You can have my stalker. Collect the whole creepy set. I'm getting out of here."

Without waiting for a response, I stride to the desk. It doesn't have a chair, which suits me just fine. Swinging a leg up, I haul myself onto the surface, ignoring the sharp protest from my bruised arms where the alien grabbed me too tight. Overhead, the ceiling tiles form a patchwork of matte panels, the seams just wide enough to spark a little reckless hope.

Reaching up, I press against one of the tiles. It lifts in my hand and excitement flares through me at the success, but the moment I try to shift it aside and push upward, something inside snaps. The tile slams back into place with a metallic click that echoes through the room.

A startled yelp bursts out of me as I scramble to keep my balance, nearly toppling backward off the desk.

"Are you serious?" I hiss, rubbing my elbow where it hit the wall.

Jumping down I cross to the exam table and kneel down to yank open one of the drawers. Empty. The next has a stack of sterile cloths. The next has a foot-long metal cylinder. I grab it and flip it end over end.

"What is that?"

"Do I look like an alien tech expert?" In a moment of clarity I remember I'm locked in a room with an actual locksmith. "Hey, you're the locksmith. Go unlock the damn door."

Naia lifts her arms and glances down at herself. "Gee, Nerrisa, I seem to be fresh out of lock-picking tools. Must've forgotten to stash one in my *cooter*, in case of alien abduction."

I thrust the metal cylinder toward her. "Use this."

"I'm not touching ET's sex toy. Who knows where that thing's been." She tucks her hands into her armpits and leans away.

"You are absolutely no help. Are you seriously planning to sit here and wait to find out what they've got planned for us?"

"Yeah. Pretty much."

"I love you, but you're exhausting." I resume pacing, faster this time, looking for a way to escape. "I don't know how you're so calm."

Gripping the cylinder with both hands, I give it a shake, then with a snarl, I slam it against the door panel.

Metal crashes against metal, sharp and brutal, echoing off the sterile walls with violent finality.

"We have to get out of here," I snarl, slamming the cylinder harder with each word. "We need to find the others. Adeline, Astrid, Pearla… even Phoebe. They were all with us on the yacht. And now they're trapped somewhere."

This can't be happening. I'm a damn test pilot, not some lost girl in a cage. I've survived jet flights that shredded everyone else's nerves, outmaneuvered military drones, walked out of that last meeting with Colonel Harris with my head high and my record clean.

And now I'm trapped in a bright white box with one calm woman and somewhere outside, is one massive bastard who thinks I belong to him.

"They could be anywhere on this freakshow planet. Locked up, alone. Can you imagine Adeline waking up in one of those glass tubes? She's claustrophobic, Naia. She panics in a freight elevator. If she wakes up in one of those..."

My voice fractures.

No.

I don't care what this place is, who he is, or what the hell he thinks I am.

I'm getting out.

Even if I have to tear this room apart piece by piece.

After hours of waiting, Naia grumbles, "Alien hospitality sucks."

"Please place your hand on the lit square on the wall near the door," a male voice comes from a speaker in the ceiling.

Naia and I glance at each other and at the glowing square on the wall.

"I don't know about that," Naia says, shaking her head. I walk over to the indicated square. It looks like a simple backlit section of the wall.

"Please place your hand on the lit square on the wall near the door. Once your blood has been tested for malfunctioning nanos, and replacement ones can be injected, you will be released to your mates," the voice repeats.

"I don't have a mate!" I shout at the ceiling. "What I have is a stalker with horns and no sense of boundaries."

Naia jumps down from the exam table, walks over, and slaps her hand on the square. This woman has lost her mind.

"What is wrong with you? They might electrocute you or implant some alien mind control chip."

"If they do, my giant new mate will probably rip the walls down and decorate the room with their entrails. He seems the type."

She's got a point.

A few seconds later, the voice returns. "Analysis complete. Nanos activated. Remove your hand."

She steps back and gives me a pointed look. "Your turn."

"Next female, place your hand on the lit square," the voice repeats.

"FINE! Freaking aliens. I'm only doing this because I want out of this damn room." I slam my hand on the panel and glare at Naia.

The only thing the square does is get warm. After a few minutes, the voice says the test is complete. I remove my hand, look it over and find nothing different. I resume pacing until the door slides open.

The giant that hauled Naia here fills the entire opening. He leads her away, and I'm left looking up at the towering male who dragged me here.

He must be at least seven feet tall.

"Come, we will walk to the palace where you will stay for the foreseeable future." He gestures for me to walk with him. I hesitate for a moment before falling into step beside him.

When we leave the medical center, I'm able to get a good look at the wide boulevard. On one side, the vast black ocean reaches the distant horizon. The view is partly blocked by trees with black bark and vivid blue leaves.

On the right are quaint multi-storied buildings that remind me of the small Irish villages back in my home country.

I could almost imagine myself on Earth if not for the pale lilac sky overhead and the odd-colored trees and flowers.

The sound of crashing waves and the briny scent of the ocean do some good in calming my jangling nerves as we walk.

"King Jakvar said the Ulae'Zep didn't negotiate mate contracts with you as agreed upon before bringing you here. Please accept my deepest apologies and allow me to introduce myself. I am Frakyss." He glances down at me from his towering height.

"What kind of mate contracts? Can you explain that? Because I woke up on this alien planet and have no idea how I got here!"

"Again, I am sorry. The Abrauxian females all died in the Grievous Plague seventy-five years ago. As a species, we will go extinct with my generation unless we find compatible mates from somewhere else in the universe.

We hired the Ulae'Zep, a species that collects DNA samples from across the universe, to find our mates."

He pauses for a moment before continuing. "In the past, bonding happened in person through intimacy, but due to the circumstances, your contracts needed to be negotiated, and our DNA combined to trigger the grith bond. That's why I am marked with this design." He gestures at the tattoos on his bare arms and chest.

"In exchange for accepting my mate proposal, I provide you with a domicile, new conveyance, and funds all in your name only. I don't know your name yet, but everything will be transferred as soon as you tell me, and I can finalize the transactions."

"I'm Nerrisa Byrne of Earth," I respond as we walk around the end of the large hangar I woke up in earlier.

Ahead of us, up a slight hill, is a huge black castle with multiple round towers. I'm taken aback. It looks like something straight out of the European Renaissance.

The dark stone reflects the bright sunshine, and as we go through imposing wrought iron gates, I'm surprised by this architecture on an alien planet.

"What's the deal with this castle? Is this where I'm supposed to stay?"

"This is the Royal Palace of the King and Queen of the Ioneus Asteria Galaxy, Auriqae Solar System," he says, his voice calm and annoyingly steady, like this is the most normal conversation in the world.

My stomach flips.

Palace? Galaxy? What in the actual hell?

"You'll stay in a suite here while you read your mate contract and review the compensation I provided when you accepted my mate bond."

My jaw drops.

"Accepted? I didn't accept anything. You aliens dragged me here like a duffel bag with legs."

He pauses, and I'm not sure if he understood a word I just said, then continues, "You'll be able to decide where you want to live, and we can spend time getting to know one another."

I blink at him.

"Getting to know one another? What is this, some intergalactic dating app from hell?"

He stands there like a wall of calm certainty, as if he hasn't completely hijacked my life. My pulse hammers in my ears. I don't even know what half of those words mean. Ioneus Asteria Galaxy? Auriqae? Royal Palace?

I was supposed to be flying missions, not starring in a sci-fi version of *The Bachelor: Abduction Edition*.

I cross my arms tightly over my chest, every nerve in my body screaming to run. To punch. To *do something.*

Instead, I glare up at him.

"Let me get this straight. You want me to read some alien contract that magically makes me your 'mate' after I've been kidnapped, dragged across stars, and locked in a medical clinic for hours with no food, water, or restroom facilities?"

He has the nerve to nod.

My eyes narrow into slits.

I don't say another word. I keep my eyes locked straight ahead and put a few paces between us as we walk.

The path winds through a courtyard bursting with vivid alien flowers. There are blooms the size of my head. Others glow faintly like bioluminescent sea creatures. It should be beautiful, breathtaking even.

But it feels like walking through a well-tended cage.

I don't care how pretty the prison is. It's still a prison.

We approach a towering castle door carved from dark wood and glassy black metal. As we near it, a tall, broad-shouldered male with curled horns opens it smoothly, smiling as if this is some normal diplomatic visit and not a hostage situation.

He gestures politely for us to enter.

I step through the threshold into a massive foyer, where the air is cool and scented with something sweet and sharp, like citrus and mint.

Gold and black marble pillars rise to a domed ceiling painted with constellations I don't recognize. Everything looks expensive and gleams. But it's eerily quiet.

I don't belong here.

Just as I open my mouth to say as much, a small figure glides toward us.

She's maybe four feet tall and blue-skinned, with delicate fingers and smooth amphibious features. Her wide, silvery eyes blink slowly as she looks up at me, studying my face with open curiosity and no hint of fear.

"I am Panshe," she says in a soft, lilting voice that brushes across my ears like silk.

"Please follow me to your suite."

I hesitate.

She's not threatening. Nothing about her says danger. But that doesn't mean I trust her or any of this.

I glance up at Frakyss, narrowing my eyes.

He watches me quietly, giving nothing away.

I want to demand an explanation of who she is and what she wants. She's likely just another polite face meant to soften the blow of captivity. But the anger is rising so hot in my throat I can't get the words out without screaming.

So I nod once, stiffly.

Fine. Let's see what this "suite" looks like.

Maybe I'll find a window to jump out of.

Or something sharp.

Either way, I don't plan on staying long.

She must sense my hesitation because she adds gently, "You are safe here. Frakyss will attend this evening's formal welcome dinner."

Safe? I almost laugh. He nods like that's some kind of reassurance.

I don't respond. I just grit my teeth and follow the little blue alien into a cavernous hallway off to the right. My bare feet make no sound on the glossy floor as we start up a wide, sweeping staircase that feels like it was designed to impress royalty or intimidate intruders.

Gold pillars rise on either side of the upstairs corridor, and chandeliers the size of cars dangle overhead, spaced at perfect intervals. Every wall is covered in elaborate tapestries and vivid paintings I don't understand.

Crystal-covered tables display strange artifacts locked beneath glass, that hum faintly with energy.

I keep my arms folded tight across my chest.

We stop at the second door on the right. Panshe touches a panel, and the door swings inward without a sound.

The room inside looks like something out of a dream I would never have.

Silver and soft blue stretch across the walls and floor. The bed is massive, draped in fabric that glows faintly silver. Silk curtains pool on the floor at one wall made entirely of mullioned windows. They offer a sweeping view of an alien town that's illuminated by the confusing purple sun.

My breath hitches before I can stop it. Not because it's beautiful. Because it's disorienting and overwhelming.

"This will be your home while you are here," Panshe says, her voice warm like she actually believes that's a good thing. "And we have much to do in preparation for tonight's formal dinner."

Home. Right. Like I signed a lease.

I don't move.

She walks calmly into an adjacent room and gestures for me to follow. I step in and find myself surrounded by mirrors, light panels, and what looks like some high-tech closet from the future. In the center of the far wall is a sleek embedded device, its surface pulsing with faint light.

"This will scan you and create your clothing," she says, as if that's a totally normal sentence.

I stare at it, then at her.

"Great. So I'm being dressed by a vending machine now."

Panshe just smiles like I didn't say it with enough venom to melt steel.

And I seriously consider jumping out the window.

She gestures to a silver disc embedded in the floor. It pulses softly as if waiting for me to obey. I step onto it with a sigh, because really, what choice do I have?

The platform rotates me in a slow, smooth circle, completing one full spin before coming to a stop. Panels inside the mirrored walls flicker, and suddenly the closet spaces around me bloom to life. Fabric sways into view on sleek silver hangers. Silks. Satins. Materials I cannot even name, each more extravagant than the last.

"Choose what you like," Panshe says, her voice bright and utterly sincere.

Her eyes sparkle like she's offering me a birthday gift, not dressing me up for some intergalactic dinner I never agreed to attend.

I reach out and run my fingers over something that looks like liquid woven into fabric. It's soft and impossibly light. I pass over pale blues and silvers and stop at a gown of deep emerald green.

The color catches the chandelier light, shifting like sunlight through forest leaves. The off-the-shoulder neckline drapes down into tiny puffed sleeves. It's elegant, and the exact opposite of everything I've been wearing for months.

I pull it from the rack.

"Excellent choice!" Panshe says, producing a matching green lace strapless bra and panties set like it's part of a magic trick. I take them without comment since she's clearly immune to my sarcasm.

I peel off the shapeless white mini dress they shoved me in when I was kidnapped and toss it onto a nearby ottoman.

Panshe snatches it up and drops it into a tall cylindrical hamper in the corner. The surface flashes blue, then goes dark.

I narrow my eyes.

"What is that?"

"The recycler," she says with a gentle nod. "Once you're done wearing something, you place it in the recycler, and it's broken back down into molecules. The material is then used to make something else."

I stare at her.

"Impressive. If the clothes are that high-tech, I can't wait to see what kind of aircraft you've got stashed around here. You wouldn't happen to have something that scrubs the bottoms of feet, would you? I walked here from the medical clinic barefoot."

I lift one foot and glance at the filthy sole.

Without missing a beat, Panshe crosses to the adjoining bathroom and returns with a soft damp cloth. No judgment. Just calm, eerie efficiency.

I sit on the dressing table stool and clean my feet in silence, scrubbing until the cloth is filthy and my skin looks normal again. I stand, flick the cloth toward the recycler, and watch the flash of blue with a strange sense of satisfaction.

Panshe steps in again, this time with a small brush in one hand and a glint of something in the other.

"May I?" she asks, gesturing to my hair.

I consider arguing. Saying no. Demanding space.

But my mouth doesn't open.

Instead, I nod once and sit back down.

She sweeps my long red curls into an elegant twist, pinning it in place with delicate emerald-tipped sticks that sparkle when they catch the light.

I sit rigid, hands on my knees, as she brushes a fine dusting of powder across my face, barely-there makeup applied just enough to blur the edges of exhaustion from under my eyes.

When she finishes, I turn slowly toward the mirror.

And freeze.

I don't look like me.

I look *refined*. Soft where I've spent months trying to be sharp. Beautiful, even.

I barely recognize the woman staring back.

I haven't worn makeup since Colonel Harris started circling like a predator and I learned the fastest way to disappear was to dull every part of myself that might draw attention. I had been pulling my hair into a bun so tight it ached, and hid behind shapeless clothes, and added steel in my voice.

But this?

This is definitely not camouflage, and I don't know what to do with it.

"You look beautiful," Panshe says, stepping back to admire her work.

I glance at her through the mirror.

"Thanks," I murmur, surprised when a small smile sneaks past the edge of my anxiety.

She helps me step into the gown, and it settles around me like water; cool, smooth, and dangerously soft. The hem brushes the floor, and the bodice hugs my curves in a way that feels far too noticeable.

I walk carefully to a row of shelves lined with shoes, each pair more impractical than the last. I find a pair of elegant green heels that match the gown and slide them on.

They fit like they were made for me.

Which, apparently, they were.

I follow Panshe into the bedroom, and she stops at an ornate writing desk carved with unfamiliar symbols. A polished device waits there, a slim band of silver and green.

She picks it up and fastens it around my wrist.

"This will allow you access to all approved areas of the palace," she explains with that same gentle clarity. "If you need directions, speak to your communicator. Your nanos will display a map. You can also say the name of someone you'd like to contact. A green light means you're connected. A red one means they're unavailable."

I nod once, absorbing the flood of information. She hands me a datapad next.

"You can access anything here that you might want to see. Eventually, once you're comfortable, your nanos will allow you to pull the same information directly with your thoughts. It's all about how much control you want."

Thought-activated data, smartwatch door locks, and fabric printers. That's great, but where do I find the spaceships?

Chapter 2 - Nerrisa

Then the Ceiling Falls

Before I can ask another question, the sound of laughter filters in through the door, familiar voices carrying a rhythm I have not heard since the yacht. I turn toward the sound, heart thudding.

"That must be the other females assembling for dinner," Panshe says with a small smile. She crosses to the door and opens it wide.

There they are.

Naia. Pearla. Demi... everyone is dressed up in alien gowns and draped with elaborate jewelry, glowing softly in the overhead lights. For a second, I don't breathe.

Then they spot me.

Before I can say a word, arms wrap around me from every side. Laughter bubbles up as we cling to each other, squeezing tight like we can make up for lost time all at once.

Unfamiliar scents of a new world cling to their skin, weaving together into something both familiar and new. Wide eyes shine with excitement, low whistles sound in appreciation, and compliments fly through the air like bright, sparkling confetti.

"From the Caribbean to an alien castle, ladies," I say with a grin, forcing strength into my voice. "Are we ready?"

Every one of them nods, unwavering. No one hesitates and no one steps back. A force moves between us, silent but undeniable, binding us together with something stronger than words. It is determination, it is survival, it is the unbreakable bond of sisterhood.

Another small amphibious woman appears at the end of the hall and beckons. We follow her in a line down the wide staircase, our heels clicking in sync.

The air in the entry hall shifts the moment we arrive.

Two horned males in ceremonial armor pull open the massive wooden doors. Light, music and the murmur of conversations spill out.

And then, the Great Hall opens before us.

It is massive, shining, and almost too perfect to be real. Crystal chandeliers hang from the vaulted ceiling like constellations turned upside down. Marble trees line the sides, tall and gleaming with their branches intertwined overhead.

Everything sparkles around us, from the walls to the floors to the massive windows that stretch all the way to the ceiling.

A low hum pulses through the room.

I feel it before I see the group of large, powerful males standing near the bar. Their predatory eyes snap toward us the second we step inside.

The air goes still.

Every eye is on us.

The butterflies in my stomach morph into something sharper.

Not fear, but focus.

A female alien with a goat-shaped face, weaves gracefully through our group, balancing a round tray of filled champagne flutes on one hand.

Her movement is effortless and her expression serene as she offers the drinks to each of us. I take a glass, watching the pale bubbles rise and burst like starlight trapped in crystal.

I take a cautious sip, and the flavor unfolds slowly, sweet and crisp with a delicate hint of something floral. It blooms across my tongue and settles with a warmth that feels almost dangerous.

For a moment, I close my eyes, savoring the aftertaste as it lingers like a memory I am not ready to let go.

"Oh wow, this stuff is amazing, Nerrisa," Arabella says next to me. Her smile is wide, eyes already gleaming with ideas. "I don't know where they came up with this, but I'd kill for a few hours in their kitchens with all those alien ingredients."

She glances toward a pair of side doors just as they swing open. An army of the goat-faced servers emerge, wheeling out floating trays topped with domed silver cloches.

An unfamiliar scent trails after them, rich with spices I cannot name and sharp enough to cut through my discipline. It stirs something primal, something that reminds me I have not eaten in far too long.

Arabella practically glows. She's one of the best chefs I've ever met, and her new Manhattan restaurant just earned a Michelin star. If anyone can reverse-engineer alien cuisine, it's her.

The smell of roasted meat and warm spices curls around me, tightening the knot in my stomach. I cannot remember the last time I ate. It was probably dinner on the *Seaduction*, though I have no idea how many days or weeks have passed since then.

Whether it's the lack of food or the adrenaline hasn't worn off, my stomach clenches tight.

I glance toward the cluster of towering males across the room.

Frakyss is watching me.

His red eyes are steady and unreadable. His face is a roadmap of old scars, some deep, some faded, but all brutal.

And yet, he's handsome. Undeniably so. Not polished, not pretty, but he exudes power in a way that commands space without asking for it.

I wonder, briefly, what happened to him.

Then I shut that thought down.

It does not matter. I have no interest in powerful men with haunted eyes and big strong hands that think they can shape my life.

I have carved out my own path, piece by brutal piece, and I will not let anyone take it from me. I owe no one my trust or freedom.

"Can you believe we're here?" Layla murmurs, stepping up on my other side and interrupting my dark thoughts. Her voice is soft, her eyes wide as she takes a sip from her flute. "An alien palace, on an actual alien planet?"

I force a smile. I want to feel that wonder. I really do. But it's buried under layers of survival mode.

"I can't wait to explore the medical facility," Layla adds brightly. "Maybe they've finally cured the common cold."

That gets a laugh from all three of us. It's small but real.

I glance back toward the males.

"I'm not sure any of them have ever had a sick day in their lives," I say, raising an eyebrow. "If I were a germ, I'd run the other way."

"Or drop dead from a scowl," Layla adds with a laugh. "That giant one with the weapons strapped all over him scares me to death."

I follow her gaze. She's talking about the one who hauled Naia around earlier like she weighed nothing. He's at least a head taller than any other male there, his shoulders broad enough to block out the light behind him.

"That one's Naia's," I say dryly. "Of course. It's always the biggest and the smallest."

"Oh goodness, I bet she's eating that up," Layla says, grinning as we glance at Naia, who's standing near the edge of our group with a glass in her hands and hearts practically floating out of her eyes. She's staring at the brute like he hung the stars.

Everyone in the Second Sister Consortium knows Naia has always been the one dreaming of her Prince Charming. Fairy tales, soulmates, destined love, she believes in all of it. She used to doodle wedding dresses in the margins of her homework.

Personally, I've never understood her fascination.

All I can think about is how much I despise the idea of someone claiming me. Mate, bond, or destiny... whatever they choose to call it, the very concept makes my skin crawl. It's not just Frakyss. It is any male who thinks he can own me because some alien biology says so.

"Which one is yours, Arabella?" I ask, mostly to distract myself.

She tips her chin toward a striking male with sleek dark hair and a perfectly tailored black jacket. His stance is graceful and composed, less of a soldier and more royalty.

"Governor Godefray of Silvergate Cay," she says. "We're going there after this dinner."

Of course she is. Arabella's always been elegant enough to match a governor. She belongs in glass halls and candlelight. Me? I belong in a cockpit.

Before I can respond, the enormous entry doors creak open and the sound slices through the crowd like a blade. A hush ripples over the room.

Everyone turns.

Striding through the doorway is a stunning male, tall and regal, with my friend Astrid on his arm. An Abrauxian standing near the entrance slams his spear against the floor with a deep, resonating *bang*.

"I present His Majesty, King Jakvar of Abrauxia, and Her Majesty, Queen Astridia Akselsen of Earth."

All around me, the male guests press their right fists to their chests and bow low.

I glance at the women near me, and we bow too, our motions clumsy and stiff.

Astrid is radiant, her gold gown reflecting every shimmer of light in the hall. A delicate crown rests atop her platinum waves, and she walks like someone born to it. In truth, each of us is the daughter of a queen on our own planet, something we frequently forget.

All eyes follow her. Rightfully so.

Beside her, the King's gray skin not covered by a brocade vest, glints with black tattoos that trace his muscles like war paint. His glowing eyes sweep over the crowd with calm authority.

The two of them move into the room with grace and purpose, and the crowd parts like a tide. The other women and I move to meet Astrid, forming a ring around our friend, drawn to her like gravity.

One by one, we take turns hugging her. There's laughter, whispered congratulations, and happy tears.

She looks like a queen.

And I feel like a fraud in borrowed silk.

I smile, hug, and nod along with the excitement rippling through the group.

But deep down, my chest tightens.

This isn't a fairy tale for me. It certainly doesn't feel like a celebration. It's a cage, gleaming and beautiful, locked so perfectly that escape feels impossible.

I have no idea how I am going to break free.

Near the edge of our group I catch a glimpse of Layla, beaming up at an alien. He looks down at her as if she strung every star across the sky. I envy her, the effortless way she shines here, as if this strange new world had been waiting just for her.

She doesn't know what it's like to feel trapped. To have your body treated like a bargaining chip, and your choices stolen with a sneer. She believes in this mate bond thing. Maybe it'll work out for her. I hope it does.

She deserves a dream.

I'm not so sure about mine.

The room hushes as the king steps toward us, every inch of him steeped in authority. His presence pulls the air taut, and our little circle of women goes still.

He walks to Astrid, and I watch the way she stands, tall and composed, radiant in a way that feels almost untouchable. She looks as if she has always been meant to wear a crown.

Their eyes meet with no hesitation or fear.

He offers his arm, and with a graceful smile, she takes it.

He leads her to the foot of the long table and pulls out her chair with quiet ceremony. She climbs up onto the plush seat, and when she settles in, the whole room seems to breathe out. The light catches her gown and the gleam of her crown.

She shines.

The King circles the table and takes his place behind his own towering chair at the far end. He doesn't pause, doesn't falter. This is his world, his rhythm, and he was born to command it.

The other males move in sync, finding their mates, offering their arms, mirroring their King.

I feel him before I see him.

Frakyss.

His presence hums next to me, heat radiating from his skin like he's built of fire and stone. I glance up and find him watching me, his expression unreadable, his thick, black hair catching the golden light and shimmering like ink.

"Nerrisa," he says, and his voice is low and smooth, rich like Connemara whiskey by a fire on a cold night.

"Frakyss," I answer, matching his calm tone with one of my own. My voice doesn't shake. My fingers twitch, but he doesn't need to see that.

He extends his arm toward me.

For a heartbeat, I stare at it.

A part of me screams to walk away. To say no, to make a scene, to remind every single person here that I do not belong to anyone.

But I don't move.

Not because I've given in. Not because I trust him.

But because for now, it's easier to play along.

I place my hand on his arm. His skin is warm, solid, and unnervingly smooth beneath my fingers.

He leads me to the seat just beside Astrid. I climb up using the footrest and settle onto the soft cushions, heart pounding, jaw tight.

He slides me in, then takes his place beside me. I focus on the table.

Silverware that gleams like starlight. Goblets catching the candlelight and throwing it in every direction. Plates edged in fine metallic script I can't read.

Across the table, a tall gold male stares at Demi like she's his entire reason for existing. She looks ethereal in her Victorian goth ensemble, dark and dramatic, like midnight dressed for a vampire court.

The king lowers into his seat with a smooth, practiced motion, and the rest of the males bow together. A wave of power rolls across the hall as they take their chairs.

Frakyss settles in beside me, and I swear the temperature around us spikes. He's a furnace, all tightly coiled strength and heat.

Silence falls.

Everyone watches.

The King and Queen lift their forks and take a bite of food.

And then, at last, the room exhales.

Laughter rises. Glasses clink. Voices spill across the hall like music.

But under the hum of celebration, my pulse keeps time with something else.

Escape.

Or war.

Whichever comes first.

I glance at Astrid. She's already cutting into the blue filet on her plate, the texture flaking like fish.

Beside it, a pile of seaweed salad glistens under the lights.

That, at least, I recognize. I take a cautious bite. It's briny and citrusy, a strange but familiar mix that settles like a small peace offering on my tongue.

Just as my shoulders begin to ease, I feel a warm hand on my arm.

The peace vanishes.

Every muscle in my body tenses. A flare of heat burns beneath my skin, but not the good kind. It's sharp and defensive. I yank my arm back like I've been scalded.

My heart thunders.

I whip my head toward Frakyss. He looks startled, his brows drawing together, his mouth parting like he wasn't expecting a reaction at all.

"You can't just touch me like that," I snap, keeping my voice low. I don't want to make a scene, but the tremor behind my words betrays how close I am to unraveling.

He tilts his head slightly, his expression creased with confusion. "But I am your mate," he says, voice soft, as if the title explains everything.

It doesn't.

He gestures toward the intricate markings on his arms, the bold swirls and symbols that stretch across his skin, glowing faintly under the light.

"These are proof of our bond."

I stare at the tattoos. They *are* beautiful. Sharp, elegant, full of meaning I don't understand. But they're not a contract I signed.

"They don't give you the right to touch me," I say, voice steady now, sharper. "I didn't choose this. I didn't choose *you*."

The words hang there between us, heavy and raw.

His mouth opens slightly, then closes again. His red eyes blink once, slowly. I can almost see the weight of my rejection land. It knocks something loose in his expression.

Around us, the soft clink of silverware and quiet laughter continues, but I feel the shift. A few people glance our way. They're pretending not to listen, but they are.

"Please," he says after a beat, his tone gentler now. "I'm not trying to offend you. I just want to understand you. I want this to work."

I believe him. I *do*. And it makes this harder.

I sigh and press my palm flat to the table, grounding myself.

"Getting to know someone doesn't start with putting your hands on them," I say, quieter this time. "I need space. Physical touch doesn't feel safe to me. That's not your fault, but it's still real."

He leans back, giving me more distance. I can see it in his face. He's listening. He's trying. But the disappointment there is unmistakable.

A long breath passes between us.

Then, barely above a whisper, he says, "I'm sorry. You must find my scars unpleasant to look at."

My gaze sharpens.

"Is that what you think?" I ask. "That I'm repulsed by you?"

He doesn't answer.

I let my eyes trace over him slowly. His face. His arms. The lines etched into his skin. Scars and strength and sorrow, all visible.

"You are an attractive male," I manage, forcing the words past the tightness in my chest. "Your scars do not bother me. They are not the reason I flinch." I swallow hard, hating how my voice wavers. "This is not about you. It never was."

A breath shudders out of me before I can catch it. "Something happened. Back on Earth. Something I have not figured out how to leave behind."

His jaw tenses slightly. He nods once, not pressing further.

I glance down the table.

The other women are smiling. Laughing. Leaning into the warmth of the males beside them. They look like they belong here, like the bond has offered them something they didn't know they were missing.

I feel outside of that.

Like I'm watching through a window, unable to step in.

I take a slow breath and let it fill the space in my chest that had started to close. Around us, the room is alive with quiet joy and connection. I try to let it soften me, even just a little.

But I don't reach for him.

And he doesn't try to touch me again.

For now, that's the closest thing to peace we have.

Suddenly, the sharp scrape of a chair cuts through the laughter like a blade. I freeze.

My heart skips a beat.

The King is standing, his towering form rigid, his silver eyes narrowed. A ripple of confusion sweeps the room.

I glance at Astrid. She shakes her head and gives a small shrug, her brows drawn in confusion. It's obvious she doesn't know what's happening either.

The males react instantly, rising as one, their chairs groaning against the marble floor, the sound multiplying until it becomes a thunderous roar. Bodies shift. Heads turn. Unease blossoms fast and hard in the pit of my stomach.

Frakyss stands unmoving behind his chair, eyes scanning the room.

I scramble to do the same, but my legs tangle in the long gown. My chair won't budge because it's wedged too close to the table and too heavy for me to budge. Panic claws up my spine.

The chandeliers above us begin to sway.

Then, without warning, the world detonates.

The blast hits before I even understand what is happening.

A roar tears through the hall, erupting from somewhere inside the room itself. Heat punches into my chest, and the shockwave slams me backward. My chair rocks but rights itself.

The long table shatters apart in an instant, sending plates, goblets, and shards of marble screaming through the air. Windows crack and explode, raining jagged glass.

The ceiling groans overhead.

A second explosion, closer this time, sends a violent shockwave down the length of the hall.

Crystal chandeliers, each easily the size of a car, snap free of their anchors and plummet.

One crashes into the broken table with a shriek of metal and glass, the impact spraying razor-sharp fragments across the room like bomb shrapnel.

I throw my arm over my face, but it only provides minimal protection. The pieces cut through the air with terrifying speed, biting into my skin, slicing fabric, and embedding into walls and bodies.

My chair jolts hard. I try to duck, but I'm pinned between the arms, locked in place by a slab of tabletop.

A beam above us splits with a sound like a bone cracking.

Then the ceiling falls.

Chunks of carved stone and ancient gilded plaster rain down. I hear the sickening crunch of it striking flesh. Furniture shatters beneath the weight. Screams become sobs. The scent of fire, blood, and scorched silk floods the air.

I curl into myself, desperate for cover, with my pulse roaring louder than the chaos.

And for a terrifying moment, I think this is it.

This is how it ends. Barely hours after arriving on an alien planet, dressed like someone I don't recognize, beside a male I didn't choose, in a palace that already felt like a trap.

Chapter 3 - Frakyss

Chasing the Flame

Darkness envelops me, heavy and suffocating, as I struggle to comprehend what's happening. The last thing I remember is shouts echoing in the Great Hall, the sound of explosions and the ceiling crashing down, and then everything went black.

Now, I'm trapped beneath a mass of debris, the weight of the collapsed ceiling pinning me down. Panic rises within me as I shift my body, but the rubble is unyielding, and I can't see anything.

The distant wail of an alarm pierces through the silence, a stark reminder of the damage outside my confinement.

I hear frantically muttering alien voices I can't quite understand, and the crunch of footsteps moving nearby. My hearts race. I need to get to Nerrisa.

I struggle to free myself to no avail. "Hello!" I call out, my voice strained and muffled. "Is anyone there? I need help!"

My words are swallowed up by the mountain of rubble trapping me. I strain my ears, hoping for a response, but all I hear is the alarm and the shifting of the damaged structure. Time stretches painfully as I wait, my heart pounding in my chest.

Then, I hear it, Abrauxian voices calling out. "Is anyone trapped? We're here to help!"

"Over here!" I shout, my voice rising to be heard. "I'm trapped. I need help!"

The sounds of movement grow closer, and I feel the vibration of footsteps. Moments later, I hear the crunch of rubble being shifted.

"Hold on! We're coming!" Determined voices call out as they dig through the debris.

I feel the crushing weight above me shift. "Keep talking!" one of them calls out. "We need to know where you are!"

"I'm near the Queen's end of the table!" I shout back, trying to keep my voice steady.

After what feels like an eternity, the last of the weight is pulled off, and light floods in, blinding me for a moment. I shield my eyes from the heavy-duty flashlight.

A warrior reaches down, grasping my other arm and helping me out of the wreckage. My body is sore and battered, but I manage to pull free, gasping to breathe in the dust-filled air.

"Are you injured?" the male asks, concern etching his face as he helps me stand.

"I'm fine," I manage, though I can feel bruises and cuts all over my body. "But I need to find my mate!"

The Great Hall is destroyed, debris strewn everywhere, thick plaster dust swirls in the air around us. I search each plaster-covered face as people emerge from the wreckage.

"Where is she? Where's Nerrisa?"

The warrior shakes his head, his expression grim. "We don't know. We need to focus on getting these people out."

"No!" I protest, panicked desperation clawing at me. "I won't just leave her! She could be trapped!" I glare at the warrior, towering over him and fixing him with my red glare.

I lean in flaring my nostrils aggressively. I'm not called Frakyss the Scary by chance, and I will not be deterred in my search.

The warrior's eyes widen when he realizes who he's talking with, and he backs up, chastened. "I'm sorry, sir. Can you help us load the injured onto the stretchers as we look for her?"

My anger eases, and I nod. I dig through the detritus surrounding me, pulling free an injured and weeping brown-haired female and placing her on one of the hovering stretchers.

There's no sign of Nerrisa in the rubble near me where she should be, and I realize she's gone.

We move through the devastation, gathering the injured onto the stretchers that glide above the littered floor. Halfway down the room I find the crushed body of Elder Gisun, the poor old fellow.

I didn't always see eye-to-eye with him but what a miserable way to go. I lift his broken body onto a stretcher and cover him with a thin sheet, giving his remains the respect he deserves. I gesture to a nearby warrior to take the remains out of the ruined hall.

As I work, my mind races with fear for Nerrisa. I steal glances around me, hoping to spot her shimmering copper hair or the flash of her green eyes, but she's nowhere to be found.

A warrior calls out, "We need to get the injured to the clinic! Everyone able to help, please guide a stretcher."

With a single hopeful glance back into the ruined building, I guide the last stretcher out of the wreckage. The procession moves down the small hill past the space pad and marina to the medical center. One of Lukbos's assistants is directing the line of injured to the mass casualty ward.

When I enter, I look around, hoping my mate is already here. Lukbos is busy treating a whimpering Earth female with a compound fractured arm.

The majority of the injured are Grasheta who were in the hall serving the banquet. I see only six Earth females, but Nerrisa is not among them.

I swallow hard, pushing back on the rising tide of panic threatening to overwhelm me. I can't stay here, not without knowing where she is. I'm about to turn on my heel and head back to the Great Hall when the door slams open with a force that reverberates through the clinic and about takes it off its hinges.

Grizlor strides in, his towering figure drawing immediate attention. His piercing gaze sweeps over the injured. The room falls silent as he takes in the scene.

"Do you need treatment, General Grizlor?" Lukbos asks from where he's treating the female. Grizlor looks down at himself. Like me, he is covered with blood and plaster dust from the collapse.

He picks a couple of large shards of glass and metal from his thick hide and drops them to the floor. A cleaning bot zips over and vacuums the pieces away before racing back across the room to its docking station.

"No. I am searching for my mate. Was she injured?" He asks.

"She was not among those brought in. We lost four guards at the entrance to the palace, and Elder Gisun perished. Witnesses say that a group of Zugunu entered the ruined building and carried away King Jakvar and two of the females. We believe one was Naia, and the other was Frakyss's mate, Nerrisa."

Panic turns my blood to ice in my veins, and next to me, General Grizlor lets out a ferocious roar. The entire ward goes silent, and everyone stares at the giant with open fear.

"General, you are disturbing my patients. I believe rescue efforts are being coordinated at the marina." Lukbos responds and turns back to the injured female.

Grizlor races out of the clinic, and I walk to Lukbos. "Who said the Zugunu took my mate?"

He glances up at me, then continues setting the female's arm before running the healing wand back and forth to knit the bones together. "One of the wounded guards told Trustram."

"Where is he so I can talk to him?"

"He died of his wounds shortly after," he comments. "I suggest you go take a shower so we can see if you need shrapnel removed from your carcass."

I look down at myself, and I might as well be encased in cement; so much filth clings to me.

Nodding, I follow the long hall to the large open shower area at the back of the clinic. I peel off my torn leather pants and step under a shower head, and water begins to beat down, the steam enveloping me.

As the hot water rains down, I scrub away the caked-on blood and grime. I focus on picking out the embedded glass and a large sliver of marble from my thigh.

All the while, my thoughts keep drifting to Nerrisa. Why would the Zugunu attack the royal palace and more importantly, what are they doing with my mate?

Once I'm finished and dried, I grab a fresh pair of pants and boots from the replicator, feeling a little better as I pull them on. With a deep breath, I walk back into the mass casualty ward.

But the moment I enter, I'm met with a flurry of activity. Lukbos's mate rushes over to me, her eyes wide with excitement. "Frakyss! Nerrisa just got Lukbos to retrieve the King from a Zugunu shuttle she stole!"

The news hits me like a jolt of electricity. "What? She's alive?" I'm filled with an overwhelming wave of relief, but it's mixed with anxiety. How did she rescue the King and what is she doing flying a shuttle?

Without a second thought, I race out of the clinic, almost colliding with Lukbos and his assistants, bringing the unconscious King in on a stretcher.

"Watch it!" Lukbos snaps, but I barely register his words. My focus is laser-sharp as I run past them, scanning the area for Nerrisa.

And then I see her. She's standing a short distance away, her fiery hair a beacon in the bright sunshine. But her green dress is shredded, and she's smeared with filth and dried blood. Relief floods through me, but before I can reach her, she pins me with a fierce expression.

"Don't touch me!" she yells, her voice echoing down the boulevard. "Stop bothering me, Jerk!"

I freeze, taken aback by her sudden outburst. "Nerrisa, I..."

But before I can explain, Grizlor strides up, his formidable presence demanding her attention. "Female, have you seen Amoranaia, my mate?" he asks, his tone urgent.

Nerrisa nods, her expression serious. "Yes, she stayed behind on the Zugunu ship. She blew the shuttle bay doors open so we could rescue the

King. She was going to jump in the water as soon as we were clear."

My heart races at her words but before I can say anything else, Nerrisa turns and grabs the hand of the small Omatu beside her, and they leap into the shabby Zugunu shuttle behind them.

The engines roar to life, and within moments, they are soaring over the ocean, a flash of yellow disappearing into the vast sky toward Silvergate Cay.

I stand there, stunned, the rush of adrenaline still coursing through me. I can't believe she just left like that without saying another word to me. My frustration boils, and I turn away, heading toward the dock for my ship, cursing under my breath.

"Still having mate problems?" Grizlor asks when I catch up to him.

"Blasted Ulae'Zep. The female is impossible. She won't even talk to me," I grumble.

"I heard her talk very loudly to you," he replies, flashing a frown my way.

I shoot him a glare, my patience thinning. "You're not funny, Grizlor!" I turn at the first pier and head to my ship.

"I wasn't trying to be!" he shouts at my back, but I'm already halfway to my boat and ignore him. I don't like this feeling that everything is spiraling out of my control.

The only person I want to talk to is the one who just flew away, and I'm left to stew in my own dark thoughts and frustration.

Once aboard The Helysh, I head to my office. As I walk across the command bridge, I feel the familiar weight of Bruud land on my head and clutch my right horn. The small Meeve chitters and scolds me for being gone for so long.

"Not now, Bruud; I'm having a rough day."

As I drop into my chair, he glides to my desk and jumps back and forth through the holographic screen hovering there. I tap in commands, and a satellite image shows the small Zugunu shuttle carrying my mate.

Bruud reaches up and tries to touch the small boxy shape as it hovers above my desk before the image pans out to a higher altitude.

Despite Nerrisa's difficult nature, I feel pride for her skill in piloting the vessel. We were led to believe Earth didn't have advanced aeronautics, not that the shuttle is more than rudimentary technology.

I grab a new communicator from my desk drawer.

"Call Godefray."

He answers immediately. "Frakyss, my friend, how are you? No major injuries from the bombing, I take it."

"No, how are you and your mate? Are you back in Silvergate City?"

"Yes, we arrived a couple of hours ago. I got Arabella out of the side doors before the whole ceiling collapsed. We flew straight here."

"The Zugunu took my mate along with the King and Grizlor's mate, but they escaped, and my mate is flying toward Silvergate in a Zugunu shuttle. An Omatu female is with her. Would you please make sure she receives a new communicator and gets whatever she needs? She is struggling with the whole mate situation, so I'm not sure how much you should tell her about me being involved."

"Of course, anything you need. I'll keep you apprised of her status."

I sign off and pick up Bruud. "Little buddy, let's head to Silvergate."

Chapter 4 - Nerrisa

The Pilot and the Sprout

The engines thrum beneath me as I grip the controls of the shuttle. Kishi sits wedged beside me in the cramped cockpit, but her presence is reassuring.

The ocean below becomes a blur as we race toward the nearest large landmass, marked on the primitive alien mapping system as Silvergate Cay.

"Just a little further," I coax the ship with my gaze fixed on the display, watching the fuel cells drain with every passing moment. They've got just enough charge to get us there, I hope.

As the shuttle slices through the air, I feel my shoulders hunch with the weight of everything that happened fresh in my mind. I took this shuttle from our kidnappers and flew the King and Kishi out of harm's way.

When we reach civilization again, I need to find a way to regroup and make the most of my freedom by finding Kishi and me a place to live and a pilot job.

"Approaching Silvergate Cay," Kishi affirms, her lilting voice comforting me amid the stress gripping my mind and worry over a water landing. I glance out the windshield, and the sprawling silver futuristic city comes into view, its towering structures gleaming against the amethyst horizon.

With a deep breath, I guide the faltering shuttle toward an open, marked space where similar small shuttles are arranged. My heart pounds as we descend until the landing gear thuds against the surface, and I exhale a shaky breath. We made it. I power down the engines, the hum fading into a heavy silence.

As we disembark, we're met by a team of port workers who assess the shuttle, their eyes wide with curiosity and surprise. "Nice flying," one of them comments.

"Thanks. Is there a place I can catch a taxi?"

He nods and points a short distance away where a shiny red vehicle hovers. As I approach, the small orange driver greets me with a nod and opens the back door. I climb in, and Kishi follows, sitting close.

The driver settles into the front. "Where to?" he asks.

"The governor's residence," I reply, my voice steady even though my insides feel like they're twisting in knots.

The pilot nods, adjusting course. The sleek skimmer banks gracefully, slicing through the sky over Silvergate's glittering skyline. The flight is short but surreal.

Flying vehicles dart between towering buildings in a silent, choreographed dance. They move like they've rehearsed this a thousand times. Maybe they have.

Everything below pulses with color and movement. Buildings shaped like blown glass and laced with chrome twist toward the sky, catching the sunlight in shimmering hues. Public squares burst with alien flora, with petals like stained glass and trees whose leaves shimmer like scales.

The city hums like a living organism.

I should be awed.

Instead, I feel tightness in my chest, and hopeful in the most fragile way.

I am heading to the governor's mansion with no real plan, only instinct. I am hoping Arabella and her mate made it there after the bombing on Epree Island. I have not heard from them since the explosion, just static on every channel and a crawling dread in the pit of my stomach.

If they are not there, I will figure something out. Even if it's only a bench, hallway, or a garden alcove I can borrow for a while. Some corner of the world that feels like I won't be immediately told to leave.

Somewhere that feels remotely safe.

Because I'm not alone anymore.

I glance down at Kishi, curled beside me on the plush seat, her tiny form barely disturbing the fabric. She is so small, only three feet tall, and impossibly delicate, with skin like mossy bark and long white hair that tangles like windblown threads of silk.

She looks like something born from the roots of an enchanted forest.

Right now, she's sleeping, her green lashes resting on her cheeks, one small hand curled around the hem of my sleeve. Her breathing is light, almost soundless. But even in rest, she doesn't let go.

She trusts me. Completely.

That trust terrifies me more than anything else I've faced since leaving Earth.

I rest my hand gently on her back, careful not to wake her, and turn back to the window as the skimmer begins to descend. The tower rises elegant and sprawling in the middle of the city.

This planet is vibrant. Alive in ways I don't understand, and I have no idea how to exist in it.

When the taxi lands on top of one of the highest buildings, I step out. Kishi joins me and hurries to the entrance doors before the strong wind on the roof can sweep her away. I follow close behind.

The doors swing open, and we're met by the handsome Abrauxian I recognize from the ill-fated welcome banquet.

He steps up to the taxi and pays the driver before leading us into a lavish, colorful interior filled with art and décor that speaks of wealth and power. His sharp eyes size us up in an instant. "Nerrisa, I presume?" he asks.

"Yes. Thank you for seeing me, Governor," I reply, my voice steady. "I need your help."

"Of course. I see you have been on the move since the palace bombing," he says, his expression shifting to one of concern as he looks me over. I glance down at the shredded remains of my gown.

I'm filthy and covered with cuts and dried blood. I can only imagine what my face and hair look like.

At that moment, I spot a familiar woman enter the room. "Arabella!" I exclaim, rushing forward to embrace my friend. "I'm so glad you are safe." I release her, realizing I'm getting her pretty white dress dirty.

"Are you okay, Nerrisa? You look like you've been to hell and back."

"I think I have. Aliens kidnapped King Jakvar, Naia, and me. The King called them Zugunu. But we got out, and he is safe on Epree Island again."

She nods. "We saw on the news he was back, and Astrid amassed an ocean army to take out the ones responsible for the bombing and kidnapping."

"Our friends have been very busy," I reply, my mind racing with plans. "Is there a place in the city where I can rent an apartment? And I'm looking for a job as a pilot. Do you know of any opportunities?" I glance between her and her mate.

The governor's brow furrows, but he nods. "There are indeed places to rent. I'll call my realtor friend right away. Once you've showered and eaten, he can take you out to look for a place.

As for piloting, I can assist you in finding a position. We need skilled pilots. After the attack on the palace, many of our freight and transit pilots have already transitioned temporarily to the warships patrolling the galaxy."

"Thank you," I respond, a wave of gratitude washing over me. "I appreciate any help you can provide. I just need to get on my feet and figure out my next steps."

Arabella leans in closer, her expression shifting to one of concern. "You're not thinking of going back to Earth, are you?"

I shake my head. "No. I have nothing to go back for. I was scrubbed from the Mars Mission by my boss, the degenerate Colonel who sexually harassed me for the past six months and whose advances I rejected."

She and the Governor both look at me aghast.

"Are you serious? He harassed you, and when you turned him down, he kicked you off the program?" Arabella asks.

"Yes, the day before we left for our vacation in the Caribbean."

"Oh, Chica, I'm so sorry. That's terrible. I know your heart has been set on traveling in space since we were little girls at school. At least now you can travel a lot farther in space without dealing with a pervert."

Governor Godefray nods in agreement next to her.

Arabella leads Kishi and me to an elevator that takes us several floors down. The corridor is adorned with vibrant artwork and lush plants.

"Your new home is beautiful, Arabella. I bet you love it here."

"I do. Everything is amazing, and I couldn't have asked for a better mate than Godefray." She opens a door into spacious guest quarters.

It's exquisitely decorated, with a wall of windows that offer a breathtaking view of the city sprawling below. The shimmering lights and bustling streets, are a stark contrast to the Renaissance-era royal palace on Epree Island.

"Make yourself at home," she says with a warm smile lighting up her face. "Let me show you how to use the replicator! You need something new to wear," she adds, glancing down at my ruined gown with understanding.

I nod, grateful for her guidance. She demonstrates how to program the machine, explaining the various options available. "Your measurements are in the system from being scanned at the palace. The machine reads the information from your nanos. Just tap in what you want, and it'll create it for you," she explains.

I'm left marveling anew at the technology, feeling excited to be in such an advanced society where anyone can fly into outer space or program what they want to wear into a machine.

After Arabella leaves, Kishi urges me to shower first. I let the steaming hot water wash away the stress of the past day.

For a moment, I simply close my eyes and allow the tension to melt from my body. After a few deep cleansing breaths, I scrub myself and step out, feeling refreshed and almost back to my usual self.

Kishi walks in, her eyes sparkling with excitement as she waits for her turn in the shower.

"Your turn, Kishi." She hurries in, yanking her soiled dress over her head and jumping in the shower immediately.

I program my clothing request into the information screen of the replicator and order cream-colored wide-legged trousers in a soft flowing fabric, pairing them with a matching silk blouse. I've finished dressing when Kishi emerges from the shower, looking radiant.

"Look!" Kishi exclaims, her voice trembling with excitement as she twirls in front of me. Bright green leaves unfurl across her skin, vibrant and full of life where her moss-like flesh once looked dry and brittle. A soft pink flower blooms among the wild tangle of her white hair, its petals open and trembling as if breathing for the first time.

She presses a tiny hand to one of the new leaves, her fingers brushing it with reverence, as if she cannot quite believe it is real.

"I only received a few sips of water a day during my months on the Zugunu ship," she says, her voice catching. For a moment, her bright eyes shimmer with unshed tears. "I thought I would wither away. But now..."

She trails off, smiling through the emotion, and lifts her face toward the overhead light like a flower finally free to grow.

She taps her clothing request into the replicator and pulls out a pretty spring green dress that matches the color of her leaves. She pulls it over her head and twirls, and the knee-length fabric flares around her.

"Beautiful!" I say, impressed with her changed appearance.

Once we're both ready, we leave our room to find a droid waiting to escort us to the dining room, where Arabella and her mate are waiting.

The room is stunning, with a wall of windows overlooking the city on the opposite side from the guest room. A huge ringed purple moon lights up the city's spires in magical splendor.

"Come, sit!" Governor Godefray greets us, gesturing toward chairs on his left. "I hope you're both hungry."

"We are. This is my new friend Kishi. She's been with me since I woke up in the Zugunu shuttle."

"It's a pleasure to meet you, Kishi," the governor says, his tone warm and inviting, and Arabella echoes his words.

As the meal progresses, I allow myself to relax and live in the moment. The governor is an entertaining dinner companion, and the conversation flows.

"Bella, what do you plan to do without your New York restaurant? Have you thought about it?"

She gives the governor a quick, mischievous glance. "I would love to open a restaurant here. The ingredients are incredible, and I cannot wait to start experimenting."

Her smile widens as she adds, "But I will probably have to put someone else in charge, since Godefray seems determined to drag me all over the planet. On Earth, I used to work sixteen to eighteen-hour days, seven days a week. Things are a little different now." She laughs softly and blushes as she gazes up at her mate, the warmth in her eyes unmistakable.

After the meal, Governor Godefray hands me a sleek smartwatch. "This is for you," he explains. "Frakyss set aside funds for you, and they're accessible through this unit. It will help you rent your apartment and purchase furniture and a replicator."

I feel a rush of gratitude. "Thank you so much. That's very thoughtful of him, and this means a lot."

"You might want to consider getting a synthetic housekeeper," Arabella adds. "With your new job, you'll be traveling a lot. You'll want to make sure Kishi doesn't get lonely while you're gone."

"That's a great idea," I agree, envisioning how much easier it would make things. Unlike Arabella, I'm a terrible cook and have no desire to be tied to an apartment when I can be flying.

After dinner, the rooftop doorbell chimes, and we follow the governor. A striking tall blue male with majestic horns and vibrant, sparkling eyes introduces himself.

"I am your realtor, Stel'Xon. I have several apartments to show you this evening."

"Thank you. I appreciate you coming out during the evening hours to take us around. This is Kishi, and I am Nerrisa Byrne."

"It's my pleasure." He gestures for us to follow him out to the landing pad, where his shining white vehicle awaits. I give Bella a quick goodbye hug and thank her and Godefray for their hospitality.

Stel'Xon takes us to see several apartments, each more beautiful than the one before. But when we arrive at one right next to the spaceport, in a building called the Celestial Spire, I know we've found the perfect place.

It's a show unit on the 107th floor, all glass and chrome, situated near the top of the building. The view is breathtaking, and the included furnishings are modern, minimalist, and sleek. I feel at home as soon as I walk through the door.

"This is it," I whisper, my heart racing as we view the multi-level unit. "What do you think, Kishi?"

"I love it. The windows are amazing. I can't wait to see the bright sunshine lighting up this whole place."

"Me too. Stel'Xon, we'll take this one."

"Excellent. Please review and sign this contract and transfer the fees." He holds out a small digital tablet, and I review the simple document, sign the agreement, and pay the fees. As soon as I finish, a weight is lifted from my shoulders.

"Welcome to Silvergate Cay. You can order a replicator and housekeeping bot from this tablet." He flicks through several screens to show me what's available, and I make my selections. Within an hour, the replicator and robot are delivered and set up.

Feeling a wave of satisfaction, I make a quick video call to Arabella, eager to let her know how things are going. When she picks up, her face lights up with a smile. "Did you find a new place?"

"Yes, it's gorgeous! It's also right next to the spaceport, so when I get a job, I can walk to it. Kishi and I are settling in already. Thank you for all your help."

"Of course! It's what friends are for," she replies before Godefray enters the screen next to her.

"I'm sending you the contact for a potential pilot job," he says, a proud smile creeping onto his face. "You can start in two days. The word is already out that you piloted that junky Zugunu shuttle all the way from Epree Island. Several shipping companies have been fighting over who got the first chance at hiring you."

My heart leaps at the news, a rush of excitement flooding through me. "Thank you, Governor! I can't wait to get started."

As I end the call, I turn to Kishi, who's already exploring our new replicator with wide eyes. "We did it," I whisper, a smile breaking across my face.

Chapter 5 - Frakyss

Close Enough to Burn

"Governor Godefray, thank you for helping Nerrisa get settled in. I trust you kept our conversation private?"

"Of course, my friend. I am glad you gave us a heads-up that she would be arriving."

He leans in slightly, lowering his voice. "She has no idea you will be her new boss. She is scheduled to start in two days, just like you asked. Her contact is your operations manager, Evruik."

He pauses, his mouth tightening. "At dinner this evening, she told us her previous boss on Earth made unwanted advances toward her. When she pushed him away, he kicked her off a major project to a nearby planet. It happened not long before the Ulae'Zep took them."

His jaw clenches. "I can only imagine the damage that left behind. No wonder she is running from you."

I feel my claws dig into the polished wood surface of my desk. If I find out who harassed her, I will fly to Earth and end him myself.

"Thank you for that information. That explains her aversion to being touched. Did Stel'Xon handle her apartment needs?"

"Yes. Thank you for giving me his contact information. He took her to view the properties, and she took the one near the spaceport for convenience. It came furnished, and she and the Omatu are already settled in. She said they rescued the Omatu from the Zugunu ship. I thought they were extinct! We should ask the Ulae'Zep if they know of any others hidden away."

"That's a good point. I'll talk with King Jakvar about it tomorrow during our call. Keep me posted on anything else that comes up." I sign off and lean back in my chair with my fingers steepled under my chin.

At least Nerrisa is safe. I take deep, calming breaths to stave off the rage that creeps up when I think about that disgusting human male trying to force himself on her.

I picture his face for only a second before the blood rises so fast, I see red. Not even space would be far enough to shield him from me if I ever laid eyes on him. I would make him understand what it feels like to be powerless under a stronger hand.

I stand at my office window, gazing out at the bustling spaceport below. The sleek ships coming and going are a testament to the thriving interstellar trade that's the lifeblood of our planet. The tang of ion fuel hangs in the air even through the thick glass.

The low hum of cargo loaders and incoming transmissions vibrates faintly through the floor, a reminder that life moves forward whether or not my heart keeps pace.

But today, my mind is far from business matters.

This morning, Nerrisa will walk through my company's doors, ready to start her new job as a pilot, unaware I'm behind her employment or that I've orchestrated this opportunity to keep her close while giving her the autonomy she craves.

The irony isn't lost on me. I'm manipulating circumstances to be near a woman who abhors me.

I turn from the window, my reflection catching in the polished glass. The scars etched across my skin tell a painful story of my early youth, a battle for survival that I fought and won.

If I don't win this skirmish with Nerrisa, the new scars will cut much deeper and be more agonizing.

Bruud shifts restlessly on his perch, his tiny claws digging into the branch of the Jinlu tree as he watches me. His thick white fur fluffs up slightly, a sure sign he senses my mood. He stretches his limbs and glides down in a slow arc, landing lightly on the edge of my desk.

I reach out and let him nose at my fingers, his violet eyes wide and unblinking.

"You feel it too, don't you, little one?" I murmur. "She is close, but still so far away."

Bruud chitters quietly and presses his small head against my knuckles, a soft reminder that I am not as alone as I feel.

"What do you think? Shall we get some work done before our female arrives for work?"

Chapter 6 - Nerrisa

No Longer Grounded

I wake early, with excitement buzzing through me as I prepare for my first day on the job. The past two days have been a whirlwind of settling into the apartment and exploring Silvergate City with Kishi. Now, as I stand in front of the mirror, adjusting my black flight suit, I feel a surge of pride. This is it, my chance to prove myself in this amazing new world.

"Good luck today!" Kishi calls from her seat at the breakfast bar. Her leaves are vibrant green in the morning light and pink buds are popping up on the thin branches on her arms. She's sipping a seaweed smoothie, and her thin frame is already starting to fill out after her long imprisonment.

"Thanks, Kishi," I reply with a grin. "Hold down the fort while I'm gone, okay?"

I grab a quick breakfast from the replicator and head out, my steps light as I make my way to the spaceport. The day is sunny and breezy with the briny tang of the ocean in the air. The walkway is filled with a variety of aliens in all shapes, sizes, and colors. I smile and nod, unable to hold back my joy.

The entry terminal bustles with activity as I weave through the crowds. My heart races with a mix of excitement and nervousness. It's been a long time since I've started a new job, and I'm determined to make a good impression.

I spot a tall, lanky Abrauxian male holding a datapad with my name on it. As I approach, he gives me a polite nod. "Nerrisa Byrne?" he asks, his voice a low rumble.

"That's me," I reply, trying to keep my voice steady.

"I'm Evruik, operations manager for Galactic Freight. Welcome aboard." He gestures for me to follow him into a glass and steel private section through a series of security checkpoints, each more advanced than the last, before arriving at a nondescript door marked 'Galactic Freight - Employee Entrance.'

He slides his communicator against the security pad, and the door slides open. As we step inside, I'm struck by the contrast between the chaos of the spaceport and the calm efficiency of the office. Holographic displays flicker with flight paths and cargo manifests, and various aliens focus on the data from their workstations.

"This way," Evruik says, leading me down a corridor. "We'll start with a quick tour, then get you set up with your credentials and ship assignment."

My heart skips a beat at the mention of my own ship.

He shows me dispatch, the crew lounge, and a bustling maintenance bay. "This is where all the magic happens," he says, leading me into the main control center. It's a vast room filled with screens and consoles, each one displaying real-time information about the fleet.

"Wow," I breathe, my eyes wide as I take in the sight. "This is amazing."

"Just wait until you see your ship," Evruik grins, enjoying my reaction. "Let's get your credentials from the security office, and we'll go see *The Tabris*. She's a real beauty."

We take an elevator up a level and enter the security offices for Galactic Freight. A huge leonine female approaches. "Welcome Nerrisa, I am Eri. Would you please fill out this form and press your thumb on this button so we can get a nano download for your personnel file? Then we can issue your credentials and company access."

I take the datapad she holds out and settle into one of the chairs in the small lobby. The furniture is sleek but surprisingly comfortable. Across the room, Evruik stands chatting with the stunning feline woman, their voices low and easy.

I focus on the screen in my hands.

A series of questions appears, asking for my educational history, flight background, family connections, length of time on Abrauxia, and reason for being here.

The last question makes me pause.

My thumb hovers over the screen as I weigh my options. I cannot exactly type *'kidnapped from Earth and genetically bonded to an alien'* without raising a few eyebrows.

But my instincts from my time in the Earth military kick in. Honesty matters, especially in official records. Lies have a way of surfacing when you least want them to, and the last thing I need is to ruin this opportunity or get myself sent back to Earth.

Slowly, I type the truth, even if it tastes bitter. *Bonded mate of Frakyss.*

Once I finish the last of the form, I press my thumb to the glowing button. A sharp prick stings my finger, quick and clinical. The unit chimes, and I stand, handing the datapad back to Eri.

She disappears through a side door, leaving Evruik and me waiting in the quiet lobby. The silence stretches, heavy enough to tighten the muscles across my shoulders.

When she returns, she carries a sleek black card between her fingers.

"Here you go," she says with an easy smile. "This will give you access to everything you need. Hold it against your communicator to transfer the access. That way you will not always have to carry the card."

I take it carefully, the smooth surface cool against my fingers.

My training whispers caution in the back of my mind. Anything that grants access can also track movements, monitor activities, and report back to someone higher up. Nothing is ever given without strings.

Eri does not seem to notice my hesitation. She presses the card firmly into my palm and says, "Welcome to the team," her voice bright and genuine.

I offer a smile in return, but it feels tight around the edges.

One step forward. Eyes open. Walls up.

I take the card from her furry gold fingers and can't stop the grin on my face. "Thank you so much, Eri. It's a pleasure to meet you."

"The pleasure is mine, Nerrisa." She responds. I nod and follow Evruik to the elevator, and we go down multiple floors to the hangar level. My heart hammers in my chest as the elevator doors open.

There it is, gleaming in the bay. A huge sleek black ship, aerodynamic and futuristic, better than anything I could ever have imagined. Evruik leads me closer, and I gaze up. "She's beautiful," I whisper, awe filling my voice.

"She's equipped with everything you need for intergalactic freight. You'll love flying the Gen5-Axiam. Let's take a quick look inside,"

Evruik suggests, leading me up the crew stairs to the cockpit.

I sit in the comfortable black leather pilot's seat. The controls are laid out in an organized way, backlit, and ready for me to take her out. I feel relaxed and at home for the first time in months.

After touring the rest of the enormous ship, Evruik explains the training schedule. "You'll spend the next five days in the simulators to get familiar with the controls and operations of The Tabris. We also have a nano memory upload to install the information into your brain before you start training."

"Excellent. I can't wait to get started."

"You'll be flying in no time," he assures me. "I heard how you piloted that junky Zugunu shuttle all the way from Epree Island. I can't believe you made it this far."

The blush creeps up my face. It's going to be nice having a boss who is proud of my accomplishments and not trying to grope me at every turn.

As the days unfold, I immerse myself in the training protocol. The simulators are as impressive as I expected on an advanced planet.

I spend hours learning the ins and outs of The Tabris. I navigate through various scenarios, from routine cargo runs to emergency situations, each simulation pushing me to adapt and grow as a pilot.

The nano memory system works seamlessly, advancing my knowledge with each day. My confidence builds as I become more familiar with my new ship's systems and controls. All my past experience with test planes on Earth pales in comparison to what I'm able to accomplish in a few short days on Abrauxia.

On the fifth day, I finish my last simulation, exhilarated and exhausted. I step out of the unit, a sense of accomplishment washing over me. I've learned as much as I can, and now I'm ready to take *The Tabris* out into space.

I walk through the hangar doors and just stand, staring up at my ship.

Is it possible to fall in love with a machine?

Chapter 7 - Frakyss

Wings He Gave Her

I stare at Nerrisa's blissful expression as she gazes at her ship. I shouldn't be jealous, but I wish she looked at me like that. Even if she knew I purchased the ship for her as part of her mate package, and it's not just an assigned company vessel, I know she wouldn't.

I heave a frustrated sigh.

I've watched her on the video feeds for the past five days, and I'm proud of her accomplishments as a pilot. She's got uncanny instincts, and I've already asked Dyebarth to work on a neural interface between her and *The Tabris*, and the half dozen cargo shuttles and two Shadowstrikes in her ship's bay.

Evruik steps into my office, a quick grin flashing across his face.

"Nerrisa finished her training today. Sharpest pilot I have seen in a long time."

He hands me a datapad, already queued up with the details.

"We have a couple of options for her first assignment, but I recommend starting simple. A supply run to Roxus. Construction materials for rebuilding the Royal Palace Great Hall."

He taps the screen once for emphasis.

"She will need to align and secure *The Tabris* at the Qirath Drift space dock, then ferry the cargo down to the landing pad using the shuttles. Straightforward, but a good test under real conditions."

He looks up, waiting.

"Your thoughts?"

"Yes, that's a good idea. It will give her hands-on experience with the ship, to help her gain confidence for larger hauls from other planets and stations. Why don't you assign Eri as her ship's security officer? Eri requested a role on a ship so she can travel. They will make a good team."

"Excellent idea. I'll make that assignment now and get Nerrisa set up for the delivery tomorrow."

He leaves my office, and Bruud glides to my desk and stares at me. I take a freeze-dried zucress out of my top desk drawer and hold it out to him. His little eyes light up, and he snatches the small pink fruit, gliding away to enjoy it in his tree.

As I settle back into my chair, the communicator on my desk chimes with an incoming call. The holographic display flickers to life, revealing King Jakvar's regal visage. His silver eyes gleam with their usual intensity, and the intricate mate marks adorning his face and neck seem to shimmer in the light.

"Frakyss, my friend," he greets, his deep voice resonating through the room. "I hope this call finds you well."

I incline my head respectfully. "Your Majesty, it's good to see you. How may I be of service?"

The King's expression softens slightly. "I wanted to tell you I took your suggestion to heart. I contacted the Ulae'Zep about locating more Omatu. It seems your mate's little friend isn't the last of her kind after all."

My hearts quicken at the news. "That's excellent, Your Majesty. Kishi will be overjoyed to hear she's not alone."

"Indeed," Jakvar nods, a rare smile playing at the corners of his mouth. "The Ulae'Zep already located a small colony on a distant moon. They're arranging for their transport to Abrauxia, where they can thrive safely."

I lean forward, intrigued. "That's wonderful news. I'm sure they'll adapt well to our world. The climate should be perfect for them. Have you decided where on the planet they will settle?"

"Romrey or Epree would be best with their temperate climates. I've asked Governor Vrens to propose a 50-acre inland tract on Romrey for settlement."

The king's gaze sharpens, his silver eyes seeming to pierce through the hologram. "And speaking of adapting, how is your mate? I understand she's begun her new role as a pilot for Galactic Freight."

The familiar surge of pride wells up in me. "Nerrisa is excelling, Your Majesty. Her skills in the cockpit are extraordinary. She's completed her training in record time, mastering our most advanced systems with an ease I've never seen before."

Jakvar raises an eyebrow, clearly impressed. "High praise indeed, coming from you, Frakyss. I look forward to seeing her capabilities firsthand."

"You won't have to wait long. She'll be docking at the Qirath Drift space station tomorrow and using cargo shuttles to bring down supplies to rebuild the Great Hall. It's a complex operation, but I have no doubt she and her crew will handle it with ease."

The king's eyes narrow slightly, a knowing look crossing his face. "You speak of her with great admiration, Frakyss. Yet, if I recall correctly, there were some initial difficulties between you two."

I sigh, the warmth in my chest cooling slightly. "Yes, Your Majesty. Nerrisa is resistant to the idea of our bond. She fiercely protects her independence, largely due to her superior commander on Earth trying to physically force himself on her. When she rebuffed his advances, he kicked her off the space travel program she was a part of.

King Jakvar nods thoughtfully. "Are you thinking of paying that male a visit?"

"I am."

"Good. In the meantime, don't keep your role as her boss a secret for too long. Better to start earning her trust with honesty."

Chapter 8 - Nerrisa

Roots and Wings

"Kishi, I'm done with my training and have my first cargo pickup tomorrow! I'm flying to Roxus for construction materials to rebuild the Great Hall on Epree Island."

"That's exciting. I can't wait to hear about it. I have news too!" She gets up from her seat in front of the windows and follows me up the stairs to my bedroom.

"I start my new job tomorrow." Her beautiful little face is alight with happiness.

I yank my tank top over my head and stare at her. "You got a job? I didn't even know you wanted one."

"Of course I do. I have many skills. Did you know there is an amazing botanical garden right in the middle of Silvergate City? One of the largest buildings houses plants from all over the universe.

The facility is in desperate need of a botanical specialist to focus on the cultivation of rare plants. It's my dream job!" She's never looked so happy and animated.

"Kishi, that's wonderful. I'm so excited for you. How will you get to the city center?"

"A small shuttle transports employees and guests multiple times a day. It will pick me up every morning on the roof of our building and will bring me back in the evening. It's included in my employment package."

"That's perfect!" I embrace my small friend. "I know you're going to love being among all the plants. When I have a day off, I'll come visit you at work."

"I look forward to that."

We order dinner delivered to celebrate our new careers and sit at our fancy dining table for the first time.

"This is so exciting. Do you mind me asking a personal question, Kishi?"

"Ask anything."

"How old are you? You don't have to answer if you don't want to. Women on Earth are offended if you ask their age." I grin at her.

"I am six hundred and fifty-two UPC years old."

I feel my eyes bulge out of my head. I snap my jaw shut when I realize it's hanging open. Kishi giggles at my expression.

"Why are you surprised? How old are you?"

"Twenty-five! I'll be twenty-six in a few months."

She ogles at me. "What? You are a child!"

I laugh. "No, my kind is quick to mature, and our average lifespan for an Aquar'thyn is about two or three hundred years."

"That's so sad. I hope your life will be prolonged living here on Abrauxia."

I nod, though I can't imagine the small youthful creature sitting next to me is over six hundred years old. It boggles the mind.

"Do you mind telling me about yourself? Where you're from, and how you ended up on Abrauxia?"

"The short version is the Zugunu attacked Sylvaris, our planet, about seven years ago. They learned that the blood of Omatu creates a powerful and addictive hallucinogenic to many alien species, and they killed most of my people within a couple of years, draining away our life's blood. They ravaged our planet for resources in the process. Small pockets of us hid in remote areas, but they captured me several months ago."

I stare at her, unable to process the horror. "Kishi, I am so sorry. I don't know what to say."

"Why are you apologizing? You and your friend rescued me. The Zugunu were taking my blood and giving it to the Ven'aens so they could try to make a synthetic version."

"I guess it's an Earth thing. We apologize when something horrible happens to a friend to let them know we care."

"Then thank you. Thank you for rescuing me, and thank you for being my friend and letting me live with you in this beautiful city and apartment." She reaches out and puts her hand on mine. There's an unusual vibration of energy through her touch.

"Kishi, you don't have to thank me. You are my friend, and I love having you here. Now, let's eat this amazing food. Maybe I ought to become vegetarian like you, see if I live to be over six hundred years old."

I flash her a grin.

The Tabris' engines provide a steady hum beneath me as I navigate her through the clear morning sky of Abrauxia. The lilac hues fade to purple and finally black as I leave the planet's atmosphere behind.

For the first time, I'm piloting a ship into outer space, and the thrill is everything I thought it would be. It might be a routine cargo run for the Abrauxians, but to me, this is the culmination of my lifelong dream.

As I approach Roxus, the horizontal rings of the moon below me look almost solid enough to walk on.

Soon the moon's surface comes into view, the majestic spires of Whitevale Citadel rising like a crown against the stark pink icy landscape. I take a moment to admire its beauty before lining up for my descent.

The air traffic controller directs me to a landing pad near the row of enormous warehouses a short distance from the Citadel. I guide the enormous ship down with measured precision.

Once we're on the ground, I initiate the cargo loading sequence. The main areas of the ship are sealed from the cold atmosphere of the moon, which lacks enough oxygen to support the lifeforms on my ship. I watch lumbering yeti aliens lift giant stacks of construction materials and carry them into the cargo bay.

Eri, my security officer, told me the gravity on Roxus is much lighter than on Abrauxia, and that's why it's a great shipping hub for this quadrant of the universe.

A familiar face pops up on the screen for the airlock into the ship.

"Adeline!" I exclaim, surprised. "What are you doing here?"

"When I heard you came to Roxus for a shipment, I wanted to see you!"

"Enter the airlock, and I'll be right there to let you in." I flick the control to open the door for her and close it, triggering the airlock sequence. I race through the ship to let her in.

"Nerrisa, it's so good to see you." She embraces me and I feel the chill from her coat through my flight suit.

"Wow, you're freezing!"

"I'm getting used to it. Minus twenty Fahrenheit today. A balmy summer day on Roxus."

She grins and removes the breather from her nose and tucks it in her pocket.

"Come on, let me show you The Tabris!" I lead her through the ship, showing the passenger sections as well as my living quarters and ending at the cockpit. "Isn't she beautiful?"

"Absolutely! I love the sleek design, and she's gorgeous inside. From outside, she looks like a giant Manta Ray with those two fins sticking out on the front."

"You're right! I didn't even think of that. How appropriate for an aquatic pilot."

"You know, the Abrauxians are aware that we're shifters. They didn't think anything of it. That's kind of refreshing, considering the secrecy required on Earth."

I nod, mulling over her words. "It's nice to be accepted. Here, we can be ourselves, and no one considers us strange."

We meet Eri in the hallway, and Adeline gapes at the feline female in her black security uniform.

"Adeline, this is Eri, my security officer for The Tabris. Eri, this is my dear friend Adeline, who came here from Earth at the same time I did."

"It's a pleasure to meet you, Adeline." Eri nods at my friend. "Captain, loading is complete. We can depart when you are ready."

"Thank you. I'll escort Adeline to the airlock."

"Oh, did you hear that Astrid and Jakvar are going to have an Earth-style wedding in two months when the Great Hall is rebuilt? We're all invited to attend. I'm so excited, and it's the first official wedding from the surprise bondings."

"That's great news. I guess since I'm the one hauling the construction supplies for their venue, I better get them delivered." I hug her tight. "I've missed you."

"I've missed you too. We'll probably see each other a lot more often now that you'll be coming to the Citadel as part of your job. Maybe next time, you'll be here long enough to come in and see the marketplace. It's probably one of the seven wonders of Abrauxia."

She flashes me a grin before entering the airlock. She pulls the breather out of her pocket, places it at her nostrils, and nods for me to cycle the unit for her to exit.

Chapter 9 - Frakyss

The Royal Wedding

"Nerrisa, you look radiant," I approach my mate as she walks through the palace gates with Kishi at her side. "Kishi, it is a delight to see you again."

"Frakyss," Nerrisa acknowledges me, and the little Omatu waves. I fall into step next to them, and we enter the newly completed Great Hall through the side doors.

"Our seats are near the front." I gesture toward the second row, already filling with Abrauxians and their Earth mates.

Kishi leads the way, her small frame slipping easily into an open seat beside Arabella. Nerrisa follows, brushing her hand over the back of the chair before settling in. I slide into the next seat, the polished material cool against my legs.

Dyebarth drops heavily into the spot on my right, the chair creaking under his weight, and his mate settles in beside him with a soft rustle of fabric. Around us, the low hum of conversation and the occasional scrape of chairs fills the air, a steady rhythm of a gathering coming to life.

The new Great Hall is much like the old one but more modern, with windows on all sides that extend up to the steeply pitched ceiling. It's almost twilight, and the chandeliers cast a warm glow over the burgeoning crowd.

Video drones zip through the air, and one follows King Jakvar and his brother, Prince Theovesh, onto the raised platform in front of us.

I glance at Nerrisa sitting next to me, watching the crowd with wonder. She is even more beautiful in person. My hearts swell with pride. It's been a struggle to keep my distance these past two months, but I watch the company video feeds to catch glimpses of her coming and going.

She's the best pilot I have on staff and a dedicated worker. She turns and catches me watching her, and her pale cheeks darken.

"How are you, Frakyss?" she asks.

"I am well, Nerrisa. It's good to see you." Before I can say more, a hush falls over the crowd, and everyone stands. Queen Astrid walks up the center aisle, dressed all in white. When she reaches the steps onto the platform, Lord Chyrgog guides her up, then returns to his seat in front of us.

Elder Xirsid tells everyone to be seated, and I watch the ceremony with interest, wondering if this is something Nerrisa wants. They repeat vows to each other and exchange rings. "I now pronounce you husband and wife. You may kiss the bride." The elder pronounces at the end. Jakvar wraps his arms around Astrid and presses his lips to hers.

My blood heats as I glance down at Nerrisa, imagining my lips on hers.

Everyone around us jumps to their feet, clapping and cheering. I stand and watch the newly married couple leave the great hall.

Grashetas open the large glass doors along the north side of the room, and the courtyard is filled with small round tables and chairs arranged in the center. At one end is a large banquet and at the other is a wooden platform connected to a stage with avian musicians playing soft music.

Nerrisa's eyes are sparkling as she takes in the trees hung with twinkling lights. A Grasheta female guides us to one of the tables near the center and we take our seats along with Dyebarth and his mate.

"Makena, it is so good to see you!" Nerrisa comments to the female.

"It's good to see you too, Nerrisa. Where have you been keeping yourself? I haven't seen you since that ill-fated welcome dinner."

"I got a job piloting the most beautiful ship in the galaxy. Mostly hauling freight but sometimes passengers too. You wouldn't believe how amazing all the planets in this galaxy are and the diversity of beings on them."

"That reminds me," Dyebarth says. "The neural link for you to connect with your ship is complete. It can be installed right away."

Shize, I forgot to tell Dyebarth to keep that secret, and now Nerrisa is staring at him, confused.

"What neural links?"

"The ones Frakyss requested several months ago. He was so impressed with your abilities as a pilot that he felt a neural link to your ship would be appropriate." Dyebarth glances at me, and I give an almost imperceptible shake of my head.

"Why would Frakyss make that request, and how does he know what kind of pilot I am? We haven't seen each other since right after the Great Hall was bombed." She narrows her green eyes at me with suspicion, and everyone at the table stares at me, awaiting my explanation.

This is not how I intended to tell her everything. Certainly not at the party to celebrate the royal wedding. Now I've been outed and need to explain before we've had time to build a better rapport.

I clear my throat. "I asked Dyebarth to design the neural connection between you and *The Tabris* because she's your ship. I own Galactic Freight."

Her confusion slowly morphs into understanding and anger flashes in her expressive eyes.

"You are my BOSS?" she shouts.

I nod, sitting there embarrassed as people at the surrounding tables glance our way.

"When were you planning to tell me this tidbit of news?" she glares up at me.

"I don't know. I guess after you settled in on Abrauxia and hated me less." I hang my head feeling ridiculous now for misleading her. You can't build trust with someone by hiding the truth. "I'm sorry. I really didn't think it through. But I didn't think you'd accept the job if you knew, and you're an amazing pilot. The best in the company."

"I can't believe you were so sneaky and didn't just talk to me."

"I did try to talk to you. You took off with Kishi and refused to listen to anything I had to say."

"That's no excuse!" She jumps up and stomps toward the gates of the courtyard. Kishi gives me a sympathetic glance and runs after her friend.

"I am sorry. I didn't realize your request was secret, Frakyss." Dyebarth apologizes. His mate has her small, graceful hand on his arm and is nodding her head.

"Don't worry, it's not your fault. It was going to come out at some point. I hadn't figured out a way to tell her. Though I did hope there'd be time to get to know her better before I broke the news."

Makena gives me a sympathetic nod. "Be patient with her. Nerrisa has always wanted to be a pilot more than anything else since we were young girls. She lived and breathed flying. She jumped off the dormitory roof when we were ten and broke her collarbone, positive she could fly."

"I'm glad she at least does her flying in a ship now. I'd hate to see her jump off the roof of her one-hundred-and-eight-story apartment building." That breaks the tension, and we all laugh.

"Evruik, please bring Nerrisa to my office when she arrives this morning." I stand at my office window, watching ships coming and going from the spaceport.

"Yes sir," he responds. "I expect her anytime. We'll be right up."

Bruud chitters from his perch in the Jinlu tree, no doubt picking up on my tension. "It's fine little one. No reason for you to be stressed too."

I'm at my desk reviewing transport contracts when I hear a tap at the open door. I glance up, and Evruik stands there with Nerrisa by his side.

"Come in, Nerrisa, please have a seat." Evruik nods before leaving.

As usual, my mate's flight suit does nothing to hide her beautiful figure, and her hair cascades down in thick waves. She sits at the edge of the chair on the other side of my desk, glancing around. After a few moments she looks up at me, fear in her eyes.

"Is something wrong, Nerrisa?"

She nibbles her bottom lip and clenches her hands tight together. "Are you going to fire me?"

I'm surprised by her question, mistakenly having thought her nerves were from being alone in a room with me despite the open door. "No, of course not. Why would I fire you?"

"Because I keep rejecting you."

"Nerrisa, I am not dishonorable like your boss on Earth. Your employment does not hinge on our relationship. I'm actually quite angry a male treated you in that way, and I'll end him if you tell me where to find him."

Surprise lightens her expression, and she lets out a relieved laugh. "I'm sure you can find him on Mars within a year or so." I file that information away for future reference.

"I called you to my office to apologize for not being upfront when you came for your first day.

I didn't want you to feel you owed me anything for hiring you. I understand you felt trapped when you woke on Abrauxia to find you had a bond mate after your past experience. The Ulae'Zep were supposed to allow a UPC representative to negotiate our bond, and you would have had the option to accept or refuse. Unfortunately, once our DNA was combined and my mate marks appeared, refusal was no longer an option. That oversite is already being addressed with them by King Jakvar."

"I appreciate that, in addition to you providing my employment and keeping me on despite this relationship mess." She waves her hand between us, emphasizing her point.

A flash of white passes over her shoulder and Bruud lands on my desk in front of Nerrisa and flicks his fluffy tail while staring up at her startled face.

"Bruud, come here. You scared Nerrisa." He glances over his shoulder at me but turns toward her again and doesn't move. Nerrisa leans forward and is almost nose to nose with the little Meeve.

"Aren't you the cutest little flyer?" She coos at him, and he sits up on his hind legs. "Can I pet him?"

"Of course. Here's a zucress treat for him." I hold out the pink fruit and the brush of her fingers when she takes it, sends sparks shooting up my arm.

She gasps as she yanks the treat away and gives me a suspicious frown. Bruud taps her hand with his small paw to get her attention back on him and the treat. She opens her hand to let him take it and strokes his soft fur while he munches and purrs.

"What a sweet baby you are, Bruud." Once finished eating, he stretches out on his stomach, his limbs fully extended, and closes his vivid violet eyes.

My communicator chimes and a few seconds later, so does Nerrisa's. We both glance at the caller and are surprised to see King Jakvar is requesting a meeting. He and Queen Astrid have barely started their honeymoon on Roxus.

I glance at her and we both accept the call and find ourselves seated at a holographic round table with other Abrauxians and their mates.

"We didn't expect to hear from you so soon." Prince Theovesh comments. The rest of us chime in with our agreement.

"When we were in the market this morning, a starving young Shassa cub approached Astrid. A Shike had gotten him at an orphanage on Coprinus-LV3. XVR-2 was able to trace their movement. They stowed away on a Zibarth cargo ship.

During the forty-two-hour flight to Roxus, the Shite stole credits and jewelry from the crew. He ate and drank in their cafeteria but withheld both water and food from the child." Jakvar explains. My blood boils at the thought of that poor child.

"Ladies, can we organize a children's center somewhere on Abrauxia, where we can house the children from the orphanage?" Queen Astrid asks. "XVR-2 discovered the orphanage director and several of his workers have been selling the children!"

Arabella responds immediately. "Godefray and I will house the children on Silvergate Cay. We toured an unoccupied manor house and grounds just yesterday that would be perfect for children."

Nerrisa pipes up, "Frakyss and I will transport the children." She glares at me as if daring me to argue, but I nod in agreement. "Please send the coordinates to my ship, The Tabris, and clear the way for our arrival on Coprinus-LV3."

Nerrisa's communicator pings within moments, and she glances at her wrist. Her gaze goes distant before she adds, "We will arrive there in forty hours. Nerrisa Byrne, out." She taps her device and disconnects from the call, standing and looking at me expectantly.

I disconnect and stand too. Bruud jumps up and glances between us before jumping on Nerrisa's shoulder, gripping the collar of her flight suit.

"Traitor," I mutter at him, and I catch Nerrisa grinning as she walks out of the room ahead of me.

Chapter 10 - Nerrisa

The Hidden Ones

As I stride out of Frakyss's office, my mind races with preparations for the rescue mission. The weight of Bruud on my shoulder is oddly comforting as I make my way to *The Tabris*.

"Eri," I call out as I enter the ship. "We have an urgent mission. Can you get the standby crew onboard and have them gather supplies for potentially malnourished children? We're heading to an orphanage on Coprinus-LV3 to evacuate the children. Arrival, forty UPC hours. Contact XVR-2 for further details about the children."

Eri's eyes widen, but she nods. "Of course, Captain. I'll get right on it."

I head to the cockpit, settling into the pilot's seat with practiced ease. As I begin the pre-flight checks, I hear heavy footsteps behind me. Frakyss enters, ducking slightly to avoid hitting his horns on the doorframe.

"Mind if I take the copilot's seat?" Without waiting for my response, he sits beside me, and Bruud jumps to him to dangle off one horn, chittering with excitement.

"Nice hat," I wink at him and finish programming the trip coordinates into the navigational system. He chuckles and watches the video feeds showing the last of the crew entering the ship and sealing the door.

He triggers the drone to pull *The Tabris* to the authorized take-off pad while I complete the flight check sequence, and after a short wait for clearance, we ascend through the layers of lilac sky.

As we break through Abrauxia's atmosphere, the vastness of space unfolds before us. I engage the warp drive, and the stars stretch into streaks of light.

The familiar hum of the engines settles around us, and I lean back in my seat, allowing myself a moment to breathe.

"You handled that well," Frakyss says, his deep voice breaking the silence. "Your quick coordination for the rescue mission."

I glance at him, surprised by the compliment. "Thanks. I couldn't bear the thought of those children in danger at the hands of those who are supposed to be taking care of them. I have some experience with rescue missions back on Earth, in the military."

He nods, his expression somber. "It's admirable. Your compassion, I mean."

As an awkward silence falls between us, I focus on the control panel, double-checking our course despite knowing it's unnecessary. Finally, I can't take the tension anymore.

"Look, Frakyss," I say, turning to face him. "I know I've been difficult. But I appreciate you giving me space and not pushing things. This whole situation has been a lot to process."

He meets my gaze, his red eyes intense but not unkind. "I understand, Nerrisa. I never meant to deceive you about the company. I just wanted you to have the chance to fly, to pursue your passion without feeling obligated to me."

I nod, considering his words. "I get that. But in the future, I'd prefer honesty. Even if you think I won't like what you have to say."

"Agreed," he says, a small smile tugging at his lips. "No more secrets between us."

As if to punctuate the moment, Bruud chirps and glides from Frakyss's horn to land on my lap. I chuckle and stroke his soft fur. "I think someone approves of our truce."

Frakyss laughs, the sound warm and rich. "He's always had good instincts about people."

We settle into a more comfortable silence, the endless expanse of space stretching out before us. As the hours pass, we talk intermittently about the mission and our respective roles on Abrauxia and even share a few stories from our pasts. It's friendly, and not once does he try to touch me. I find myself relaxing bit by bit in Frakyss's presence.

Three-quarters of the way through our journey, Eri enters the cockpit. "Captain, we've prepared the open passenger seating section for the children with age-appropriate meals programmed into the replicators. Datapads, headphones, and bedding have been placed on each seat. XVR-2 sent details that there will be 47 children total ranging from five years to teens. The medical team is on standby as well. I reprogrammed the flight assistant bot with the nanny module. I don't have a clue of how to care for children unless they are delinquents needing to be arrested."

I laugh. "Let's hope that won't be necessary. Great work, Eri. " I say, impressed by her efficiency. "We're making excellent time and should arrive in ten more hours. Make sure everyone is rested and ready to go. We probably won't get much sleep once the children are onboard."

"I'll let the crew know, Captain." She leaves the cockpit, already talking to the crew on her communicator.

"You should get some rest too, Frakyss." I glance at him. He's only been up a few times over the past thirty hours.

"Abrauxians don't require much sleep. I'm happy to stay here while you rest, though."

"I'm good. I can doze for a while here.

As we approach Coprinus-LV3, the planet comes into view...a swirling mass of greens and browns beneath wispy white clouds. I begin the landing sequence, guiding *The Tabris* through the atmosphere with ease.

We touch down on a landing pad near several dilapidated buildings surrounded by a large rusty wire fence. My heart clenches at the sight. What kind of life have these children been living?

"Ready?" Frakyss asks, his voice gentle.

I nod, steeling myself. "Let's go."

We disembark with Eri and a small team, and we're met by a tall, thin, official-looking alien with orange and turquoise mottled skin, multi-jointed arms, and the head of a hornet.

"I am Miazi, the UPC representative. Thank you for helping evacuate the children." He gestures to dozens of youngsters of various species sitting cross-legged in the dry grass at the edge of the landing pad, eyes wide with fear.

My throat tightens as I take in their thin, dirty, and poorly dressed bodies. The passenger bot moves toward them, her bright voice sweet and motherly.

"Look at you beautiful children. I can't wait to meet each of you. Please follow me into the ship." She organizes the children into two lines and leads them into the cargo bay, where the medical team waits to check each one.

"King Jakvar explained you will be taking the children to a new facility on Silvergate Cay on Abrauxia. Please have them notify me when the children arrive. We are still coordinating the rescue of those missing," the UPC leader advises us. "Any children rescued will be transported to Abrauxia."

"Thank you, Miazi. We will take great care of these children. I'll let the center know to stay in contact with you." I nod to him and walk back to the ship with Frakyss at my side.

Once inside the cargo bay, he closes the ramp and seals the exterior door. Three medical crew members are scanning children with handheld units.

A small furry child is in the healing pod behind them. A series of sonic cleansing booths are along the back wall and Eri is helping children in and showing them how to work the controls.

A larger blue teen wearing multiple bulky layers hangs at the back, shuffling his feet and looking as suspicious as I've ever seen anyone. I put a hand on Frakyss's arm and nod my head in the teen's direction. He strides across the bay and towers over the kid, who stares up at him and me as I near them.

"Son, what is your name?" Frakyss asks him.

"Isyarhi, sir," he responds, his large almond-shaped black shimmering eyes carrying a hint of panic. The two long, thick antennae rising majestically from his head turn white and tremble. It's obvious he's terrified of the giant red-eyed Abrauxian. I step between the two and smile at the boy, who is almost as tall as me.

"Hi Isyarhi, I'm Captain Nerrisa from Earth. We're here to help you and the other children. Is there something you need?"

Isyarhi's antennae quiver as he glances between Frakyss and me. "I...I'm fine," he stammers unconvincingly.

I notice how he clutches his baggy clothing as if hiding something. A suspicion forms in my mind. "Isyarhi, if you're trying to protect someone or something, you can trust us. We want to help all of you."

His eyes widen, and he takes a step back. "I don't know what you mean!"

Frakyss moves to stand beside me, his imposing presence softening as he kneels. "Whatever it is, Isyarhi, you're safe here. We will protect all of you with our lives. I promise no harm will come to any of you."

Isyarhi's resolve seems to crumble. With shaking hands, he slowly opens his coat. Nestled inside is a tiny Omatu child, no more than three or four years old. The little one blinks up at us with large, frightened eyes.

"Oh, sweetheart," I breathe, my heart breaking. "You've been so brave protecting him. My friend and roommate is an Omatu."

"You know what he is?" the boy asks, surprised.

"Yes, we were captured and held by a crew of Zugunu and escaped. Now we live in Silvergate City. That's where we're taking you and the rest of the children. We found out about all of you from Taji, a Shassa boy brought to Roxus."

"You know Taji?" His antennae return to their beautiful turquoise color and no longer tremble.

"No, but my dear friend Astrid does. He is safe now, and if you like, I bet we can visit him."

Chapter 11 - Frakyss

A New Chapter

I watch as Nerrisa holds out both hands and gently coaxes the frightened Omatu child from Isyarhi's protective embrace. Her compassion and patience shine through as she speaks to both children, reassuring them of their safety.

"Let's get you both checked by our medical team," Nerrisa says, cuddling the small green child and guiding Isyarhi toward the waiting staff. "They'll make sure you're healthy and comfortable for the journey."

As they walk away, I trail behind, stopping near the healing pod.

"What is wrong with this Wollokan?" I ask the medic monitoring the pod's display pad.

"He crashed as soon as he entered the hold. Truthfully, I'm surprised he's still alive. He has numerous broken bones, a collapsed lung, a fractured skull, and a brain bleed. We need to find out who did this so they can be dealt with."

"I agree. I'll notify King Jakvar immediately."

"Captain," Eri approaches Nerrisa, her feline features set in a serious expression. "All children are accounted for and have been medically cleared. We're ready for takeoff whenever you give the word."

Nerrisa nods, her demeanor shifting seamlessly into the capable pilot I've come to respect. "Excellent work, Eri. We'll be ready for departure once the medics move the healing pod to the med bay. Please make sure all children are settled in the passenger area and belted in for takeoff. Let the passenger bot know once we're in warp, the children should be given all the food and drinks they want throughout the trip."

Nerrisa walks through *The Tabris* to the cockpit, and I follow, taking my place in the co-pilot's seat again. She begins pre-flight checks before the familiar hum of the engines fills the air.

"Med bay ready for take-off."

"Passenger compartment ready for take-off."

The Tabris lifts smoothly off the planet's surface and out of the atmosphere. Once we've reached the warp lane, Nerrisa engages the drive. The stars stretch into streaks as we accelerate to faster-than-light speed. I watch her deft movements at the controls, once again admiring her skill and confidence. I can't believe she never traveled into space before she came to Abrauxia."

"I'm impressed by the way you handled those two children."

Nerrisa glances at me, a small smile on her lips. "Thanks. I can't imagine what they've been through. Especially Isyarhi keeping that little Omatu hidden."

I nod, understanding her concern. "They're safe now, thanks to you and this mission."

She's quiet for a moment, her gaze fixed on the screens. "I keep thinking about what Kishi told me, about how the Zugunu nearly wiped out her people for their blood. How many more Omatu children are out there in danger? How many other species of children are being exploited?"

"It's a sobering thought," I agree. "But we're making a difference. And now that we know, we can work to find and protect more." My thoughts turn inward for a moment as the nightmare memories of my lost childhood surface. I push them back deep into the recesses of my mind where they belong.

Nerrisa nods, her expression determined. "You're right. I just wish we could do more."

"We will. King Jakvar and the UPC are working on locating more children in danger, including those still missing from Coprinus-LV3. They'll let us know when we're needed."

She reminds me so much of the guardian angel who rescued me when I needed her most. "I'll be back. I want to check on our passengers." She nods and continues monitoring the ship.

When I enter the passenger compartment, the children wear matching white T-shirts and black shorts and are in their seats with boxed meals on their lift-up trays. Drinks with straws are secure in the cupholders, and the children's expressions are relaxed and happy as they chatter among themselves.

Isyarhi is seated in the aisle seat with the Omatu toddler next to him and another teen on the far side.

The passenger bot is busy removing empty food containers and refilling drinks. As I pass down the aisle, I see a young Drecril fumbling with his datapad, and I kneel next to his chair. "Let me help you." I turn the device right side up and place it back in his furry gray hands, pointing at the on button. The screen lights up, and I get a quick grin of sharp teeth.

"Have you got it from here?"

"I think so. Thanks sir."

I get to my feet and continue down the hall to the med bay.

The single healing pod is locked in place, the head securely against the wall. Two of the medics are standing at the monitoring station discussing the boy's status.

"Will the child be okay?"

The medic I spoke with before nods. "In addition to all of his injuries, he has severe malnutrition and stomach parasites. I've injected him with healing nanos that are repairing his body. It will take longer for him to recover from the malnutrition. He should be out of the pod in about twenty hours, and I'll take him to join the others so he can eat his fill, the poor youngling." I nod, and I walk back to the cockpit, angry over what these children have endured, and wanting to get my hands on those who abused them.

After I'm settled into the co-pilot's seat, I glance at Nerrisa. Her brow is furrowed in concentration as she monitors our course.

"How are they doing?" she asks, not taking her eyes off the controls.

"Better than expected," I reply. "They're eating well and seem to be relaxing. The passenger bot is doing an excellent job keeping them comfortable and entertained."

Nerrisa nods, a small smile tugging at her lips. "That's good to hear. They deserve some comfort after everything they've been through."

We fall into a comfortable silence, with the hum of the engines a soothing backdrop. After a while, I notice Nerrisa stifling a yawn.

"You should get some rest. I can handle things here for a while."

She stubbornly shakes her head. "I'm fine. We'll be arriving at Silvergate City soon enough, so I'll rest then."

"Nerrisa," I say, my tone firmer this time. "You've been going non-stop since we left Abrauxia. A fatigued pilot is a dangerous pilot. Please, just a few hours of sleep."

She looks at me, her green eyes searching my face. She sighs. "Alright. But wake me if anything happens, no matter how small."

I nod solemnly. "You have my word."

As she stands to leave, she pauses, her hand resting on the back of her chair. "Frakyss... thank you. For everything."

Before I can respond, she's gone, the door sliding shut behind her. I lean back in my seat, with warmth spreading through my chest. It's a small step, but it feels like progress.

The rest of the journey passes uneventfully. True to my word, I don't wake Nerrisa until we're about ten hours away from Abrauxia, triggering the chime on her communicator. I see her on the internal monitors when she enters the passenger compartment.

She walks among the children who mill around the back of the open space, laughing and chatting with them. She returns to the cockpit, looking refreshed, and takes over the ship's controls.

When we're finally ready to begin our descent to the Silvergate Cay Space Port, I announce over the speaker system that it's time for everyone to stow their belongings, take their seats, and prepare for landing.

These children are about to start a new chapter in their lives, one filled with hope and opportunity. And perhaps, in some small way, this mission has also opened a new chapter for Nerrisa and me.

The spires of Silvergate City come into view, glinting in the bright sunlight. Nerrisa guides *The Tabris* onto the landing pad. As we touch down, I see a group waiting to welcome us... Kishi, Arabella, Godefray, and a team of caregivers.

Nerrisa stands and turns to me, her eyes bright. "Ready?"

I nod, standing to join her. "Let's get these kids taken care of."

Together, we join the rest of the crew, helping organize the children with their new backpacks, datapads, and other belongings. Their hollow-eyed fear has been replaced by relaxed smiles and laughter. The Wollokan teen is bumping shoulders with Isyarhi and the two are joking as they follow the Omatu hurrying to the exit.

As the children step out into the bright clear morning, they stare around in wide-eyed wonder at the spaceships landing and taking off and the enormous silver-spired city beyond. Kishi rushes forward and scoops up the Omatu while Isyarhi shuffles uncomfortably close by. His antennae wave back and forth, as if he's unsure about intervening.

Chapter 12 - Nerrisa

The One I Didn't Miss

I watch as the children disembark, their faces filled with wonder at the sight of Silvergate Cay. Kishi rushes forward, lifting the little Omatu child in her arms. The toddler's eyes widen in surprise, then delight as he reaches out to touch Kishi's leaves and flowers.

"It's okay, Isyarhi. Kishi is the friend and roommate I told you about. She's also an Omatu."

Isyarhi's antennae settle, but he looks stricken. "Is she taking him? Will I ever see him again?"

"Of course," I assure him. "You've done an amazing job protecting him. That bond doesn't just disappear. Maybe you would like to stay with us too."

Arabella approaches us, her smile warm and welcoming. "Welcome to Silvergate City," she says to the children. "We have a beautiful home prepared for you, with plenty of space to play and grow. You're safe here."

The caregivers begin to guide the children toward the waiting transports. I feel a presence beside me and turn to see Frakyss, his expression a mirror of my own emotions. "They'll be okay. Arabella and Godefray have put together an excellent team."

I nod, surprised at the comfort I feel from his words. "I know. It's just... I wish we could do more."

"We will," Frakyss assures me. "This is just the beginning."

As the last of the youngsters board the transports, Kishi approaches us, still holding the Omatu child with Isyarhi hovering close by.

"Nerrisa," Kishi says, her eyes shining with excitement. "I'd like to adopt Brier. Is that okay with you?"

I smile, not surprised by her request. "I'm not in charge of adoptions, but I think it's a wonderful idea, Kishi. I've also invited his big brother Isyarhi to live with us."

Isyarhi clears his throat nervously and gives her a small wave. "Um, hi."

Kishi wraps an arm around his waist and hugs him from the side. "You're Brier's brother?"

He nods and gives a small grin.

"Then I'll adopt you too, Isyarhi. If you want to have me as a mother, that is."

His mouth drops open. "Really? You don't think I'm too old or too ugly to adopt?"

Tears pool in my eyes. Oh my goodness, this poor child. What horrible things has he been told?

"Of course not; what gave you that idea? You are perfect and everything I would want in my first son." He turns and envelops her and the toddler in his arms.

My heart swells and I turn away as a tear escapes down my cheek at their exchange. I catch Frakyss watching me, a small smile on his face. For the first time since I've met him, I don't feel the urge to pull away or put up my defenses. Instead, I find myself returning his smile.

"Aunt Nessa, are we really going to the Royal Palace on Epree Island?"

"Absolutely, Isyarhi. We were all invited to the baby shower for the new princesses. Are you excited for the trip?"

"Yes, I'm already packed and ready to go. Mom is getting Brier packed and ready. Do you need any help?"

I pat the tall young man on the shoulder, hardly able to believe he's grown so much in the past seven months. "I'd love some help. Frakyss will be here soon to pick us up. Would you carry our bags up to the roof-level lobby?" I hand him my small carry-on bag.

"Sure! I can't wait to see Uncle Frakyss!" He shifts his backpack to a more comfortable position and heads for the elevator, his long antennae waving happily in the air.

I hear a shriek of laughter behind me and turn just in time to see Brier race down the hall, stark naked, with Kishi close behind.

"Brier! Come back here, you little rascal!" Kishi calls out, her leaves rustling as she chases after the giggling toddler. I laugh at the scene. In the months since she adopted Brier and Isyarhi, our apartment has been filled with more joy and chaos than I ever could have imagined. "Need some help?" I ask, moving to intercept the streaking green blur.

"Please!" Kishi pants. "He's too fast for me."

I crouch down, arms outstretched. "Come here, you little troublemaker," I call in a playful voice. Brier squeals with delight as he races toward me. Just as he's about to dart past, I scoop him up in my arms. "Gotcha!"

The little Omatu squirms and giggles in my grasp. "No clothes! No clothes!" he chants.

"Oh yes, clothes," I counter, tickling his belly. "We can't have you running around the Royal Palace in your birthday suit, can we?"

Kishi approaches, holding up a small outfit. "Thank you, Nerrisa. I don't know where he gets all this energy."

I hand the squirming child over to her. "Probably from all that sunlight he's been soaking up. He's growing like a dandelion."

As Kishi wrestles Brier into his clothes, I hear the apartment's communication system chime. Frakyss's deep voice comes through. "I've arrived. Are you ready to depart?"

"We'll be right up," I reply, feeling a flutter of anticipation in my stomach. Over the past months, Frakyss and I have been slowly building a relationship. He's been patient, respectful of my boundaries, and genuinely supportive of our unconventional family. I find myself looking forward to seeing him more and more.

"Alright, troops," I call. "Let's move out. We don't want to keep Uncle Frakyss waiting!" I grab the large bag from just inside Kishi's suite and set it to hover so I can stack it high with the multitude of pink-wrapped baby gifts we've amassed. As we make our way to the roof, I follow Kishi, making sure nothing is dropped along the way.

Frakyss is piloting a gorgeous, sleek silver transport that reminds me of a space-age conversion van. By the time the small orange building valet loads our luggage into the back compartment, and I've climbed in and sealed the side door, Isyarhi is standing between the two front seats chatting with the big Abrauxian about navigation systems and multi-dimensional routing.

"If it's okay with Frakyss, you can take the copilot's seat for this trip, Isyarhi."

The boy's face lights up with eagerness, and Frakyss nods warmly. "Of course, I'd be happy to have you as my co-pilot, Isyarhi. Take a seat."

As Isyarhi excitedly straps in, I settle in the back with Kishi and Brier. The little Omatu bounces in his seat, his pointed ears quivering excitedly. "Princesses, Auntie Nessa?" Brier asks, his big dark eyes wide with wonder.

I chuckle. Since learning about the birth of the two princesses a month ago, he has chattered about nothing else. "Yes, sweetie, we're going to visit the princesses. They have a natatorium... it's a covered pool where they spend a lot of time. Do you want to swim with them?" He nods.

The quick flight to Epree Island is filled with Isyarhi's questions about piloting and navigation, Brier's constant chatter about princesses, and Kishi's gentle reminders to use our "inside voices." It's chaotic and loud and absolutely perfect.

As we approach the island, the gleaming black towers of the Royal Palace come into view. Brier presses his face against the window, his mouth open in awe. "Pretty!" he exclaims.

We land smoothly on the space pad, where several other transports have already arrived. As we disembark, I spot Arabella waving to us as she steps from her own ship.

"You made it!" she calls out, rushing over to hug me. "Did you have a good trip?"

"A little noisy," I laugh, "but wonderful. Didn't Godefray come with you?"

"No, he had some issues with the baggage handlers at the spaceport threatening to strike."

Frakyss comes up to stand beside me, pushing a luggage cart filled with our bags and the baby gifts. "Shall we head to the palace?" he asks.

I nod, suddenly feeling a bit nervous. It's our first big social gathering since the royal wedding. As if sensing my anxiety, Frakyss gives me a reassuring smile.

"Are you okay? I hope you're not worried about security. Jakvar promised there would be no more bombings at the palace. He's got a family to protect now."

We stroll up the slight hill to the palace, Brier riding on Isyarhi's shoulders and Kishi walking arm-in-arm with Arabella. I glance up at Frakyss walking next to me, keeping just the right amount of space between us so I don't freak out from being touched.

When I search my feelings, I realize I'm no longer repulsed by the idea. We've spent so much time together, and he's always been very careful of it. I reach out and take his hand. His step falters for a moment, and the gaze he fixes me with is shocked.

Most of the of the Second Daughter Consortium is gathered in the grand vestibule with a number of Grashetas guiding hovering tables laden with food. Layla is holding the handle of a large pink wagon with a 'Welcome Babies' sign on the side. XVR-2 holds his hands up for silence, and as soon as the chattering dies down, he opens the double doors.

"Your Majesties, The Second Daughter Consortium to see you." He steps to the side, and we rush through the door, shouting, "SURPRISE!"

We surround Astrid and take turns hugging her, offering our congratulations on her twins.

"We wanted to give you time to get settled in at home before we had your shower. I hope you don't mind." Princess Kateryna tells Astrid, putting her arm around the Queen's waist.

"Not at all, Kat. This is wonderful! I love you all, and it's great having everyone together in one place for a change."

Sunlight pours through the arched windows, scattering gold across the polished floors and fluttering silk banners overhead. Laughter floats through the air, sweet and easy.

The baby shower is in full swing. Gift tables brim with boxes wrapped in soft pastels, delicate ribbons trailing down to the floor. The scent of warm cakes and sweet fruit carries on the breeze.

I spot Frakyss stepping into the bright space, his arms loaded with the pile of gifts we brought. He moves quietly, placing them with care on a long table against the wall before crossing to join the other Abrauxians already gathered near the king.

General Grizlor strides in behind him, his massive frame filling the doorway as he ducks beneath the arch. The other males greet him with booming backslaps and grins, their voices rumbling through the chamber like distant thunder.

Nearby, Isyarhi crouches beside Brier near the raised pool. The little boy smacks his chubby green fists on the transparent wall, giggling as the twin princesses on the other side wave and splash. The scene is warm and safe.

And then Astrid speaks.

"General Grizlor, it's good to see you back. Where's Naia? We thought she'd return with you."

Grizlor frowns, confused. "Why would she be with me? I've just returned to the planet. I haven't heard from her once during my deployment."

Silence sharpens.

King Jakvar steps forward, eyes tight with concern. "She's not here. We haven't seen her since you left. We assumed she'd joined you for the mission."

Grizlor's face darkens. "No, she was not with me. She is missing, and no one noticed? You let her vanish," he growls, stepping forward, fists clenched at his sides. "You all stood here celebrating while my mate disappeared, and no one even asked where she'd gone?"

He shouts the last part, and the noise in the room dies instantly. A high-pitched alert wails from his communicator. He lifts his arm, scowling at the message flashing across the screen. Jakvar leans in to read it with him, their expressions hardening in unison.

Without another word, Grizlor turns and storms out.

The room buzzes behind him with whispers and stares, but I can't hear them. I can't move.

Naia's missing. Seven months. Gone.

And I didn't even notice.

I didn't ask. I didn't call. I never even checked.

The realization hits like a gut punch. Cold, sharp, and nauseating.

My stomach churns, twisting hard.

I press a hand to my abdomen, trying to keep it together as guilt crashes through me. I've been so buried in my own resentment, my own slow-burning fury at this world, this bond, this entire life, that I never even looked outside my own orbit.

Naia was bright, loyal, and always believed in the best of people, and she vanished without me even noticing she was gone.

I feel sick.

All the sweets, the laughter, and the decorations blur together. The sunshine suddenly feels too hot. Too harsh. The edges of the room feel like they're closing in.

I swallow hard.

She was my friend. And I abandoned her without even realizing it.

Chapter 13 - Frakyss

Celebrations and Shadows

The joyous atmosphere of the baby shower evaporates instantly as General Grizlor storms out of the room. King Jakvar's face is grim as he turns to address the stunned crowd.

"My friends, I apologize, but we have an urgent situation. It appears that Naia has been missing for some time without our knowledge and the General has just been notified she was rescued by the patrol ship from the head of the troqel. I need to attend to this matter immediately."

Astrid rushes to her mate's side, concern etched on her face. "What can we do to help?"

Jakvar places a reassuring hand on her shoulder. "For now, continue with the celebration. The princesses shouldn't be deprived of this moment. I'll update everyone as soon as I have more information."

As the King hurries out with Layla close behind, a tense murmur ripples through the room. I catch Nerrisa's eye across the space, and she nods, understanding passing between us without words.

We both move toward Astrid, who looks shaken. "Your Majesty, perhaps we should continue with the party. The children seem eager to swim with the princesses. Give your mate time to find out what's going on."

Astrid nods gratefully. "Yes, that's a good idea. Thank you, Frakyss."

The party continues, but the air is thick with unease. I'm left unsettled, wondering where Naia has been all these months. Remembering the attack on the palace adds to my fears.

I hastily send messages to Godefray, Evruik, and Eri, instructing them to increase security measures immediately. My mind races with thoughts of the worst-case scenario as I try to protect my people from any potential danger.

The females have taken seats and chat among themselves while watching the twin princesses zipping through the water with several Maiamoni children. Isyarhi and the furry blue Shassan prince are sitting at the shallow end with Brier between them, splashing happily and calling to the twins. Nerrisa stands at the edge of the pool, keeping a watchful eye on the children.

I approach her. "Are you alright?"

She turns to me, her eyes filled with a mix of emotions. "I'm worried about Naia," she admits. "How did no one know she had been missing for seven months? I feel like a terrible friend. None of us were alarmed when we didn't hear from her for so long."

I nod, understanding her concern. "I'm sure Naia will be fine."

A small smile tugs at her lips. "Thank you, Frakyss. I appreciate your support. In everything."

Before I can respond, Astrid calls out, gathering everyone's attention. "Friends, I want to thank you all for this wonderful surprise. Despite the concerning news about Naia, your presence here means the world to Jakvar and me. Let's enjoy this moment together, and hopefully we'll get an update about Naia soon."

When the next morning arrives, we're surprised by the news Princess Kateryna shares at breakfast.

Her eyes are shadowed and as she leans forward, her voice hushed but filled with concern.

"I spoke with the troqel late into the night," she begins, capturing everyone's attention. "His name is King Zaphre Kragmals from Gillis XPM, and he told me about his adventures with Naia."

She pauses, looking around at our surprised faces before continuing. "It turns out that Naia has been exploring the deepest parts of Abrauxia's oceans with Zaphre as her guide. They've discovered things beyond our wildest imagination... bioluminescent forests of kelp that stretch for miles, underwater mountain ranges teeming with life we've never seen before, and caverns that echo with the songs of creatures older than our civilization."

Kateryna's hands move animatedly as she speaks, painting vivid pictures with her words.

"But the most astonishing find was several days ago... an old hidden Ven'aens facility. Naia went inside and when she came out, she told him they needed to destroy the place.

The Ven'aens had been experimenting on humans from Earth and creating a plague to release into the environment. Naia used her powers to freeze the building to kill the virus and Zaphre crushed the installation and killed two of the horrible Ven'aens monsters as they tried to escape."

Those of us seated around the table are stunned into silence. My mind tries to process the implications of their discovery.

"Naia managed to send information from the facility's servers in a download to my system, and I've been busy reviewing that information. They are responsible for the Grievous Plague that killed the Abrauxian females, and there is a second facility somewhere in Abrauxia's oceans where they are growing the pathogen that is intended for human women. The Ulae'Zep are already on their way to Abrauxia with more than two-thousand human females who signed up for the bride program. They won't be able to offload until the threat is neutralized."

"What steps are being taken to locate the second facility?" Nerrisa asks.

"Dyebarth and Makena are already working to find it. We'll let you know if there's anything you can do to help."

"Freaking aliens," Nerrisa shakes her head. "What did they hope to achieve by killing all the females?"

"I believe they planned to make Abrauxians extinct so they could take the planet for themselves. By only killing the females, they made it look like an environmental event so the UPC wouldn't investigate." I add to their conversation.

Princess Kateryna looks surprised at the thought and nods. "Good point Frakyss. We've already forwarded the files Naia managed to send from the hidden facility to the UPC so their scientists can start unraveling the pathogens. I want to make sure hybrid children aren't susceptible to the original virus if it still survives in the environment."

The thought of any future children Nerrisa and I might have, being lost to the Ven'aens' treachery, heats my blood. I can feel my eyes blaze even brighter, and I struggle to contain my rage. The last thing I want is to frighten the females and children.

With nothing left for us to do, we gather our belongings and say our goodbyes in the Grand Vestibule.

"Thank you for inviting us, Kateryna, and allowing us to stay overnight at the palace. Would you please keep us updated on Naia's condition and anything we can do to help with the Ven'aens problem?" Nerrisa asks the Princess and gives her a hug as we prepare to leave.

"Of course. Thank you for coming to the baby shower. I know Astrid appreciates you being here." The children and females take turns giving goodbye hugs to the Princess before we walk to the space pad.

Having those I've come to love near me in the sleek shuttle helps me remain calm on the return trip to Silvergate City.

I drop everyone at their building and head to my own private retreat near the barren north point of the island. A Ryze bird hunts the ocean waters below my home, and I admire his pale blue form as he dives into the turbulent waves below.

Once I've left my transport in the phantom bay beneath the house, I take the lift to the main level. Bruud glides from the open level above and lands on my head, chittering and scolding me for leaving him at home alone overnight.

"Sorry, Bruud, I don't think you would have enjoyed the really long, loud trip with a small child. He would likely have tugged on your tail and eaten your snacks. Or maybe the reverse." I enter my office and sit, picking up my mother's photograph from the edge of my desk and staring at her beautiful light gray face.

I don't remember her. The Ven'aens plague took her right after my birth. Long before my own miseries were wrought by the hands of aliens who wanted to control me for my gift.

The frame is cold in my hand, the corners smooth from years of wear. I trace the edge with my thumb, the way I always do when my thoughts wander too far.

Her face stares back from the photo, forever caught in stillness.

I set it down gently on the desk and press my elbows into the wood. My eyes close. I draw in a slow breath, deep enough to still the throb that's started at the base of my skull.

The ache isn't just a headache. It never is.

The air shifts, cooler now, quieter. The pressure builds behind my eyes, not painful, but deep, like standing on the edge of something ancient and endless.

Then the darkness opens.

I don't see with my eyes. I feel it. A map of stars and time stretching around me. Lights flicker in the void, each one humming with memory, possibility, truth.

One pulses bright and sharp ahead of me. New. Future.

I reach for it, and the vision pulls me in.

Nerrisa stands on the bridge of an enormous freighter. Her shoulders are squared, chin tilted up just enough to show she's not here by choice. A hologram shimmers into view at the front of the command deck, casting pale light across the controls.

The Ulae'Zep commander's face is almost human, delicate and symmetrical, unnervingly perfect. But there is something beneath the beauty that does not belong to anything born of Earth or Abrauxia.

Long, thin filaments of flesh wind around her head, shaped into elaborate curves and spirals like sculpted ivory. They glow softly from within, as if lit by bioluminescence. Her "hair" is the same.

Those same fibers flow weightlessly in the air, too slow, too graceful, as if underwater or unbound by gravity.

Her eyes, huge and glittering like cut diamonds, catch every light in the room and throw it back tenfold.

She's breathtaking in the way lightning is beautiful from a distance. Too perfect and alien.

Nerrisa tightens her grip on the console. The projection flickers faintly, but the commander holds her gaze with crystalline calm.

"I'm only here because I agreed to see the troqel safely to Abrauxia," Nerrisa says, voice steady. "Not because I trust the beings who thought kidnapping me and my friends was acceptable policy."

She doesn't raise her voice, but every word strikes like steel. The Ulae'Zep doesn't flinch.

I tense. This is still to come. Too far ahead to act on now.

I release the vision, letting it fade like fog. The light drifts back into the void.

Another star waits behind it. Dimmer and closer. Heavier.

Past. Recent.

I reach again, deeper this time. And I find them.

The air tightens. The temperature drops. This one comes fast and hard.

The vision slams into me.

A cell—dark, filthy, stinking of mold and fear. The floor is slick with leaking pipes and old blood. Metal walls, sweat-streaked and rusting, press in close. There's no light, no comfort, and no sense of time.

Two girls huddle in the corner, limbs wrapped around each other. One older, her jaw tight, her arms protectively braced around the younger. The little one shivers, her face buried in her sister's shoulder. They're barefoot, soaked from the leaking ceiling, and their clothes are clinging damp and filthy to their skin.

A sound cuts through the dark. A low, mechanical groan.

The door.

The older girl lifts her head, eyes wide and furious.

A moment later, the bulkhead creaks open and the Cegnu slithers inside.

It's enormous. Tentacles dragging wetly across the threshold, mouth hidden behind a breathing grate that hisses with every step. Its eyes are wrong—bulbous, too many, unblinking. They gleam as it steps forward, slow and hungry.

The older girl moves fast. She shoves her sister behind her, shielding her body.

The creature looms, scanning them like livestock. One long, slime-coated appendage reaches out.

Then—a spark of light. A short in the panel. A chance.

The door seal falters.

The girls move.

They're out of the cell and running barefoot through the dark hallway before the Cegnu can react. The corridor hums with failing power. Warnings blare in three languages. The girls round a corner, one of them hauling open a maintenance grate with shaking hands.

They vanish into the shaft.

Inside the duct, it's narrower than breath. Elbows scrape raw. Knees bruise. The metal is hot in some places, frozen in others. They crawl without speaking, the only sound the rasp of their breath and the hiss of something behind them too far to see and too close to forget.

The Cegnu follow, pounding through the corridor beyond the wall, tentacles battering against the ducts, trying to rip them open.

They can't fit.

But that doesn't mean they stop.

The girls crawl faster.

The younger one sobs once, a sharp, scared sound that echoes down the metal tunnel. Her sister squeezes her hand. "Quiet," she whispers. "We're not done yet."

The duct groans under pressure, but it holds.

The vision ends.

When I open my eyes, the desk is solid beneath my hands. The room is still. But the weight of what I've seen presses against my chest like a storm held behind glass.

These are not dreams. They're not guesses.

They are real.

At first, I feel disbelief, struggling to reconcile the familiar face with the passing of years. Its features are just as I remember... cold, calculating eyes that gleam with malice, a cruel growl that reveals hundreds of small sharp teeth.

The sight sends a shiver down my spine, memories flooding back unbidden: the sounds of shouting, the suffocating darkness of the room where I, too, was held captive, the echo of my own terrified and pain-filled screams as the creature flayed the flesh from my face and body.

I tear myself from the vision with a gasp so sharp it burns my throat.

The room tilts. My stomach clenches.

I fall hard onto my hands and knees, the granite floor of my office cold beneath me. My palms slam against the stone, slick with sweat. I can't breathe. My pulse thunders in my ears and my vision swims.

It was the same place.

The same stinking cell. The same bloodstained floor, and the same thick silence broken only by the hiss of breathing through grates.

I was seven.

I feel it in my bones—the jolt of pain as they took strips of flesh from my arms. The sting of air hitting raw muscle. The way I screamed until I couldn't speak anymore. The way *he* screamed beside me.

Gereph.

My best friend. My brother in all but blood.

Gone.

We were nothing to them. Flesh to be pulled apart. I'd almost buried the memory deep enough to forget the details. Almost.

Until I saw it again.

The Cegnu.

The same one who stood over me in that cell, scalpel-bright tentacle hooks gleaming, eyes like polished coals, unblinking and unfeeling. The same who reached into my body and carved something that never healed. The one whose presence burned itself into my nightmares for years.

The one who lit my eyes red from the inside out.

I gag, my chest heaving.

And then I retch.

Nothing comes up, but the dry heaves shake my ribs, and I press my forehead to the floor, trembling like a dying thing.

Chapter 14 - Nerrisa

Crowns and Cracks

"Evruik, have you seen Frakyss?"

"No, why?" He turns from the flight assignment screen in the company control hub to face me.

"I haven't seen him since we got back from Epree Island yesterday. There's a special ceremony at the palace this evening that we were invited to attend."

The tall gray Abrauxian rubs his chin thoughtfully. "That's odd. I can't imagine him missing an important event, especially with you."

"The invitation came late last night. I thought for sure I'd hear from him last night or today. Can you take me off the roster for today and tomorrow? I'll take one of the *Phantoms* from *The Tabris* to attend the event."

"Of course. I'll let you know when I hear from Frakyss," he responds, punching commands into his communicator.

"Thanks. I'll just take Isyarhi with me to the event as my plus one."

"Your plus one? What's that?" he gives me a puzzled look.

I smile, forgetting not everything translates between English and Abrauxian. "I'll take him as my guest. I'm supposed to bring someone else with me. I'm sure my nephew would love a chance to be my copilot.

Evruik nods, grinning. "I'm sure he would. What teenager wouldn't want a chance to drive a phantom?"

I leave, sending a quick message to Kishi, asking if she minds Isyarhi traveling with me to the formal event so I don't have to go alone.

By the time I've guided the sleek shuttle from the bay of *The Tabris*, she's responded that he's already dressed, packed and waiting for me on the roof.

I laugh, the boy reminds me so much of myself at that age, already with my pilot's license at sixteen and my friends calling me a flying fish.

I focus on landing in the buffeting wind and trigger the passenger door to swing up for him when I see his face outside the window.

He climbs in and I'm hit with a blast of cold wind. "Hi, Auntie Nessa; thank you for inviting me!" He shuts the door and pulls the safety harness over his shoulders.

"Thanks for coming, Isyarhi. I hope you don't mind such a quick trip. There's a ceremony this evening for Naia. We'll come back home right after the event. We can enjoy the warmer weather the short time we're there." I guide the *Phantom* straight up and point us toward Epree Island.

"I can't believe how cold it's getting here. Where I'm originally from on Earth, it gets cold and damp, but nothing like this." I guide us high enough to avoid the buffeting wind.

"It wasn't cold like this on Coprinus-LV3 either. That horrible place was mostly warm and dusty. Nagoria, my home planet, was vibrant with lots of trees and warm rainy weather."

"Do you miss it?" I ask the solemn teen.

"Yeah, but it wasn't safe anymore after the Zugunu started showing up. Maybe someday we can visit. I might have some relatives still alive."

"I'd like that. Now that we're out of the worst of the wind, do you want to take the controls?"

"Really?" he exclaims, his antennae perking up with excitement. "You'll let me fly?"

I smile at his enthusiasm. "Of course. You've been practicing in the simulators, right? This is a great opportunity for some real flight time."

Isyarhi nods eagerly, his hands already hovering over the controls. "I've logged over 100 hours in the sims. I won't let you down, Aunt Nessa."

"I know you won't," I say, activating the co-pilot controls. "Just remember, smooth and steady. We're not in a rush."

As Isyarhi takes control, I feel a swell of pride. He handles the *Phantom* with a natural ease. His antennae tremble as he concentrates, making minute adjustments to our course.

"You're doing great," I encourage him. "How does it feel compared to the simulator?"

"The ship feels alive," he says, a note of awe in his voice. "I feel every little movement, every air current. It's amazing!"

We fly in comfortable silence for a while, the clouds parting to reveal the vast dark ocean below.

As Epree Island comes into view on the horizon, I notice Isyarhi's grip on the controls tightening.

"Nervous about landing?"

He nods, his antennae droop. "A little. I've never landed anything but the sim before."

"Don't worry," I assure him. "I'll talk you through it. Just remember your training and trust your instincts."

As we approach the island, I guide Isyarhi through the landing procedures. His movements are a bit jerky at first, but he soon finds his rhythm. We touch down on the palace's lawn with only a slight bump.

"Well done!" I exclaim, giving him a proud smile. "That was an excellent first real landing."

Isyarhi beams, his whole face lighting up with pride. "Thank you, Aunt Nerrisa. I couldn't have done it without you talking me through it."

As we disembark, I notice a Maiamoni female waiting for us. "Captain Nerrisa, young Isyarhi, welcome," she greets us. "I am Asha. Please follow me. Captain, I'm guessing you would like to change? The ceremony will begin soon."

"Yes, thank you. I have my dress and bag." The sun is dropping below the horizon beyond the royal palace when we enter through the side door into the east wing.

Asha opens the door to an elegant first floor sitting room with an attached restroom and dressing space. I change into my dark green silk evening gown and spend a few minutes touching up my makeup and piling my curls on top of my head.

Isyarhi gives a low whistle when I emerge. "I have the most beautiful aunt in the universe."

I give him a side hug.

"Thanks, sweetheart. I have the most handsome nephew and escort in the universe." He pulls himself taller and extends his arm. "Where did you learn that?"

Uncle Frakyss. He told me when you escort a female, extend your arm so she can choose to take it or not." I'm surprised that's something Frakyss thought to teach the boy. I take his arm, and he leads me into the corridor where Asha awaits us.

We follow her to the crowded Great Hall to our seats in the second row, and we slide in next to Layla and her mate. The air is filled with a buzz of happy conversation, and as the outside sky darkens, the chandeliers cast their dazzling glow over the space.

King Jakvar and Queen Astrid are seated on elaborate thrones at the front on a dais, their faces a mixture of happiness and pride. Prince Theovesh and Princess Kateryna are seated to their right, deep in conversation. Everyone's attention is drawn to the back of the room as a herald hammers his long spear to the floor with a reverberating boom.

"Announcing Amoranaia Kalakaua of Earth." We all stand and clap while small silver drones circle overhead among the chandeliers. We're surrounded by quite a few Abrauxians, so we can't see Naia until she is led past our aisle by an elderly white-haired male.

The applause dies down, and the room grows quiet. King Jakvar's voice booms through the Great Hall. "Welcome Amoranaia Kalakaua. We have asked you here this evening to honor and recognize you for your heroic actions that exposed and destroyed the Ven'aens facility in Zone K4791 of the Itos Ocean. With great peril to yourself, you saved future generations on Abrauxia from another plague and discovered the cause of the

Grievous Plague that wiped out the Abrauxian females."

He pauses a moment before continuing. "It is our honor and privilege to hereby declare Amoranaia Kalakaua a landed Baroness by the three thousand and thirty-seventh Royal Court of Abrauxia."

I peek between the two towering males in front of me and see Astrid place a vivid blue crown on Naia's head.

"Please accept this jeweled collar of office that reflects your elevation." Astrid puts a heavy ornate collar of jeweled plaques on Naia's shoulders. Naia curtseys low.

"Rise Baroness Amoranaia. Turn and face the citizens of Abrauxia who thank you for your service to the planet," King Jakvar announces.

Everyone in the audience cheers, and the big Abrauxians stomp their booted feet, causing the marble floor to tremble. After a few minutes, everyone in the hall sits and I can now see the dais again.

"Because of his brave service and assistance to Baroness Amoranaia, we recognize King Zaphre Kragmals of Gilles XPM. He has served the

Royal House of Abrauxia by guarding our planet's oceans for the past four thousand years. In honor of his service, the Ulae'Zep will assist Pilot Nerrisa Byrne of Earth in locating and retrieving a mate for the great troqel from Gilles XPM and transporting her to Abrauxia at the earliest opportunity."

Naia leaps up from her chair in the front row and claps, and everyone else stands and joins her.

"The UPC and Abrauxia will make every effort to bring the Ven'aens to justice for the extermination of the Abrauxian females. They will also be held accountable for their attempts to poison the planet's waters to slaughter current and future females from Earth, and for their recent experimentation on and murder of humans."

Everyone cheers and stomps. XVR-2 steps forward on the dais and raises his hands for silence. "This concludes the Royal Court of King Jakvar and Queen Astridia, the Thirty-Seventh Rulers of Abrauxia." The attendees jump to their feet and the room starts to empty from the front.

While we await our turn to depart the Great Hall, my communicator vibrates. I tap the message from Evruik.

"I found Frakyss at his north cliffs home and is ill. Please come at once." The house coordinates appear at the bottom of the note.

Our row starts moving, and I stop and turn to Isyarhi behind me. "We need to go out the other way, through that side door." I nod my head toward the large glass doors at the other end of the row.

Phoebe blocks our way, deep in conversation with another couple. I tap Phoebe shoulder urgently. "Excuse me, we need to get through. It's an emergency."

She turns, her eyes widening as she takes in my expression. "Of course, sorry, Nerrisa!" She and couple step aside, creating a gap for us to squeeze through.

We hurry down the row, weaving between clusters of chatting attendees. The ornate side doors loom ahead, flanked by two stern-faced Abrauxian guards. I flash my credentials as we approach, and they nod, swinging the doors open.

The cool night air hits us as we step onto a moonlit terrace. In the distance, I can see our *Phantom*, its sleek black form gleaming under the starlight. We rush across the courtyard, our footsteps echoing in the quiet night.

"Aunt Nerrisa, what's wrong?" Isyarhi asks, his antennae quivering with concern.

"It's Frakyss," I reply, my voice tight. "He's ill. We need to get to him quickly. Message your mom and let her know we're going to be at Frakyss's house at the north end of Silvergate Cay."

We reach the *Phantom*, and I initiate the startup sequence. The engines hum to life as we strap ourselves in. I guide the ship off the landing pad and into the night sky.

The journey seems to stretch on forever, even though I'm pushing the phantom to its limits. The dark ocean rushes by beneath us, occasionally illuminated by flashes of bioluminescent sea life. In the distance, the lights of Silvergate City grow steadily larger.

As we approach Frakyss's secluded home at the north end of the island, I see Evruik standing on the wide parking space. My heart races as I bring the phantom down for a landing. Before the engines have powered down, I'm already unbuckling my harness.

"Stay here," I tell Isyarhi, my hand on the door release. "I'll come get you when it's okay."

I rush toward the house, the wind whipping my dress around my legs. As I near the entrance, I can hear crashes and roars coming from inside. Evruik stands nervously by the door, looking unsure of how to proceed.

"What's happening?" I demand, approaching quickly.

"Nerrisa, it's not safe," he warns. "Frakyss is not himself. He's delirious and violent. I can't get near him."

I take a deep breath, steeling myself. "I'm going in."

"Do you want me to go in with you?"

"No, just me." I push past him, entering the house. The interior is a mess with furniture overturned and claw marks scoring the walls. Bruud is darting around the room, frantic and wide-eyed with fear. I follow the sounds of destruction to Frakyss's office.

The sight that greets me makes my heart clench. Frakyss is crouched in a corner, his massive frame shaking. His red eyes are wild and unfocused, darting around the room as if seeing deadly enemies.

Deep, ragged claw marks score the walls and floor around him, and the remnants of his desk lie in splinters on the floor.

"Frakyss," I call from the doorway, taking a cautious step forward. His head snaps toward me, a feral growl rumbling from his chest. I ca see the muscles in his arms tensing, ready to lash out. But there's something else in his eyes too, a flicker of recognition, quickly overwhelmed by terror.

"It's me, Nerrisa," I say, keeping my voice calm and steady despite the fear coursing through me.

"You're safe. You're home on Abrauxia."

He shakes his head, his claws digging into the floor. "No... no... they're coming. Can't let them... can't let them use me."

I take another slow step forward, my hands raised in a non-threatening gesture. "No one's coming, Frakyss. It's just me. You're safe here."

His breathing is ragged and his chest heaves with each gasping breath. Sweat glistens on his scarred skin, and I can see him trembling. "They... they want to make me see. Make me tell them... I won't. I won't!" His voice rises to a roar, and he slams his fist into the wall, leaving a sizable hole.

I flinch at the sudden movement but force myself to remain calm. "Frakyss, look at me. Really look. You know me. You're not there anymore. You're here with me."

His eyes lock onto mine, and for a moment, I see a glimmer of clarity. "Ner... Nerrisa?"

"Yes, that's right," I encourage, taking another step closer. "I'm here. You're safe."

He blinks rapidly, confusion washing over his features. "But... the Cegnu... they were here. They were trying to..."

"They're not here," I assure him, now close enough to reach out and touch him if I dared. "It was a memory, a nightmare. But it's over now."

Frakyss slumps against the wall, the fight draining out of him. "A memory," he repeats, his voice hoarse. "It felt so real." He glances around him. "Where am I? This isn't Starlight Hall."

I kneel beside him, careful not to touch him without permission. "You are at your home on the north end of Silvergate Cay. Do you want to talk about it?"

He's quiet for a long moment, his gaze fixed on some distant point. When he speaks, his voice is a whisper. "I was seven when they took me, the Cegnu. Somehow, they found out about my gift."

Moving next to him, I sit close enough to feel his body heat without touching. "Do you want to tell me about it?" I extend my hand to him. He stares at it for a few moments before gripping it like a lifeline.

"Sometimes I can see things before or while they are happening. My mother was ill with the Grievous Plague when pregnant with me, and the doctor thought that's what caused it. He called me an anomaly, a throwback to the original winged Abrauxians we descend from, who had special powers."

I give his warm hand a gentle squeeze.

"My father was wholly devoted to me after losing my mother. He called me his good luck talisman, a small part of my mother that stayed with him when she could not." His breathing is returning to a normal rate. He is silent for so long that I wonder if he will say more.

"The dragon season of my seventh year, I was playing with my friend, Gereph, on the beach of my family's estate, Starlight Hall, on Romrey Island. That's where I was born and spent my early childhood." he rubs his beard, making a faint rasping noise.

"We were sitting in the warm sunshine laughing, and the next thing we knew, we were dragged into the water by dark red tentacles wrapped around our legs. I regained consciousness in a small dark cell, with Gereph shaking me, pleading for me to wake up because he was scared. A dark red monster stood watching us from the opposite side of thick bars that trapped us in the room."

His hand grips mine, and he shudders as the memory envelopes him. "The Cegnu are like nightmares made flesh. They didn't care about our innocence; they only wanted my gift. They tortured us, Nerrisa. Day after day, they sought to extract the oracle from my very being, flaying our flesh as if it were the only way to uncover the truth."

My heart aches for him; the image of him and another small child tortured in such a horrific way that it would leave the kind of scars that mark his flesh even now.

"Gereph was my best friend. We shared everything... our dreams and our fears. But after three months in that hell, he succumbed. I watched him fade away, his laughter silenced by agony. I thought I would follow him into the next life, but thoughts of my father had me clinging to the hope that someone would come for me."

He takes a deep breath. "It was a warrior female who rescued me, her wings slicing through the darkness like a beacon of hope. She brought me back to Abrauxia, but it was too late.

My father had perished from grief, having lost the son he cherished so deeply. Even now, my ancestral home sits as he left it, waiting for my return."

He heaves a shuddering sigh. "When I returned, I was not the same child who had left. My eyes, once filled with the purity of white light, now glowed red... a mark of the darkness I endured."

I tighten my grip on his hand, my heart swelling with sorrow. "The darkness, Frakyss, does not define you. You are a warrior, an oracle. You survived when so many would not."

He turns to me, a flicker of warmth igniting within his red gaze. "I carry their memories with me, Nerrisa. I fight not only for myself but for my friend who could not endure and my father whose heart was broken. They are my guiding stars."

I allow myself to lean into him briefly before struggling to my feet in the long silky dress and tugging his hand. It's time to pull him back from the dark. As he stands, he glances around the room, and I see a grimace twist his lips. Papers lie scattered, furniture overturned and splintered, and his digital systems are in pieces.

"Come on," I lead him into the open living room, and my heart sinks at the extent of the damage. It's worse than I noticed in my rush to get to him earlier, so I lead him toward the main door.

"Let's check on Isyarhi and Evruik," I suggest, hoping that seeing the others will help pull him out of his distress at what he's done to his home. He nods, and together, we step into the cold windy night.

Evruik strides forward from near the parked vehicles, worry etched across his face, while Isyarhi's large dark eyes watch from the passenger seat of the *Phantom*.

"It's okay," Frakyss says, his voice low but steady. "I'm alright. Really." He meets the other male's gaze, and I can sense the effort it takes for him to project calm. "You can go back to the city. I'll be fine now."

Evruik hesitates, worried about the mental state of his boss and friend. "Are you sure?" he asks, concern still lingering in his voice.

"You have responsibilities there. We'll manage here."

Evruik finally nods, though the worry doesn't fully leave his eyes. He walks to his vehicle and takes off, the rear lights fading in the snow that's begun to fall.

I hurry to the *Phantom* and open Isyarhi's door. "Hurry, let's get inside. The weather is turning ugly, kiddo."

The three of us hurry through the main door and stand there, just taking in all the destruction. Just then, Bruud scampers up, his tiny feet pattering against the marble floor. He leaps onto Isyarhi's shoulder, clutches one of the boy's thick antennas, and peeks around with his little violet eyes wide and frightened.

"Hey Bruud," Frakyss calls, but the Meeve eyes the male and flicks his bushy tail, refusing to leave the safety of Isyarhi's shoulder.

I clap my hands together. "Okay, gentlemen, let's get this place put back together." We start picking up broken furniture and piling it near the door.

"Wait!" We both turn to face Frakyss. "I need to tell you something." His tail lashes back and forth, showing his agitation.

"What is it?" I ask, sensing a shift in him.

He takes a deep breath, and I can see him trying to collect his thoughts.

"I had a vision. Two Hosliens sisters... they're being held captive by the Cegnu in the same place I was. I saw it so vividly. Their fear, their whispers. It was like I was there again. All the memories came rushing back at once and," he waves his hand to encompass the room. "I did this, imagining the monsters here, after me once again."

I freeze, my heart racing. "Are they the missing Hosliens from the orphanage?"

Isyarhi steps closer, a horrified expression on his face. I put my hand on his arm. "What is it? What's wrong Isyarhi?"

"Lira is my genomia, my match. She and Elora were taken right before the UPC officers came and took the orphanage workers away."

Frakyss and I exchange glances. That's almost six and a half months. How could young girls survive that long? "I'm sure they will be fine. They might not have been with the Cegnu that entire time," I reassure him.

"Was the facility where you were held ever discovered, Frakyss?"

He shakes his head. "No, the angelic warrior put me in stasis and sent me down to Romrey Island in a small, unmarked evacuation shuttle. I don't know who or what she was or how far the Cegnu were. For all I know, they could either be in this solar system or on the other side of the universe."

He runs a frustrated hand through the front of his hair. "We've got to figure this out. We have to rescue those girls and put a stop to the Cegnu and their practice of preying on children."

"Wait," Isyarhi blurts, and we turn to him. His large black almond eyes shift back and forth between us. "Nagori are supposed to be able to find their genomia from anywhere in the universe. I remember my mother telling me a bedtime story about it. I don't know if it's true, though, or how it works."

"Frakyss, how far is Nagoria from here?" He looks at me, puzzled.

"It depends on what you're flying. Maybe about twelve hours. It's in this quadrant. Why?"

"We're going to find a Nagori adult who can explain how they locate their genomia. That's the only lead we have unless you know where to find your mysterious winged warrior woman so we can ask her where the Cegnu are holed up."

"We never found her. We don't even know what species she was, so Nagoria it is. And I have the perfect ship, tiny and mighty, just like you. Let's go."

I roll my eyes at his back as he leads us along a hall deeper into his home. I glance into the open doorways as we pass, and I realize this place is a fortress. We've left the ultra-modern glass and steel structure and are deep inside the cliff. At the end of the long hallway is a large cavern with an *LWB05 Vortex* ship.

"Are you shitting me? You just happen to have a lightweight battleship at your house? Who are you, Batman?"

The two of them glance at me. "Who is 'Batman,' Aunt Nerrisa?"

"A dark, tortured fictional character on Earth who had a hidden cave with all sorts of fancy vehicles and gizmos to help him fight crime." I meet Frakyss's red stare. "Kind of like Uncle Frakyss. Only your uncle has better vehicles. The *LWB05 Vortex* can accommodate a crew of up to ten or as few as one if a synthetic copilot is used. "

Frakyss snorts as he leads us into the black ship. He lingers to retract the ramp and seal the door before continuing to the bridge. He takes the captain's chair.

"Nerrisa, take the copilot seat there," he gestures to a seat on his left, "and Isyarhi, take the navigation station." He points out a seat to his right. He stops a moment and looks me up and down. "Do you want to change into a uniform, or are you fine? I'm not complaining about the dress, mind you."

"I'm fine for now. If we've got twelve hours of travel, I'll have plenty of opportunity to change while we're enroute. No need to waste valuable time."

Chapter 15 - Frakyss

Gifts We Hide, Truths We Share

As soon as we enter the *LWB05 Vortex*, the lights give a soft pulse, acknowledging the ship has identified me. Once seated in the command chair, I establish my neural interface with the ship.

My mind is immediately flooded with the ship's status, capabilities, and location in relation to everything near us. I check the ship's shields, tactical information, and fuel cells, finding everything optimal.

What I don't expect as I check the ship's status is the glowing mind that is also accessible through the interface. I'm drawn to that bright light, and as soon as I touch it, I realize Nerrisa is also connected to the ship.

I hear her gasp next to me and glance over to see an expression of wonder and surprise on her beautiful face. Then it dawns on me that through the grith bond, we share DNA. Hers is part of me, and mine is part of her.

"Are you okay, Nerrisa? I am sorry. I didn't consider that because we now share DNA the neural interface would recognize you and connect automatically."

"Wow, is this what you were having Dyebarth create for me and *The Tabris*?"

"Yes. It makes the need for slower manual controls obsolete. Now that we are one with the *Vortex*, it's crucial not to make abrupt adjustments or have reactionary thoughts.

You might crash the ship or accidentally shoot off a disruptor blast."

"I'll stay focused. Hopefully, you can override anything crazy I might do until I get the hang of this." One side of her mouth quirks up.

I nod and initiate the startup sequence. When all systems are green, I take the ship through the atmos shield into the snowy night beyond. The ship bucks in the turbulent air until the stabilizers activate.

Once I establish proximities, I navigate the ship in a sharp arc through the stormy atmosphere into the calm of space.

"Uncle Frakyss, how are you flying the ship without touching the controls?"

"I had a neural interface system installed. As soon as I enter the ship, it scans for my DNA, retinal patterns, and brainwave patterns. Once recognized, the ship activates the mental initiation process that allows me to accept the link. Since your aunt and I share DNA, the ship recognizes her too."

"Wow, that's amazing. I wish I had a ship with a neural link." He comments longingly.

"I'm sure you will. You are already shaping up to be an excellent pilot. The neural connection has adaptive learning, so at your age, your ship will become increasingly attuned to your way of thinking, making the connection more natural. Over time, you two would work as one."

"Do you mind another question?" His antennae are twitching with curiosity.

"I don't mind."

"How did you fly the ship out of that cavern wall? One second, we were inside, and the next, we were out! I thought we were going to crash."

Before I can stop it, I bark a laugh. "I had an atmos shield installed. It's the same tech used on spaceships to keep the atmosphere inside the ship. It's a blend of energy manipulation and quantum field dynamics used to create a seamless barrier between the interior of shuttle bays and the vacuum of space outside. The *Vortex* uses that same tech in case there's a hull breach."

"That's good news. You know, just in case Aunt Nerrisa runs into something." We both laugh.

"Yuck it up, you two. I'll get even later." Nerrisa responds, but from the amused glint in her eyes, I can tell she doesn't mean it.

It's not long before Isyarhi yawns and is drooping in his chair. He and Nerrisa had a long day with their trip to Epree Island, and back to deal with me in my distraught state. I'm embarrassed to have had my mate see me so vulnerable and out of control.

"Nerrisa, would you like to take Isyarhi to a cabin so he can get some rest? Get one for yourself too. I'm sure you'd like to wear something more comfortable than an evening gown and those shoes with spiked heels. There's a replicator in the first room on the right where both of you can get what you need."

She nods and leads our nephew out of the cockpit.

I lean back in my chair, letting out a deep breath as I'm left alone with my thoughts. The events of the past day flash through my mind - the terrifying vision, my loss of control, and now this impromptu mission. I'm grateful for Nerrisa's presence and support, even if I'm not entirely comfortable with her seeing me in such a fragile state.

The ship hums smoothly around me as we speed toward Nagoria. Through our neural link, I sense Nerrisa moving about the ship, getting Isyarhi settled.

She returns to the bridge a short while later, dressed in a comfortable black flight suit. She settles back into the copilot's chair, her eyes meeting mine.

"He's asleep. Poor kid was exhausted."

I nod, grateful for her care of the boy. "Thank you for taking care of him. And thank you for coming when I needed you earlier."

She's quiet for a moment, her gaze thoughtful. "Of course. That's what mates are for, right?" There's a hint of a smile on her lips, and I feel my eyes widen. This is the first time she's ever openly acknowledged our bond with any hint of acceptance.

"I guess so," I respond, afraid to say anything that might change her mind. She reaches over and touches my arm.

"It's okay. I'm not going anywhere..." An incoming message chimes and interrupts her. I open the communication on the large screen on our left and see a dark-haired Earth female.

"Pearla? What's going on?" Nerrisa asks her friend.

"I had one of my feelings that you were searching for the missing Hosliens girls and that I need to be there with you."

"We are! My nephew, Isyarhi is the genomia mate to the eldest Hosliens girl. His species is supposed to be able to locate their mate from anywhere in the universe, but he doesn't know how. We're on our way to Nagoria to find someone who does." Nerrisa explains and looks at me, unsure of what to do.

"Pearla, where are you?" I ask the female.

"At the Silvergate Spaceport. I came here after Naia's baronial event because the feeling was so urgent when it hit."

"Go to the Galactic Freight office and ask for Evruik. He will provide transportation for you to rendezvous with us near Nagoria." I tell her and begin the message to my operations manager through the interface.

"You believe me?" The female looks surprised and glances between Nerrisa and me.

Nerrisa snorts a bitter laugh. "Pearla, you have no idea. We'll explain when we see you in person. Do you know if you need to go down to Nagoria with us or after?"

"Definitely after. Before you actually find the Hosliens."

"Okay, we'll take care of the Nagoria part of the trip when we get there. We should be done by the time you arrive. Now hurry up and get here."

"Affirmative," she says before closing the communication.

"Your friend is like me? She's an oracle?"

"Not exactly the same. She has a very strong intuition that compels her to act or intervene. She's also like the Hosliens, able to turn invisible. And she can alter her appearance."

I furrow my brow. "She can alter her appearance? Do you mean with makeup and wigs?"

"Like this," she responds, and in a blur, Nerrisa turns into a Meeve almost identical to Bruud.

"Greezok!" I gasp and stare at the small white furry creature where my mate sat seconds ago.

Her tail waves gently back and forth, and she grins, showing her sharp little teeth. The only way I know it's Nerrisa is that her eyes are still the same beautiful green, not the violet shade of all Meeves.

She leaps to my head and swings on my horn in the same way Bruud always does, chittering. I reach up to stroke the little creature's soft fur to make sure this isn't another vision brought on by my fractured mind. She's warm and solid and completely real.

She glides off my head and in a blurred motion, is standing in front of her chair, whole and normal again.

I close my gaping mouth with a snap and stare at my amazing female. She reaches into her pocket and withdraws a smooth green pebble, holding it in her open palm. The stone lifts from her hand and dances through the air, making loops and figure eights before stopping and hovering over her palm.

I reach out and pluck it from the air between my forefinger and thumb, inspecting it for what hidden properties might make it move on its own.

"It's not a magic rock. It's one Brier gave me because he thought it matched my eyes."

"Then how..."

"Telekinesis. I can move things with my mind. Small things are easier, much larger are more of a challenge."

"Please explain." I drop the stone into her open palm, and she returns it to her pocket.

"People of my species have a variety of abilities. We all differ a little. For instance, I'm sure you heard about Queen Astrid being able to command the sea creatures and build an army to take out the

Zugunu. That's part of her powerful siren effect. Naia can mind speak. She can converse with any other living creature. And she can control the water and weather. She's quite powerful." Nerrisa explains and sits in her chair again.

"General Grizlor's tiny little mate?"

"Yes, that very one."

"Is there anything else you can do?"

"Just the basics all other Aquar'thyns can do like simple water manipulation and mild siren effect. Nothing as strong as some of the others, though. The stronger the power, the weaker it makes us." She shrugs her shoulders and reaches up to tuck a long strand of hair behind her ear.

"You're amazing, Nerrisa."

Her cheeks turn pink, and the tan dots across the bridge of her nose stand out even more. "Thank you, Frakyss. You're amazing too."

Nerrisa is humming when she returns from the galley with several paper-wrapped packets in her hands. She sits and passes one to me and tosses one to Isyarhi, who catches it midair.

"Thanks, Auntie." He unwraps it, takes a big bite and chews, moaning.

Nerrisa is already eating hers, so I unwrap mine and sniff it. The outer shell is composed of two flattened discs of grain. I peel them apart to find a thick, viscous substance with a golden hue on one side and a gelatinous purple material on the other. I push the pieces back together and take a small bite.

The rich and savory flavor explodes across my tongue, followed by a sweet fruity blast that provides a delicious contrast.

The combination is nothing short of a masterpiece. Nerrisa giggles at my reaction as I savor each bite, almost groaning with my delight along with Isyarhi. "What is this?"

"It's a peanut butter and grape jelly sandwich."

"I like this Earth food a lot. It's as good as the pancakes. Is this programmed in the galley synthesizer?"

"It is," she responds between bites.

"Good," I shove the last piece in my mouth. "I want another." I start to get up, but Isyarhi jumps to his feet first.

"I'll get it. I want another one too." He bounds out of the room, and Nerrisa snorts.

"I should have brought extras. He always eats two or three. I wasn't sure if you'd like it or not."

"I do. It's very efficient too. No mess and easy to carry."

"If you like that, I have a lot more sandwiches you'll love. Wait until you have corned beef on rye bread."

Just as Isyarhi returns and hands me two sandwiches, the navigation system indicates we are nearing Nagoria. I slow the ship as the dark green and blue planet grows larger on our main screen. I check to make sure the Vortex's cloaking system is operating and start the scanning system for lifeforms below.

"Wow, is that Nagoria?" The teen leans forward in his seat and stares at the planet and its three moons. "I've never seen it from space. The ship that took me to the orphanage didn't have windows."

"It is. Notice your natural coloration matches your planet? You blend into your surroundings to avoid the predators." He glances down at his arms and hands and back at the planet.

"I guess I didn't realize that. Is that how it works for Abrauxians?"

"Somewhat. I am lighter colored because I am originally from Romrey Island. The lighter color helped my ancestors blend into the mountains so we wouldn't be spotted by Ryze birds and other flying predators. The royal family is darker because Epree Island is mostly dark gray and black marble."

"What about the Abrauxians from Silvergate Cay?"

"Mostly medium to light gray, though there are exceptions to all. Lord Chyrgog is from Silvergate Cay, and his skin color is almost the same as Aunt Nerrisa. He has bright gold horns and eyes. Nykon is from Epree, but he is pure white with blue eyes. Some of the elders on Epree mistreated him when he was a child because he was different. It's why he and his father built Whitevale Citadel on Roxus, and he's proven himself to be an astute businessman."

"It makes me mad when adults treat kids badly," he says, his voice tightening.

I watch him closely, the way his small hands clench and his shoulders stiffen.

"The orphanage workers hurt us all the time. They told us we were too ugly and too stupid for anyone to adopt."

My chest tightens. I want to reach out, to erase those words from his memory, but I stay still and let him speak.

"Ravair, Erland the Drecril, and I tried to protect the younger kids as much as we could," he continues, his gaze dropping to the floor. "That's why Ravair was in such bad shape when you came and rescued us."

He hesitates, breathing slow and shaky. I lean forward slightly, willing him to keep going.

"He was there when the Hosliens sisters were taken. He tried to help them, but the orphanage director beat him, and kicked him until he was unconscious."

A muscle jumps in my jaw. I grip the edge of my chair to keep from moving, to keep from showing the full force of the rage boiling in my blood.

"I wasn't there when it happened," he says, voice dropping to a whisper. "I was on foraging duty with Erland. We didn't find out until we got back that night."

His hands ball into tight fists, small but fierce.

"If you and Aunt Nerrisa hadn't come when you did," he finishes, "I think he would have died."

I clench my hands harder, forcing myself to stay calm for him. But inside, I swear I will never let anyone hurt them again.

Hearing how he and the other children were treated makes my rage spike again. Nerrisa lays a calming hand on my arm and blocks me from the ship's controls before I accidentally trigger a reaction in the system.

My surprise at her ability to wrest the controls away so easily, surprises me out of my rage reaction. When I stare at her, she gives a faint shake of her head.

"I'm glad he didn't, sweetheart. The orphanage director and his workers are on the prison moon now. You and the other kiddos are safe." Nerrisa reassures him, and I an feel her mind release the ship's controls to me once more, sensing my calm.

"Isyarhi, do you remember your village name?" I ask, handing him one of the two sandwiches he brought me.

"Calcari. It's in the northern hemisphere in the great forest."

I scan the topographical map in the ship's navigation system, find the area he mentioned, and guide the ship to a stationary position over it. Three distinct settlements appear as glowing green areas. I bring the image up on the main screen. "Do you know if that is one of these places?"

He leans forward and studies the map closely before indicating the bottom right. "This one is Calcari."

Chapter 16 - Nerrisa

The Genomia Connection

"This shouldn't take long," I tell Frakyss. "I'll take Isyarhi down in one of the skiffs. We'll find an older Nagori and ask how the genomia mate link works so he can track Lira. Then we'll come right back up."

"Wait, why you? I think I should take him, and you remain on the ship where it's safe. I'm more capable of protecting him."

I raise an eyebrow at him. "Oh, I don't know, Frakyss, don't you think you'll be a little obvious walking into the middle of the village? All seven feet of you?"

I cross in front of him and stand next to my nephew. The air shimmers for a moment, and I see his eyes widen when he glances between me and Isyarhi, no doubt seeing a twin of the boy where I stand.

Focusing on the sandwich held loosely in his hand. I flip it up to bonk him on the head and drop it back on his lap with a quick flick of my mind. "Now give me a dagger and a blaster, and we'll be on our way."

"What about your green eyes? I don't think a lot of Nagori have green eyes."

"I'll put in contacts."

"Fine, but I don't like it." He gets up and follows us to the small supply room. I enter the request for black contacts to fit my enlarged eyes, and when the unit chimes, I pull them out.

They seem really large, but they pop in easily, and I blink a few times to make sure they are going to stay seated on my eye. I stare at Frakyss and Isyarhi. The boy shoots me a grin, and Frakyss shakes his head and leads us to the small cargo bay.

Once inside the room, he presses a hand on the bio reader of the weapons safe, and the door clicks open. I give a low whistle when I see the arsenal he's got stashed in there.

"Expecting a war?"

"No. I like to be prepared. Here," he hands each of us a tiny communicator that we fasten to the inside collar of our black t-shirts. When I look up again, he's holding out a small, sleek blaster in a leg holster and a dagger in a waist holster. I strap them on while the two watch me.

"Can I have those too? You know, just in case the Zugunu are still around stirring up trouble?"

I glance between the two of them and shrug. "I don't see why not. You know how to use both."

Frakyss shakes his head but reaches into his treasure trove of weapons before turning and handing Isyarhi a blaster and dagger identical to mine. We wait for him to strap them on before following Frakyss to the shuttle bay where a small two-person Shadowstrike is parked.

"Your neural connection works the same in the Shadowstrike as it does on the main ship. If something happens and Isyarhi has to fly, press this button to turn off the NIS." He points to a hidden black button that blends into the underside of the dashboard.

"If the system detects you losing consciousness, it will automatically switch off the NIS. I've added Isyarhi to the system, so we three are the only ones who can fly it."

I climb into the front passenger compartment. "Okay, thanks. Anything else about the planet I should know before we go in?"

"All the planet's data is already in your nanos, so you can do a quick review on the way down. But the basics are a higher atmospheric oxygen content, lower gravity, and only one large predator, the Rotax, you need to avoid. You're going into the tropical zone, with a temperate climate and high humidity."

He's busy getting Isyarhi strapped into the passenger section at the back of the skiff as he describes the large planet. I hear him click the rear canopy shut before he moves next to me.

"Ready?"

I nod and give him a thumbs-up. "We'll be back before you have time to miss us."

His eyes are lit with concern, but he nods and slowly lowers the canopy over me, and it clicks into place. He leaves the shuttle bay and I track him with the ship's systems as he returns to the bridge. I trigger the exterior bay door to open, and the atmos shield fills the small room. Once I'm sure the bay is airtight, I fly out and begin my descent to the planet below.

Strong wind buffets the skiff. Small elevons adjust the pitch and roll of the spacecraft, allowing for better control in the turbulent conditions as we drop swiftly, and the dark turquoise and green blur below transforms into majestic trees the size of redwoods.

I scan the real-time topography screen in front of me to find an opening to allow us to land within a klick of the Nagori village.

At last, I see a place where we'll fit and maneuver at a slight angle to avoid the grasp of large branches on either side. The twilight gloom below the tree canopy has a dreamlike quality when coupled with the foggy haze surrounding us when we land.

"It's early morning, Isyarhi. We are northwest of the village. Do you have someone in mind to speak with?"

"My uncle is one of the elders. I'm sure he'll be able to help us. His cottage is at the western edge, and I recognize this place, so I can lead the way."

With a thought through the NIS, I open both of our canopies and they swing upward. The air is thick with the scent of damp earth and vegetation, and the quiet hum of the primordial forest creates a constant white noise.

The towering trees stretch upward, with their massive trunks covered with bark that glistens in shades of deep emerald and turquoise. The canopy overhead is a tangled web, allowing only the faintest shafts of light to filter through, casting the forest floor in perpetual twilight.

I step out to the moss-covered ground, and Isyarhi slides off the wing to stand next to me. I close and secure the ship and glance around before I nod to the teen to lead the way. He sets off at a fast pace, and I follow. Thick fog rises from the ground, wrapping around our legs, and creeping higher.

It settles cool and damp on my skin. As we weave between the colossal trees, we catch glimpses of bioluminescent fungi glowing in the shadows. Their bluish hues illuminate patches of the forest floor. It's beautiful, but we can't linger. The urgency of our mission pushes us forward.

Suddenly, a low growl reverberates through the trees, sending a shiver down my spine. I freeze, glancing at Isyarhi, whose eyes are widened in fear. We crouch low, hearts pounding, listening intently as the growl transforms into a series of clicks and chittering sounds. The forest seems to hold its breath, the cacophony of life momentarily silenced.

"Rotax! Hurry," he urges, his voice barely a whisper as he gestures for me to follow him deeper into the shadows. We move silently, every sense heightened. As we navigate the thick undergrowth, the ferns part almost reluctantly as we pass.

We reach a clearing, and Isyarhi holds up a hand to stop me. Ahead, the faint outline of his village emerges through the mist, with small, organic structures that blend seamlessly into the landscape. The buildings are draped in thick vines and flowers, their colors vibrant against the muted green backdrop of the forest.

"This way," he whispers, pointing to a narrow path that leads around the outskirts of the village. I nod and follow as he slips into the shadows once more.

The narrow path winds through the underbrush, and the mist thickens around us. Nervous energy radiates from Isyarhi as we approach the clearing where a small cottage is nestled among the ancient trees.

When we near the small structure, the smell of something savory wafts through the air, mingling with the rich scent of the forest, and my stomach growls in response.

"Is this it?" I whisper, my voice barely above a breath. He nods, his eyes wide with a mix of hope and anxiety.

As we approach, I see the faint flicker of light filtering through a small window. Isyarhi hesitates, glancing back at me for reassurance. I offer him a nod, trying to show my support. He steps closer to the door, his hand trembling as he reaches for the latch.

In a swift motion, he pushes the door open, and it creaks eerily on its hinges. The interior is humble but warm, filled with the comforting aromas of food and earthy scents of wood and moss. My eyes adjust to the light, and I an see the elderly Nagori seated at a small table, a simple meal before him. I follow my nephew into the room and latch the door behind me.

"Uncle Elarin!" Isyarhi whispers, his voice breaking the stillness.

The old Nagorian male looks up, his face etched with the lines of age and wisdom. At first, confusion flickers across his features, but then shock washes over him as he gets up, sending the chair clattering backward.

"Isyarhi?" he gasps, his voice cracking with disbelief. The old man moves with surprising speed, rushing toward his nephew and enveloping him in a fierce embrace. The moment is tender, filled with the raw emotion of reunion, and I smile at the sight of their joy.

But as the uncle pulls back, his eyes narrow, and he glances warily at me where I stand behind Isyarhi. I can feel the tension in the air shift, a pulse of fear igniting his gaze. His expression morphs from joy to uncertainty, and he takes a cautious step back, creating space between him and his nephew.

"Who... who are you?" he stammers, his voice laced with suspicion. "Is this some trick? Are you... Isyarhi? But how can this be?"

I hold my hands up. "Wait, please. I'm Nerrisa. I'm here to help Isyarhi. I'm his honorary aunt through his adoptive mother on Abrauxia."

The uncle's eyes dart between the boy and me, confusion and fear mingling in his expression. He studies me closely; the resemblance between us is undeniable.

"Isyarhi, is this true?" The old man's voice trembles with a mix of hope and lingering doubt. "Is this your aunt?"

"She is," Isyarhi replies, his voice steadying as he steps protectively in front of me. "She rescued me and the rest of the kids from that awful orphanage on Coprinus-LV3. I was adopted by her friend Kishi, an Omatu. But we need help finding my genomia mate who I met at the orphanage. She and her sister are Hosliens and were taken by Cegnu. We believe they are in grave danger."

The uncle's gaze softens, his instincts as a protector kicking in. He takes a deep breath. "You've returned to me, my boy," he murmurs, his voice thick with emotion. "I searched everywhere for you and your parents between here and Mistwood."

"We were ambushed by Zugunu, a day's walk from Valnara. Father and Mother were shot with blasters, but I stayed hidden off the path, as Father told me, until the Zugunu left.

After a day of walking, I made it to Valnara, and because no one knew me, they sent me away with the Natterians to the orphanage. They wouldn't listen when I said my family were in Calcari."

As we huddle in the dim interior of the cottage, we hear the distant rumble of voices. Elarin touches his finger to his lips. "Zugunu soldiers," he breathes, and the words send a chill down my spine.

"We have to go now!" I urge, glancing at the two of them. The urgency in my voice propels them into action, and we slip out a low door in the back of the cottage. The path back to the skiff is almost invisible in the thickening fog.

We navigate the thick underbrush, every rustle making my skin crawl with apprehension. Not far from our vessel, the clicking sound of a nearby Rotax, sends us scrambling into a thicket of vines growing up the trunk of a tree.

We barely breathe, staying perfectly still, our turquoise and green striated skin blending with the tree bark at our backs. The ground trembles under the creature's footsteps. I clench my teeth together when it appears.

The Rotax creeps along on all four large, clawed feet, stopping every few yards to stand upright, towering at least fifteen feet before dropping back down.

It looks like a T-Rex and iguana had a colorful lizard offspring. One that focuses its small orange eyes in our direction. Its nose lifts into the air and sniffs before emitting that sharp clicking noise once again.

Shouting comes from the direction of the Shadowstrike, and the Rotax bolts in that direction. I let out the breath I've been holding, relief flooding through me.

Screams pierce the air. "Come on, we'll circle around and get to the ship from the opposite direction," I whisper to my companions.

We race through the tall foliage, reaching the ship and huddling behind it, watching the colorful lizard snatch up a screaming Zugunu, shaking it violently before gulping the shredded carcass down in two mighty gulps.

A second terrified Zugunu flees through the trees toward the village, and the predator follows.

I trigger both canopies to swing upwards. Uncle Elarin climbs into the passenger compartment, and Isyarhi squeezes in next to him. I seal the hatch and hurry into the pilot's compartment, closing it with a quiet click. I prepare the small ship for takeoff.

"Hold on!" I shout through the communications unit as the vehicle shoots into the air. I weave through the dense treetops until I find a gap, maneuvering into the bright clear sky, and rising through the atmosphere.

The stars twinkle as we leave the planet behind, and soon, the silhouette of the *Vortex* looms ahead, its docking bay glowing invitingly. I guide the skiff inside, and at last, the tension in my chest releases as we reach safety.

Once we land, I waste no time unbuckling myself and opening the hatch. I open the passenger section and help the two males out of the cramped space.

"Come, follow me," I say, leading them out of the bay area and up the short hall to the galley where Frakyss awaits us.

He looks toward Elarin, his expression shifting to alarm. "Who is this?"

"Frakyss, this is my Uncle Elarin," Isyarhi introduces, his voice steady despite the huge

Abrauxian's red glare. "He's the last of my family on Nagoria, and he needed to leave. There were Zugunu searching for anyone left in our village."

Elarin nods, his demeanor softening as he meets Frakyss's gaze. "Thank you for taking me in," he responds. "The Zugunu have been rounding up any remaining Nagorians for slave labor. We barely escaped."

Frakyss's expression darkens, and he moves to the food synthesizer, ordering mugs of steaming warm drinks for the four of us. "You're safe here. We'll figure out our next moves together. Isyarhi, did you have a chance to ask your uncle how the link between you and your genomia mate works so we can locate the girls?"

"We had just started discussing it when the Zugunu showed up," the teen responds.

I reach up and squeeze the dark contacts, one after the other, to pop them out of my eyes before I shift back to my normal humanoid form. Elarin rears back in his seat, almost tipping the chair over. I hold up my hand, reassuring him. "It's okay, this is how I normally look. Please continue."

Elarin leans forward, his voice low and serious. "Your connection to your mate is stronger than you realize, my boy. The bond you share is not just emotional; it's biological. You can sense her presence, her location, even across vast distances. It's not just a matter of instinct; it is a skill rooted in our biology, and it requires both focus and practice."

Isyarhi nods eagerly. "How do I do it?" he asks, leaning forward in anticipation.

Elarin takes a deep breath, collecting his thoughts. "First, you must understand the bond you share with her. It's a connection that resonates within your very genetics. The specific genome traits that bind us can be located within you by tapping into that frequency."

"Close your eyes and take a deep breath. Feel the air around you, the life within you."

Isyarhi follows his instructions, his eyes fluttering shut as he inhales deeply.

"Picture her face in your mind. Visualize her presence, her energy. You must connect with that essence," he instructs, his voice now a calming whisper.

As Isyarhi concentrates, a look of determination crosses his face. Elarin presses on, his voice steady. "This is where it becomes more nuanced. Every living thing has a unique genomic signature, like a fingerprint. Your mate's signature will feel familiar to you... warm, vibrant, and undeniably hers. You must learn to distinguish it from the multitude of others around you."

Isyarhi nods, letting the information sink in. "How will I know when I've found her?" he asks, a hint of apprehension lacing his voice.

"When you sense her, you will feel a pull, a tugging at your heart and mind," Elarin explains. "It's an instinctual response, a deep knowing that transcends logic. You may even experience a physical sensation... a warmth spreading through your chest, a fluttering in your core. Trust that feeling. It's your bond guiding you."

"But what if she's far away?" Isyarhi questions, his brow furrowing. "How can I reach her if she's light-years away?"

"That's where your innate abilities come into play," Elarin replies, a glimmer of pride in his eyes. "The bond you share is not limited by distance. With practice, you will learn to amplify your connection, helping you reach across vast expanses. It may take you time to hone this skill, but it is within you."

Elarin pauses, letting his words resonate in the quiet galley. "You must also be aware of your emotional state. Fear, doubt, and anger can cloud your connection. When you seek her, approach with love and hope in your heart. Those emotions strengthen the bond, making it easier to locate her."

As Isyarhi listens intently, I see the determination building within him. Elarin leans closer, his voice dropping to a conspiratorial whisper. "If you can achieve this, not only will you be able to find her, but you will be able to protect her, even from afar. If danger approaches, you will feel it. You must learn to trust yourself, Isyarhi."

"I will," the teen vows, his eyes clenched shut with fierce determination. "I promise to do everything I can, to find her."

"Perhaps it will help if you two go to the conference room where you can focus uninterrupted." Frakyss murmurs.

"That's a good idea. Come, nephew, let's go see if we can find your genomia mate."

We all stand and walk toward the front of the ship. Isyarhi leads Elarin into the first room on the left, and Frakyss and I continue past them to the bridge, where we take our seats. Frakyss's eyes go distant for a few minutes, and when he refocuses, our eyes meet.

"I alerted the UPC that their forces need to deal with the Zugunu on Nagoria, find the kidnapped Nagorian people, and return them to their planet. It's time the Zugunu were dealt with."

I nod, my heart aching at the thought of the peaceful villagers being used as slaves. "Do you think they'll respond in time to help them?"

"We have to believe they will," Frakyss replies, setting his jaw. "I made it clear how urgent the situation is. I also told them we are trying to find the missing Hosliens sisters being held by the Cegnu so they will be able to mobilize if we need their assistance."

"Now we wait," I say, trying to steady my nerves. "Isyarhi and Elarin will be working on locating the sisters. I just hope they find them before it's too late."

An incoming message pings the ship's communications, and Frakyss answers the hail. Evruik's face fills the screen in front of us.

"Frakyss, I am nearing Nagoria with Pearla Williams on board. Do you want me to dock with the *Vortex*?"

"Yes, I'm sending our coordinates now." It's not long before we hear the soft hum of docking clamps engaging, and the *Vortex* shudders as Evruik's ship connects to our docking bay.

We enter just as the hatch opens, and Pearla steps onto the ship. As always, she has an air of confidence, her dark wavy hair pulled back into a neat bun and her sharp pale eyes scanning the room with an intensity that speaks of her investigative background. Dressed in a neat black turtleneck, cargo pants, and combat boots, she looks ready for action.

"Hey Pearla, glad to have you join us. This is Frakyss, in case you haven't met before."

"It's a pleasure to meet you, Frakyss. Thanks for waiting for my arrival."

"Actually, we don't know where we're going yet. My Nagorian nephew and I went down to the planet's surface to find someone to explain to him how to track his mate. While we were talking with his elderly uncle, a contingent of Zugunu showed up, and we escaped back to the *Vortex* with him." I lead her to the galley with Frakyss trailing behind.

Once we're comfortably seated with cups of hot tea, we get her caught up on what's happened.

"So these Cegnu who have the girls are the ones who kidnapped and tortured you, Frakyss?" She asks and looks him over with a critical eye.

"Yes," he rumbles and boldly meets her gaze. "They killed my best friend, who they kidnapped at the same time. I was close to dying when a glowing white female warrior with wings rescued me. I don't know who she was or where she was from. I lost consciousness when she carried me out of the Cegnu cells. When I woke next, I was in the Abrauxian medical clinic on Epree Island. I had been sent down in an unmarked escape pod."

"Weren't any of the Abrauxians able to find her?" Pearla asks.

"I never told anyone what happened. I didn't talk for many years. My mind was broken, and I was so hideous no one from before wanted anything to do with me. The King sent me to live on Silvergate Cay where I could start over."

I lay my hand on his warm, solid arm. "You are not hideous, Frakyss. Far from it." I trace my index finger down a jagged scar that bisects his left pectoral. "These marks show that you survived those who would have killed you. Now that you are an adult, you have the chance to make sure they never harm another child. We can save those young girls."

Our gazes meet, and his hand covers mine. "I hope you're right, Nerrisa."

Chapter 17 - Frakyss

He Who Lit My Eyes Red

"I hope you're right, Nerrisa," I respond. When I'm touching her, my mind feels clearer. Uncontrollable rage no longer pounds through my skull, hiding just under the surface, threatening to roar to life at any moment.

I hear footsteps running in the hall, and Isyarhi bursts into the galley, breathing heavily. "I can feel Lira!"

"What do you mean, Isyarhi?" I ask, my heart racing at the sudden spark of hope.

"I feel the pull from her," he continues, his voice a mix of excitement and disbelief. "It's strong! I'm not sure how far away she is, but I know I can point you in the right direction!"

"Are you sure?" Elarin asks as he enters behind his nephew.

"Yes, I'm certain!" Isyarhi insists, his expression fierce. "It's like a thread connecting us. I can feel her energy; it's warm and bright. I just need to focus."

Pearla's eyes light up, and she exchanges a glance with me and Nerrisa. "This is it! If Isyarhi can lead us to Lira, we have to move fast."

"Can you show us on the map?" I urge, stepping closer to the teen, careful not to let my slashing tail hit any of the others in the small room.

"Right now, I can't pinpoint the exact location," he replies, his brows furrowed in concentration. "But I know the direction. Just give me a moment."

I watch as he closes his eyes, his antennas twitching as if tuning into a frequency only he can hear. The room is charged with anticipation. "I feel her," he whispers to himself.

"Do you sense any danger?" Nerrisa asks, concern etched on her face.

"No," Isyarhi replies, opening his eyes. "Not from her, at least. But we have to hurry. If she's in the hands of the Cegnu, there's no telling how long she'll be okay."

"Let's go to the bridge. We don't want to waste a moment," I urge. "Pearla and Elarin, there is only room for three on the bridge. Do you mind staying here or in your quarters?"

"We'll stay here," Pearla says and Elarin nods his agreement.

We rush to the cockpit, Isyarhi in the lead. He takes his seat at the navigation station. "I need access to the console to track the direction," he says. "I can guide you there."

I release my NIS control over the star maps and turn on the large holographic screen in front of him. The atmosphere in the room is tense, the urgency almost palpable as Isyarhi begins to run his finger along the map in the direction he feels Lira's presence. "There!" he says, his finger hovering over a point on the map. "She's around here, but I can't tell how far."

"Let's plot a course," I say, my hearts pounding in my chest. "Once we get there, we'll figure out the next step."

I lean over his shoulder, find the exact coordinates, and enter them into the navigation system. It flashes:

```
Galaxy: Zyphora Galaxy
Solar System: Nerath System
Distance: 2,500 light-years
Estimated Travel Time at Warp
Speed (100c): 25.3 hours
```

Once the system plots the route, I initiate the warp drives, and the stars elongate on the viewing screens. "We should take turns resting while enroute, so we're fresh and ready to take on the Cegnu. We don't know how many are involved or what kind of security measures they have in place."

"I'll let Pearla and Elarin know and get them set up with cabins and grab a couple of hours of sleep. Isyarhi, do you want to come with me, or do you want to stay here with Uncle Frakyss for a while?" Nerrisa says as she gets to her feet and walks to the door.

"I'd rather stay with Uncle Frakyss for a little longer if that's okay." She nods, gives us a wave, and leaves, closing the door behind her.

The moment the door shuts, I feel an almost tangible shift in the air, a mix of tension and unspoken words hanging between us.

Isyarhi's focus is razor-sharp, his eyes darting between the controls and the flickering stars on the screen. I feel a surge of protectiveness wash over me; this kid has been through hell, yet here he is, leading us toward his mate with unwavering determination.

"Isyarhi," I say, trying to break the silence that's thick as space dust. "Are you scared?"

He glances at me, his antennae twitching before he replies. "A little. But mostly determined." His lips curve into a small smile.

I nod, admiring his resilience. My tail flicks behind me restlessly. "If the Cegnu laid a finger on the girls..."

"Don't think about that," he interrupts, looking straight into my glowing red eyes. The intensity of his gaze is surprising. From a kid who seemed so fragile just months ago, now he gives off stronger vibes than some full-grown warriors I've crossed paths with. "We will get them back."

We slip into the passing hours with his words hanging in the air. The hum of the engines and distant whirring fills the space between us as we settle into our new roles: him as the developing navigator and me as the mentor overseeing him.

Isyarhi has just settled back into his seat, and as I prepare to ask him if he can still feel Lira, a familiar voice echoes from behind me. Nerrisa has returned.

"Is something wrong?"

"No. Just bonding over our mutual dread." I respond and her lips quirk at my sarcasm.

Isyarhi lets out a laugh that sounds more confident than anything I expected to hear from him today. "Okay! Maybe more determination than dread," he clarifies with mock seriousness.

Nerrisa rolls her vivid green eyes playfully at us. "Well, if we're going for alliteration, consider 'dreadfully determined.' Everyone wants to sound dramatic before plunging headfirst into danger."

"That sounds a lot like the fictional Earth entertainment Lord Chyrgog has been importing." I chuckle. The weight of our mission begins to feel lighter when we can joke about it for a second or two.

"Let me know when we're within range," she says after a beat, leaning against the wall in her black flight suit that clings more enticingly than a utilitarian uniform should. Something about the way she stands there, confident yet vulnerable, makes my blood heat under my skin.

"I will," Isyarhi promises her, turning back to his console while I attempt to focus on anything but Nerrisa's alluring presence.

The warp speeds us through space like a comet shooting toward destiny; hours fade into nothingness as anticipation mounts with every passing hour. And somewhere in that vast black void lies Lira, a tether pulling Isyarhi and the rest of us toward her with gravitational force.

A sharp beep pulls us back to reality. The navigation system alerts us that we're approaching the outer edge of the area where Isyarhi feels Lira. The stars shift as the warp slows, returning to their familiar pinpricks of light.

"Alright, everyone. Strap in," I command, my voice taking on a more serious tone. Isyarhi's fingers dance over the controls, nervous energy radiating from him. I glance at Nerrisa, catching her eye for just a moment before she takes her place in the co-pilot's chair.

"We need a solid plan," she says, her brow furrowing. "Do we know what we're walking into or have any intel on their defenses?"

Isyarhi looks up from his console, a frown crossing his youthful features. "I've been trying to tap into my Nagorian abilities. If I sense Lira close by, maybe I can also get an idea of how many Cegnu are in the area." He bites his lower lip in concentration, antennae twitching as he closes his eyes.

"What if you don't sense anything?" I ask, not wanting to add to Isyarhi's growing anxiety but needing to be prepared for all possibilities.

Nerrisa shoots me a look that says, 'Stop distracting him,' and nods at Isyarhi's efforts instead. "You got this," she encourages him.

Silence blankets the room, and we hold our breath until finally, like a light bulb flickering on in his mind. Isyarhi gasps. "I can feel her! She's close!" His voice echoes with a mixture of relief and urgency.

Fingers reaching for the navigation panel, Isyarhi begins plotting a course while my heart races with adrenaline. "There's a facility nearby.

It looks abandoned. There's an entrance on the far side that should work."

"Then that's our way in," Nerrisa declares.

"Let's not waste time," I growl with resolve, already picturing how we will extract the girls, stealthy and silent like predators hunting in twilight. But beneath my bravado is a gnawing fear: the fear of a small boy trapped by the monsters from his nightmares.

As I edge the *Vortex* closer to our target at an agonizingly slow pace, Isyarhi turns to me, a spark of concern cracking through his initial bravado. "Frakyss, you'll protect Lira and Elora, right?"

"Always," I assure him firmly masking my own apprehension

Nerrisa leans forward to see him on the other side of me. "We'll get the girls back, sweetheart."

The ship vibrates as I make final adjustments to our approach. Pearla and Elarin must have felt the change in the ship's speed because both arrive on the bridge at the same time.

We drift closer to a derelict space station that, at first glance, appears abandoned. The view outside shifts from the beauty of the hazy green Zephora galaxy to the stark, metallic structure looming ominously in front of us. Shadows flicker across the hull as if warning us away.

"Shize," I mutter under my breath. "The station looks like a death trap. It's likely impossible to detect which areas are atmospherically safe and which ones are open to the vacuum of space." So this is the place where the terrors of my childhood took place, where a tiny cell without light teems with memories of horror. I push those thoughts aside, focusing on the mission at hand instead.

Nerrisa leans closer to me for a better view of the display.

A small tremor moves through the *Vortex* as I gently anchor my ship to the side of the station, avoiding the standard gangways for a less obvious point of entry. I hope we remain cloaked from detection by any movement sensors the Cegnu might have to monitor the facility.

"What was that?" Nerrisa's voice is tense, laced with adrenaline.

"We just docked with the station," I reply. "Give me a minute to see if I can access schematics. Can you feel exactly where Lira is in there, Isyarhi?"

A quick data search identifies the facility. "This is Echo Station," I read the details aloud. "The original purpose was a communications relay center, facilitating interstellar communications across the Nerath System. It was crucial for maintaining contact between planets and trade routes. As technology improved and more efficient systems were developed, Echo Station fell into disuse and was ultimately abandoned around seventy years ago."

The three of us stare at the schematic that I bring up on the main monitor. I overlay the Vortex's life detection system, and we see three distinct larger life forms and a multitude of tiny signals that are probably the usual vermin found on old stations. Isyarhi gestures to the two red dots near the top of the station.

"These two are Lira and Elora."

"Okay." Nerrisa exhales slowly and grips the edge of the console tighter. "Let's go over the plan again."

She ticks off the points one by one. "Isyarhi will work from here to disable any security systems the Cegnu have in place. Elarin will monitor the ship's security systems to make sure no one else gains access besides us and the Hosliens."

Her voice steadies as she continues. "The three of us will go for the sisters first. Pearla will use her invisibility to scout the way, and we will follow."

She glances around the group, making sure everyone is with her. "Once we find the sisters, Pearla will lead them back to the Vortex. Frakyss and I will head to the lower level and neutralize the Cegnu threat."

Nerrisa takes another breath, her hands steady on the console now. "After dealing with the Cegnu, the team will regroup here at the ship. Once everyone is back on board, we will depart Echo Station and return to Abrauxia."

I glance at everyone crammed into the room. "Any questions?"

Elarin leans against the chair where his nephew sits, swiveled away from the console. "Are you sure you want to do this?" Elarin asks. "You're leaving your mate's safety in the hands of others."

Isyarhi nods, his jaw set. "They can get to her in ways I can't right now. If I try to go, I'll only be a distraction. I trust Uncle Frakyss, Aunt Nerrisa, and Pearla. They'll bring Lira and her sister back safely."

Elarin sighs, placing a hand on the teen's shoulder. "Then we'll wait here. But remember, you've got a connection to her. Tell me if anything feels off, and I'll inform the team."

Isyarhi nods, his jaw set as he turns and focuses on the console.

"Let's move," I say as I lead Nerrisa, Pearla, and Elarin out of the room to the docking bay. I open the weapons vault and hand Elarin a communicator. "This fits into your ear canal. Use it to communicate anything important to us. If we don't answer, it's because we don't want to betray our position." Elarin inserts the tiny unit into his ear and leaves the room. I hand out breathers and weapons to the females.

"We need to make this quick and efficient."

Nerrisa takes her weapon with practiced ease, her grip steady as she checks the blaster's charge before sliding it into her leg holster. "Right, because that Cegnu won't be eager to let us breeze in and out with its prized captives," she quips.

Pearla checks her weapons, glancing up at us. "Are you sure there's only one Cegnu?"

I nod my head. "I'm sure, but we don't know about synthetics or anyone in stasis since they don't appear on scans. They only detect organic brain waves. We'll need to keep the plan fluid and adjust as needed.

Nerrisa's eyes narrow as she scans our faces. "We find Lira and Elora first, then deal with whatever comes next."

Once armed, I lead the two females into the airlock at the rear of the docking bay. I check the display for air and gravitational levels to find them at normal limits to support our lifeforms. The heavy exterior door opens with a soft hiss, revealing a darkened corridor beyond that leads deeper into Echo Station.

As we step through, shadows cling to us, turning everything to monochromatic gray and black.

The air is stale but breathable, tinged with the stink of rust and old metal.

"Stay alert," I whisper as we inch forward, the sound of our boots muffled by decades of undisturbed dust on the floor.

With unspoken agreement, we move together as a unit, navigating deeper into the station's core. Pearla flickers to invisibility, just another shadow among shadows.

Nerrisa and I fall into step, our bodies occasionally brushing in the darkness as we inch forward.

"You got a plan for when we find the Cegnu?" she asks in a whispered voice, her pale face hovering in the darkness.

"Not really," I admit, swallowing hard. "Besides charging in and hoping we don't get our heads ripped off, that is."

"Delightful!" she responds with a playful eye roll. I notice a hint of a smile creeping in. "Let's just keep those Abrauxian protector instincts in check until we get the sisters."

I grunt an acknowledgment. "Right. Focus on saving Lira and Elora."

As we move deeper into Echo Station's heart, the oppressive silence is broken only by the faint hum of machinery. Pearla reappears out of invisibility ahead of us, her brow furrowed as she gestures for us to slow down.

"There's something up ahead," she murmurs. We stop behind a corner, and I peek around. An eerie glow spills from an open chamber at the end of the corridor.

"What do you see?" Nerrisa leans close beside me.

"There's a lit room at the end of the hall."

Pearla disappears, and I watch small boot prints appear in the heavily disturbed dust swirls on the corridor floor. They move slowly down the hall until they disappear into the lit room. We wait, silent. Eventually, Pearla reappears at the doorway and beckons us forward with a raised hand.

We move in formation, Nerrisa watching our backs while I pan left and right until we reach the doorway. I scan the room filled with machinery and unfamiliar gadgets scattered about like discarded toys from a forgotten war.

"It looks like a hangar or maybe a storage area for Cegnu tech," Nerrisa whispers.

She moves up beside me, her attention divided between the dark hall behind us and the lit room in front. I signal Pearla toward the far side of the hangar, where shadows deepen ominously around what could be another passageway.

"Let's move," I whisper, creeping into the flickering light.

As we step closer, my stomach twists at the sight: floating stasis pods line one wall. Each is labeled, but I can't read them from here.

"Lira and Elora?" Nerrisa murmurs under her breath, horror etched across her face.

"No. If they were in stasis, we wouldn't have detected them on the scans." I advance, feeling Nerrisa's steady presence next to me.

Once we reach the stasis pods, I peer inside and see a female who looks very similar to Pearla, with dark wavy hair and pale skin. When I glance at Nerrisa, she seems just as puzzled.

"Is this an Aquar'thyn?" I ask her.

"I don't think so. She looks like a regular human." Nerrisa responds and turns and looks into the pod behind us. "This one too."

"Wait!" Pearla hisses before we can make another move.

"What is it?" Nerrisa whispers.

"I hear something over there," she points to the opposite corner. The female disappears once more, and we crouch behind a large machine, waiting for her return.

Pearla's voice echoes through the air. "They're here! Lira and her sister are safe!"

We hurry across the room to find her crouched next to the two painfully thin sisters huddled in a niche created between large crates. Nerrisa crawls toward them. "Lira? Elora? I am Isyarhi's Aunt. We're here to rescue you."

The older girl's brows lift in surprise. "My Isyarhi is here?"

"Yes, he's in our ship. Are you able to walk?" Both girls nod, but as they climb out of the small, cramped space with Nerrisa, the youngest trembles and stumbles as she stands.

I reach out a reassuring hand. "I am Isyarhi's Uncle Frakyss. I will carry you, Elora, if you will permit me." The child nods, and I gather her frail body in my arms. Lira takes Nerrisa's offered hand, and they follow Pearla, who leads us to the doorway.

"What about these females?" whispers Lira. "We can't leave them. The Cegnu will harm them."

I look back at the six stasis pods. "Just a moment." I carefully place Elora in Pearla's arms and rush across the room. I tap the controls at the end of each unit, arranging them in a line. Taking a test step toward the doorway, they glide after me on their digital tether. I signal the others to the doorway, and just before we enter the dark hall, I lift Elora back into my arms.

"Pearla, lead the way," I urge the female and watch as she fades from view.

We navigate through the shadows, my hearts racing with every step. As we approach the docking bay, Pearla appear again. At that exact moment, Elarin's voice fills my ear. "The Cegnu has reached this level and is approaching your group!"

"Hurry!" Pearla urges. "We need to get to the ship!"

As we near the *Vortex* doorway, the air becomes chilled. The Cegnu is here, its bulbous eyes locking onto us. "You will not escape!" it hisses, raising a sleek, elongated Xelthar disruptor. I let Elora slide to the floor and push her behind me toward Nerrisa.

I face the creature, which seems almost anticlimactic compared to my terrified childhood memories. It's half my size in height and bulk. Clenching my fists and roaring, I draw its focus to me and away from the others. Taking a step forward, I block them from its view, so they have time to move the stasis pods into the ship.

Nerrisa orders the others through the hatchway as the dark red cephalopod before me wavers between pointing the disruptor at me and trying to angle around me to see them.

"Remember me, mud spawn?" I spit out.

Its eyes narrow as it looks me up and down, uttering a low hiss. "No. You're just another Abrauxian interfering where you don't belong. Get out of my way, and I will let you live."

"Like you let my best friend live after you stripped the flesh from his small body?"

"You are mad, Abrauxian... a monster, as evident from your red eyes."

"Yes, a monster you and your inkbag friends created sixty-three years ago." I grin, flashing my long fangs while inching closer.

As he studies me more closely, I see the exact moment of recognition. His tentacle trembles as he fires wildly, the high-pitched, pulsating hum of the weapon followed by a deep, resonant thwomp as the glowing beam strikes the wall next to me.

I spin forward on my heel, kicking the disruptor out of his grip and sending it clattering down the dark hallway behind him. He scrambles backward, trying to escape.

"The Echo Station's hull has been breached. Molecular destabilization detected," Elarin's voice crackles in my ear. "Get to the *Vortex*!"

"You've killed yourself, idiot," I smirk and race for the hatch into the *Vortex*. Just as I leap through, a tentacle coils around my ankle like a vise, the suckerbarbs digging deep, sending jolts of pain shooting up my leg. I land hard on both hands and one knee as the monster's strength drags me backward through the hatch.

I glance behind me and see the disintegrating debris from the wall of the space station swirling like a swarm of insects around the Cegnu.

With a surge of adrenaline, I yank the combat knife from the sheath on my belt and thrust downward into the thick tentacle with all my strength, feeling the blade cut deep before I drag the sharp edge upward again until I feel the resistance give way.

The severed limb snaps back with a sickening squelch, alien blood spraying like a grotesque blue fountain, splattering across the hatch and my face. The Cegnu lets out a guttural shriek, writhing and slapping its tentacles wildly. I scramble backward on my ass and kick the hatch door closed with a thunderous bang.

Nerrisa races forward and locks the door into place. "Isyarhi, detach and get away from the station, NOW!" she shouts.

The ship jolts violently, and I slide across the blood-soaked floor, hitting the corner of the weapons vault with a sickening crack. Pain lances through me, and the air in my lungs escapes, leaving me gasping for breath. Nerrisa is gripping the cargo net next to the hatch with one hand and hanging onto Pearla's arm with the other.

The floor bucks in the opposite direction, rocketing me toward a precarious stack of stasis pods. Before I crash into them, a dark meaty hand grabs my leg and lifts me up to dangle upside down.

I groan in pain and darkness invades the edges of my vision as I fight to focus on the enormous primate holding me aloft while clutching Pearla to its furry side and holding itself in place with its feet gripping the cargo net. Green eyes filled with concern peer out of the dark face.

"Please don't drop me, Starfire," I gasp and cough, sending a mist of purple blood into the air.

Chapter 18 - Nerrisa

Hunted by Angels

A loud clang reverberates through the ship as something strikes the hull's exterior. The *Vortex* shudders before becoming eerily quiet. The artificial gravity system fails, and everything not anchored down drifts weightless.

A claxon breaks the silence just as red warning lights begin flashing overhead.

An impersonal, computerized voice echoes through the docking bay.

"Hull breach detected. Shuttle bay door. Hull breach detected. Shuttle bay door."

I tighten my grip around Pearla for just a second longer, then let her go. My body shifts back into my human form, the change quick and jarring after the fight. Without wasting a breath, I kick off the wall and grab hold of Frakyss, guiding his heavy, unconscious weight down the corridor toward the med bay.

My boots skid against the slick floor as I struggle to keep both of us upright. Frakyss's head lolls against my shoulder, the heat radiating off him a grim reminder that we are running out of time.

The doors to the med bay slide open with a groan. I drag him inside, my muscles screaming from the effort, and rush to the healing pod anchored against the far wall.

I slap the lid release, the top hissing as it lifts.

Pearla glides through the doorway a second later, misjudging her momentum and bouncing lightly off the frame before righting herself. She doesn't waste time.

Together, we maneuver Frakyss onto the cushioned interior of the pod. His bulk makes it awkward, but somehow we manage, adjusting his arms and legs until he lies flat. I grab the restraint straps and buckle them into place across his chest, hips, and thighs, securing him tightly.

My hands fumble for the latch, then slam the pod lid shut with a heavy finality. The system hums to life beneath my palms, and a faint wash of cool air brushes my face as the seals lock into place.

For one long heartbeat, I can only stare at him through the transparent top, willing him to breathe, to fight, to live.

The soft glow of blue scanning lines appears, starting at the center of his torso and sweeping outward in slow, deliberate passes toward the edges of the unit.

The system is working. It is a standalone unit, untouched by the ship's failing power grid.

Relief trickles through me, thin and fragile, but I do not move away. Not yet.

Not until I see the lines pass over him again and again, a promise that he still has a chance.

"Pearla, check on everyone else. I need to lock down the shuttle bay!" I shout, not waiting for her response before kicking off the wall and shooting into the hallway.

The lights dim and brighten... the system resetting and recognizing me in the neural interface. I force myself into a calm, near meditative state, just like I learned during training for the Mars Mission.

```
Neural Interface Readout - LWB05
Vortex
Status Report: Critical
Malfunctions Detected
Location: Shuttle Bay - Hull Breach
---
[System Alert: Hull Breach
Detected]
Severity: Catastrophic
Location: Shuttle Bay
Pressure Level: Falling rapidly
Estimated Time to Compromise: 7
minutes
---
[Artificial Gravity System
Failure]
Status: Offline
Gravity Field: 0.0 G
Effects: Uncontrolled drift,
potential for collision with
internal structures
---
[Propulsion System Status]
Status: Offline
Drive Core: Unresponsive
```

Sub-system Check: Power routed to emergency systems only

[Emergency Protocols Initiated]

Deploying atmos shield in adjacent compartments.

Attempting to engage manual override for gravity stabilization.

Power rerouted to life support systems.

[Environmental Conditions]

Oxygen Levels: 22% (Critical)

Temperature: Dropping

Radiation Levels: Normal

Decompression Warning: Immediate evacuation advised

[Additional Diagnostics]

Shuttle Bay Status: Compromised

Cargo Status: Secure, but unstable due to hull integrity loss.

Crew Status: Seven accounted for in sealed compartments, must initiate evacuation protocols.

[Manual Override Activated]

Attempting to activate emergency thrusters.

Thruster Response: No power detected.

Manual engagement of emergency flotation devices... failure.

[Crew Communication Systems]

All channels offline. Attempting to restore communications.

Priority: Emergency Signal to Abrauxian Command. Emergency beacon activated.

[Final System Check]

Duration until total hull collapse: 5 minutes.

Next steps: Evacuate remaining personnel to escape pods.

Prioritize securing vital data drives and ship logs.

[Warning: Hull Breach Expansion Detected]

Compartment integrity failing. Initiating lockdown protocols.

Evacuation countdown initiated...4 minutes to failure of remaining systems.

"All passengers follow the flashing lights to the life pods immediately."

Green lights blink along the base of the walls. I follow them to the opposite side of the ship's horseshoe layout, catching up to everyone just past the bridge.

Elora and Uncle Elarin are struggling to move forward in zero gravity, so I grab their hands and tow them with me to the lighted doorway at the end of the corridor.

In the small, dimly lit room, there are five lit pods anchored upright against the inner wall. Their doors are open, so I push Elora into the first one and press the door closed.

Straps tighten around her body, holding her in place. I guide Uncle Elarin into the second, sealing it. Isyarhi and Lira are in the last two pods, leaving the center one.

"Two minutes until systems failure."

Pearla gives me a panicked look. "You take this one, Nerrisa!"

"No, I'll be fine. Get in!"

She shakes her head, pulling me forward by the hand. I use my momentum to grasp her wrist, turn her into the pod, and shove the door closed.

Her wide eyes meet mine through the glass front, and her hands press to the inside of the glass until the automatic straps anchor her in place and the sedative gas fills the pod.

I open the storage compartment on the opposite wall and find a single Abrauxian-sized spacesuit. I step into the thick fabric legs that pool around my feet, shoving my arms through the long sleeves and sealing the front closed.

I lift the synthetic helmet that reshapes to my head and connects automatically to the neck of the suit, creating an airtight, mildly claustrophobic seal. I clip the carabiner end of a tether to a loop at the hip of the suit to a horizontal bar mounted on the exterior wall.

Status readings inside the helmet visor show two hours of oxygen available.

"Systems failure imminent," warns the ship's voice.

Two hours isn't enough for another ship to reach us. I glance at the pods to verify everyone is in stasis before morphing. The helmet reshapes around me just as all moisture in the air instantly freezes and drifts in the room like snowflakes before the lights fail.

My mind claws up from the darkness. My heartbeat is slow but steady as warmth seeps into my body.

Flashes of memory.

Systems failure.

I blink my eyes. The dim glow of the operating lights of the five occupied life pods towering above me against the wall.

Artificial gravity has been reactivated.

The helmet shows one hour and forty-eight minutes of oxygen remaining. Time lapsed, six hours.

Not enough time for an Abrauxian ship to reach us. Muffled voices.

"Zar'Ka Abrauxi'thi na'korr fa'li. Na'shura vahn'keth os'ra vithar'ka thi'na keth'ra."

The door opens, and a tall female fills the doorway. She enters, shining a flashlight over the life pods before stopping before them. She has glowing white feather wings that shift against her back.

"Na'shura vahn'keth os'ra vithar'ka thi'na keth'ra. Vithar'ka two Hosliens females, vahn'keth two male Negorians fa'li and a female of unknown species, similar to the ones in the docking bay stasis pods."

I realize my nanos are learning their language.

I press my tiny webbed hand to the helmet controls, and it retracts silently. I hop away from the crumpled spacesuit and hide under the lip of its storage closet.

A second female enters the room, peering into the life pods before glancing around and noticing the empty suit on the floor.

She lifts the suit's shoulder with the toe of her silver boot and lets it drop. "Why is this empty sha'thul teth'ra to the wall?"

"I do not know," the first female responds.

"We should have destroyed Echo Station sixty-three years ago when we found the Abrauxian boy who has returned, a grown male. Leave everyone in their pods. We will repair the ship and set the autopilot to return it to Abrauxian orbit. Their people will pick them up, and no one will be the wiser about us."

"As you wish, Lyphoria."

Lyphoria turns on her heel, and her feathers sweep under the edge of the closet, brushing against my small frog body as she leaves the room.

The remaining female gives the dark room a last glance before following the other out and closing the door behind her.

Once their footsteps grow faint, I shift to my human form, shivering in the icy cold air and wishing for the millionth time that my clothes magically shifted with me.

I carefully unlatch the door, peeking down the hall to make sure the females are gone before shifting to a black feline form.

The lush black fur warms me instantly. I slink silently down the corridor, my form blending into the darkness. Ahead, I spot the two glowing females, their luminescence casting an eerie light from the bridge, where they are discussing our ship's hull repairs and system malfunctions.

"Xylara, status?"

"Kylithra is replicating the damaged components while I patch the torn hull."

"Estimated time for completion of all repairs?"

"One hour, forty-seven minutes."

"Very well. I am returning to Skyreaver Command. Keep me apprised of your progress."

The two females stride in the opposite direction, and I follow, ghosting their steps into the cargo bay, where they climb out of the open hatch.

Sticking to the shadows, I look out to see the *Vortex* is in a brightly lit cavernous docking bay surrounded by at least four magnificent ships twice her size and unlike anything I've ever seen.

They are sleek and aerodynamically designed with the silhouette of a bird in flight, with elongated wings that extend gracefully from their fuselages. The hulls are white and silver, giving them a shimmering opalescence.

My life force wanes as I shift into a wren, hopping up to perch on the hatch's bottom edge. Seeing no one around, I launch into the air with rapid wingbeats, propelling myself through the open air. I glide above the magnificent ships.

Their hulls are decorated with intricate feather designs that sparkle. I admire their aggressive design and bristling weaponry.

I tilt my wings on a thermal air current to circle over the *Vortex*. A winged female, who must be Xylara, is welding a metal patch over the large tear in our ship's side.

Another flies across the room carrying a square case, landing and climbing through the hatch. No doubt she has the components to fix the failed systems.

I soar, stretching my wings, exhilarated by the freedom of the cavernous docking bay. The mothership must be massive. I wish I had time to explore and learn about these beings.

Obviously, they are the ones who rescued Frakyss as a child, but it's a shame they didn't bother getting rid of those Cegnu bastards then.

For that failure, I'd like some answers, but it seems they don't want witnesses to their existence.

Diving swiftly, I enter the hatch and flit through the *Vortex*, finding Kylithra in the avionics bay, removing singed electronic components, and sliding new ones into place. I'm glad they're handling this part; I'm a better pilot than mechanic.

I circle back through the ship to my cabin, landing gently on the floor before returning to human form. The chill of the air bites at my bare skin, so I hurry inside, pulling on insulated leggings and a turtleneck before adding a flight suit.

Now I wait, monitoring the females' progress through the neural link as they repair our ship.

True to their word, in just under two hours, the *Vortex's* systems come back online one by one. The artificial gravity stabilizes, life support reaches optimal levels, and the propulsion systems hum to life.

I hear the hatch close as the winged female departs. Through the neural link, I sense the autopilot engaging and plotting a course back to Abrauxia. I hurry to the bridge as the engines fire up, and we begin to move.

Taking a seat at the helm, I disengage the autopilot and assume manual control. We emerge from the massive docking bay into open space, the stars twinkling around us.

As I guide the ship away from the mysterious mothership, my fingers fly over the controls, initiating a scan of the surrounding space.

The results flash across the screen... nothing.

No ships, no anomalies, just a nearby dead planet surrounded by an asteroid field and the vast emptiness of space.

Somehow, they can avoid detection by normal scans. I switch to multi-mode scanning:

```
Scanning Initiated -
Status Report: Anomaly Detection -
negative
  Gravitational - negative
  Frequency Modulation - negative
  Thermal Imaging - negative
  Magnetic Field - negative
  Subspace - negative
  Quantum - pending
  Critical Security and Cryptography
  Unauthorized Monitoring of LWB05
Vortex Systems
  Source Location: 12.8 Kilometers
  ---
```

```
[System    Alert:    Unauthorized
Monitoring]
Severity: Level 1 Security Risk
Jam Signal? Yes
Release Active Countermeasures? Yes
Initiate Stealth Maneuvers? Yes
Signal Jamming Initiated
Countermeasures Released
Initiating  Stealth  Maneuvers  in
five, four, three, two, one.
---
```

The *Vortex* unleashes a cascade of electromagnetic interference that ripples through the void. At the same time, automated countermeasures launch from the ship's flanks... dozens of sleek, decoy drones streak away into space, each emitting a barrage of false signatures designed to confuse any prying sensors in the vicinity.

I initiate the stealth tech and pull the ship into a sharp roll, diving toward the asteroid field, weaving between massive chunks of rock and ice. She responds immediately to my thoughts as I make split-second adjustments to avoid collisions.

A proximity alert blares. I glance at the rear sensors to see one of the bird-like ships seeking us, its sleek form slicing through the asteroid field with impossible grace. From its movements, they haven't been able to detect us.

"Damn it," I mutter, gritting my teeth. I bank hard around a spinning asteroid the size of a small moon, using its bulk to hide. In that split second, I kill the engines and activate the emergency inertial dampeners. The *Vortex* comes to an abrupt halt, drifting silently in the shadow of the asteroid.

The pursuing ship blasts past our position, clearly expecting us to continue at our evasive speed. I grin. They won't win a game of cat and mouse. I fire up the engines again, this time on minimal power, and creep along the asteroid's surface, using its bulk as cover.

"Computer, analyze pursuing vessels and compare to known ship types," I command, keeping my voice low despite knowing the pursuing ships can't hear me.

The computer processes for a moment before responding:

```
Analysis complete. Pursuing vessels
do not match any known ship designs
in database. Unique features include:
 - Avian-inspired hull design
 - Advanced stealth capabilities
 - Exotic    propulsion    system,
possibly gravitic in nature
 - Weapons systems of unknown type
and yield
 - Materials analysis inconclusive,
hull   composition   resistant   to
standard scans
```

I frown, processing this information. These ships are clearly far beyond standard technology levels. We're outmatched in every way.

An alert chimes softly. "Proximity warning. Pursuing vessels altering course, returning to search pattern."

My hands tighten on the controls. We can't outrun or outfight them. Our only hope is to outsmart them long enough to escape.

I guide the ship deeper into the asteroid field, weaving between chunks of rock and ice. The density increases, creating a natural labyrinth. Perfect.

"Computer, map densest areas of the asteroid field and plot a course that keeps us in heavy cover."

`Mapping complete. Course plotted.`

I engage the new flight plan, letting the computer handle the minute adjustments needed to avoid collisions while I focus on monitoring our pursuers.

They're methodically sweeping the field, no doubt confident we can't escape. But their arrogance might be our salvation.

As we glide deeper into the field, I notice a massive asteroid ahead, easily ten times the size of the *Vortex*. Its surface appears pockmarked with deep craters and crevices and an idea quickly forms.

"Computer, scan the largest nearby asteroid for any caverns or tunnels large enough to accommodate the *Vortex*."

After a moment, the computer responds: `Scan complete. Multiple suitable caverns detected. Largest opening located on the far side, dimensions sufficient for ship entry.`

I grin, the plan solidifying. "Perfect. Plot a course to that cavern, but keep us in the asteroid's shadow."

The *Vortex* glides silently through the debris, hugging the contours of the massive rock. As we round its bulk, I spot the cavern entrance, a yawning maw of darkness against the pitted surface.

I carefully back the ship into the opening. The tunnel is a tight fit, but when we slip deeper inside, the hollow interior of the asteroid opens up around us. Once we're deep within the cavern, I kill all non-essential systems.

"Computer, full sensor sweep of the cavern. Any signs of life or technology?"

Negative. Cavern appears to be naturally formed. No artificial structures or life signs detected.

"Good. Initiate passive scans only. Monitor for any approaching vessels, but keep our energy signature at the absolute minimum."

With the immediate danger averted, I slump back in the pilot's chair. The adrenaline rush fades, leaving me drained, but I can't rest yet.

I hurry to the life pod chamber, where my companions remain in stasis. I deactivate the pods one by one, helping each occupant as they emerge, momentarily disoriented.

Isyarhi is the first to fully regain his senses. "Aunt Nerrisa? What happened? Where are we?"

"It's a long story," I say, steadying him as he steps out of the pod. "For now, just know that we're safe, but we need to stay quiet and hidden."

As the others come around, I help them out of their pods. Elora and Lira cling to each other, their eyes wide with fear and confusion. Pearla immediately starts checking everyone for injuries, while Elarin steadies himself against the wall, looking disoriented.

"Is everyone alright?" I ask, scanning their faces. They nod, still groggy from the stasis.

"Where's Uncle Frakyss?" Isyarhi asks, looking around anxiously.

"He's in the med bay," I reply, leading the group out of the life pod chamber. "He was injured during our escape, but he should be healed by now."

We race to the med bay, where Frakyss is just sitting up in the open healing pod as we enter.

His red eyes lock onto mine, relief evident in his expression.

"Nerrisa," he breathes, attempting to stand. I rush to his side, supporting him as he gets to his feet.

"Easy there, big guy," I say, steadying him. "You were in pretty bad shape just a few hours ago."

He nods, wincing slightly. "What happened? Where are we?"

I take a deep breath, looking around at the expectant faces surrounding us. "We're hidden in an asteroid cavern. The ship was badly damaged during our escape from Echo Station, but..." I hesitate, unsure how much to reveal about the mysterious winged beings.

"But what?" Frakyss prompts, his eyes searching my face.

I take a deep breath, knowing I need to tell them everything. "We were rescued by mysterious beings, glowing females with white feathered wings. They repaired our ship but then tried to send us back to Abrauxia on autopilot. I regained control and escaped, but now they're pursuing us."

A shocked silence falls over the group. Frakyss's eyes widen in recognition. "The angelic warrior," he whispers. "The one who saved me as a child. It was them."

I nod. "I think so. But they seem determined to keep their existence a secret. That's why we're hiding in this asteroid."

"What do they want with us?" Lira asks, her voice trembling slightly.

"I'm not sure," I admit. "But they went to great lengths to repair our ship and send us on our way without us knowing about them. I don't think they mean us harm, but they definitely don't want us to know about them either."

Frakyss straightens, his protective instincts kicking in. "We need a plan. We can't stay hidden in this asteroid forever."

"Agreed," I say. "But we're outmatched technologically. Our best bet is to lay low until they give up the search, then make a run for it."

Chapter 19 - Frakyss

Lunarite and Life Force

"Elora, let's get you in the healing pod and make sure you're okay."

She hesitates a moment before Lira guides her forward. I lift her into the unit and settle her before closing the clear lid. Unlike me, her injuries are minor, and she remains conscious. The machine begins to hum as it scans her.

"Everyone else, why don't you go across the hall to the galley. We might as well take advantage of the downtime and eat and regroup. I'll wait with Elora."

Nerrisa ushers everyone out, leaving the door open so Elora can still see her sister across the hall. Elora's wide eyes dart nervously between me and the others and I give her a reassuring smile.

"It's okay, little one. I am Isyarhi's uncle. The pod is just healing your injuries. It won't hurt at all." I keep my voice soft and gentle. "Would you like me to tell you a story while we wait?"

She nods hesitantly.

"Alright then. Have you ever heard the tale of Starfire and the Ice Dragon?"

Elora shakes her head.

"Well, long ago, on my home planet of Abrauxia, there lived a fearsome Ice Dragon named Wraith. He ruled the northern mountains with an icy grip, freezing everything in his path. The people lived in fear of his wrath.

But there was one who wasn't afraid, a brave warrior known as Starfire. She had hair like flames and beautiful green eyes..."

As I weave the tale, Elora's eyes grow heavy. By the time I finish, she's fast asleep, her breathing deep and even. The pod chimes softly, indicating the healing process is complete. I open the unit, lift her out, and carry her to the galley, where Lira immediately rushes over.

"She's fine," I assure her. "Just sleeping now. Why don't you two rest in one of the cabins?"

Lira nods gratefully, following me around the curving hall to the empty room next to Isyarhi's.

"The facilities are through that door if you want to use the cleansing unit."

After settling the Hosliens sisters in their cabin, I return to the galley, where the others are gathered around the table. Nerrisa hands me a steaming mug as I take a seat.

"What's our next move?" Pearla asks, her eyes darting between Nerrisa and me.

I sip the hot liquid, savoring the rich sweet flavor. "We need to figure out who these beings are and why they're so intent on keeping their existence a secret."

"And why they didn't eliminate the Cegnu threat years ago when they rescued you," Nerrisa adds.

I nod grimly. "That too."

"Could they be some kind of advanced alien race?" Isyarhi suggests, his antennae twitching with excitement.

"It's possible," I concede. "But if that's the case, why haven't we encountered them before? And why go to such lengths to hide from us?"

"Maybe they're not hiding from just us," Elarin muses. "Perhaps they're concealing themselves from someone or something else. I see the appeal with the Zugunu running rampant, taking over planets and wiping out whole species."

A thoughtful silence falls over the group as we consider this possibility.

"Whatever the case," Nerrisa says, breaking the quiet, "we need to find a way out of this asteroid field without being detected. Any ideas?"

I lean back in my chair, considering our options. "The Vortex's stealth capabilities are good, but not enough to evade their sensors completely. We need something more."

Nerrisa's eyes light up. "What about the cloaking device? The one you used when we were in orbit above Nagoria?"

I nod slowly. "It might work, but it's not designed for long-term use. The power drain would be significant."

"Could we modify it somehow?" Pearla asks. "Boost its efficiency?"

"Possibly," I reply, my mind racing through potential upgrades. "But we'd need materials we don't have on board."

Isyarhi leans forward eagerly. "What if we used some of the asteroid material? There might be rare minerals or elements we could use."

I raise an eyebrow, impressed by the young Nagorian's quick thinking. "That's not a bad idea, Isyarhi. We'd need to run some scans and see what we're working with."

"I can handle that," Nerrisa offers. "I'll take the shuttle out and collect some samples."

"No," I say firmly, my protective instincts flaring. "It's too dangerous. Those ships could still be out there searching for us."

Nerrisa's eyes narrow. "I'm sure they are, but I can handle myself, Frakyss. Besides, I'm the best pilot here. If anyone can evade detection, it's me."

I meet Nerrisa's determined gaze, knowing there's no point in arguing further. She's right... she is the best pilot, and we need those samples if we hope to enhance our stealth capabilities.

"Fine," I concede with a sigh. "But take Pearla with you. Her invisibility could come in handy if you run into trouble."

Nerrisa nods, a hint of a smile on her lips. "Agreed. We'll leave in ten minutes."

As the two women prepare for their mission, I turn to Isyarhi and Elarin. "While they're gone, I want you two to go through the ship's database. See if there's any mention of beings like the ones we encountered, even if it's just in legends or myths."

"What about me?" asks a small voice from the doorway. I turn to see Lira standing there, looking uncertain.

"Lira, you should be resting," I say gently.

She shakes her head. "I can't sleep. I want to help."

I consider for a moment, then nod. "Alright. You can assist Isyarhi and Elarin with the research."

As everyone disperses to their tasks, I head to the bridge to monitor Nerrisa and Pearla's progress. Through the neural link, I can sense Nerrisa's focused determination as she pilots the small shuttle out of the *Vortex* and our hiding place into the asteroid field.

The viewscreen shows the shuttle weaving gracefully between the massive rocks. I watch anxiously as they approach a particularly mineral-rich asteroid.

"Initiating scan," Nerrisa's voice comes through the comms. "Looks promising. High concentrations of rare elements and some unusual energy signatures."

"Be careful," I caution. "Don't take any unnecessary risks."

I can almost hear Nerrisa's eye roll in her response. "Relax, Frakyss. We've got this under control."

As they begin collecting samples, I turn my attention to the long-range scanners, searching for any sign of our mysterious pursuers. So far, nothing. But that doesn't mean they're not out there.

Suddenly, an alert flashes on the console. An energy spike, just at the edge of our sensor range.

"Nerrisa, we may have company," I warn urgently. "Sector Delta-78: X: 13.87, Y:-55.67, Z: 9.89. Wrap it up and get back here now."

"Copy that," Nerrisa responds crisply. "We've got what we need. Heading back."

I watch tensely as the shuttle weaves gracefully among the asteroids. The energy signature I detected is moving closer, its trajectory intersecting with the shuttle's path.

"Nerrisa, you've got incoming at your two o'clock," I warn, my hearts racing. "ETA 30 seconds."

"I see it," she responds, her voice tight. "Pearla, get ready to cloak us."

Through the neural link, I sense Nerrisa's adrenaline spike as she pushes the shuttle to its limits, dodging and weaving through the densest part of the asteroid field.

The pursuing ship is faster, but its larger size makes it less maneuverable in the tight spaces.

"Almost there," Nerrisa murmurs, as a massive asteroid looms ahead of the Shadowstrike. For a heart-stopping moment, I think she's going to crash into it. At the last second, she cuts the engines and initiates a controlled spin, using the asteroid's gravity to slingshot around it. The pursuing ship overshoots, giving Nerrisa the opening she needs.

"Now, Pearla!" she shouts.

The shuttle's energy signature vanishes from my sensors. I hold my breath, scanning frantically for any sign of them. Long seconds tick by.

Finally, the docking bay doors open, and the shuttle glides in, shimmering into visibility.

"Quick, we need to get Pearla to the healing pod. She's drained her life force desperately low."

I run to the shuttle bay, lifting the unconscious female from the passenger compartment of the Shadowstrike.

"Grab the mineral samples. We'll run them through the analyzer once Pearla is healing."

I race down the hall to the med bay, arranging her in the healing pod and sealing the top. I press the button to start the unit as Nerrisa enters the room with the case of samples.

The healing pod chimes. A message flashes on the screen as a small drawer opens on the side.

```
-Lunarite detected.
-Place material in tray.
```

"What is lunarite?" I ask Nerrisa, who shrugs.

"Maybe it's one of the samples we brought back. Will the handheld tell us which one?"

"I don't know, but we've got nothing to lose by trying." I grab the healing wand from the drawer as Nerrisa spreads the bags across the countertop.

When I move the wand over the top of each one, the data screen on the wall shows an analysis of the contents.

"I had no idea it would analyze anything besides living matter."

"Here it is!" Nerrisa grabs a bag holding luminescent crystals that pulse with a soft glow. She shakes one of the crystals into the healing pod's drawer, and it slides shut.

```
-Analyzing vibrational frequency of
lunarite
-Calibrating   output   to   match
resonance frequency
-Creating harmonic field within pod
-Synchronizing            energy
replenishment. Stand by...
```

A deep thrum comes from inside the unit. Nerrisa lays her hand on the vibrating top. Her eyes widen in surprise.

"What's it doing?"

"It's creating pure energy... life force..." She begins to glow, her eyes losing focus. When I reach out to touch her, an energy bolt shoots through me, knocking me off my feet and into the wall.

Chapter 20 - Nerrisa

The Aetherian Enigma

The energy surges through me, every cell in my body vibrating with power. My vision blurs as the world around me dissolves into pure light. For a moment, I feel weightless, untethered from reality.

Then, as quickly as it began, the sensation fades. I blink rapidly, my surroundings coming back into focus.

The med bay materializes around me, and I see Frakyss slumped against the wall, his eyes wide with shock, and a big dent from his horn in the panel next to him.

"Frakyss!" I rush to his side, kneeling beside him. "Are you alright?"

He nods slowly, rubbing his right horn. "What happened?"

"I'm not sure," I admit, helping him to his feet. "The lunarite seemed to react with the healing pod somehow. It created an energy field."

We turn our attention to Pearla, still lying motionless in the pod. To our amazement, her skin has taken on a faint luminescence, pulsing gently in rhythm with the crystal.

"Her life force," I whisper. "It's regenerating at an incredible rate."

Frakyss leans in closer, studying the readouts on the pod's display. "I've never seen anything like this. The lunarite isn't just healing her; it's amplifying her own natural regenerative abilities."

A soft groan from inside the pod draws our attention. Pearla's eyes flutter open, confusion evident in her gaze as she takes in her surroundings.

"What happened?" she asks groggily as I open the pod.

"You drained yourself cloaking the Shadowstrike," I explain, helping her sit up. "But it seems this lunarite crystal has some extraordinary healing properties."

Pearla looks down at her hands, flexing her fingers as if testing their strength. "I feel different. Stronger somehow."

Frakyss nods, his expression thoughtful. "The lunarite appears to have not only restored your life force, but enhanced it. We'll need to run some tests to understand the full effects."

As Pearla climbs out of the pod, Isyarhi bursts into the med bay. "Uncle Frakyss! Aunt Nessa! We found something in the database!"

"What is it?" I ask, my curiosity piqued.

"There's an old Abrauxian legend," Isyarhi explains breathlessly. "About celestial beings called the Aetherian Guardians. They were said to protect the balance of the universe, wielding incredible powers and advanced technology."

Frakyss's eyes widen in recognition. "The winged females... could they be these Aetherian Guardians?"

"It's possible," I say, my mind racing with possibilities. "The description certainly matches what we saw. But if they're real, why have they remained hidden for so long?"

"The legend speaks of a great conflict," Isyarhi continues. "The Aetherians were said to have withdrawn from the known universe to protect it from some terrible threat. But the details are vague."

Frakyss runs a hand through his hair, his expression troubled. "If these Aetherians are real, and they're still out there protecting us from some unknown danger, why did they let the Cegnu continue their experiments? Why not stop them years ago?"

"Maybe they have rules about interfering," Pearla suggests. "Like some kind of cosmic prime directive."

I nod, considering this. "It's possible. But then, why rescue Frakyss as a child? Why repair our ship now?"

"Perhaps they're bound by rules, but sometimes choose to bend them," Elarin says as he enters the med bay. "Many cultures have legends of powerful beings who occasionally intervene in mortal affairs, but only in dire circumstances."

A thoughtful silence falls over the group as we contemplate this possibility. Finally, Frakyss speaks up.

"Whatever their reasons, we need to focus on our immediate situation. They still have ships out there looking for us, and we need to find a way to escape undetected."

I nod in agreement. "The lunarite we found might be the key. If it can heal Pearla and amplify her abilities, maybe we can use it to enhance the *Vortex's* cloaking systems."

Frakyss's eyes light up with understanding. "Of course! If we can integrate the lunarite into our stealth tech, we might be able to mask our energy signature completely."

"I can help with that," Pearla offers, standing up straighter. "My invisibility works by bending light and energy. If we can replicate that effect on a larger scale..."

"It just might work," I finish, feeling a spark of hope for the first time since our escape. "Frakyss, how quickly can you modify the cloaking device to incorporate the lunarite?"

He rubs his chin thoughtfully. "With Pearla's help, maybe a few hours. But we'll need to test it thoroughly before we try to make a run for it."

"Agreed," I say. "Isyarhi, Elarin, keep digging through the database. See if you can find any more information on these Aetherian Guardians or the lunarite. Anything that might give us an edge."

As the others nod and move to their tasks, I turn to Frakyss. "I'll take the bridge and keep an eye on our pursuers. We need to know the moment they get close."

Hours pass as I pour over ways in and out of the asteroid we're hiding in, star charts, and sensor data, plotting potential routes.

The ship hums with activity as Frakyss and Pearla work on the cloaking enhancements while Isyarhi, Lira, and Elarin work in the conference room. Periodically, I walk through the *Vortex*, checking on everyone.

As I return to the bridge with my steaming mug of tea, an alert chimes softly. I quickly set the mug down and slide into the pilot's seat, my eyes scanning the readouts. A faint energy signature has appeared at the edge of our sensor range, moving in a search pattern through the asteroid field.

My heart rate quickens. "Frakyss," I call through the ship's comm system. "We've got company. How much longer on those cloaking modifications?"

His voice comes back, tight with tension. "We're close. Maybe another thirty minutes. Can you buy us some time?"

I bite my lip, considering our options. "I'll do my best. But be ready to move fast if things go south."

Turning my attention back to the sensors, I watch as the energy signature slowly moves closer. It's methodical and thorough. They're leaving no stone unturned in their search.

An idea forms in my mind. Risky, but it might just work.

"Isyarhi," I call. "I need you on the bridge."

The young Nagorian arrives moments later, slightly out of breath. "What is it, Aunt Nessa?"

"I need you to take the helm," I explain quickly. "I'm going to try something, but I need to focus entirely on shapeshifting. Can you handle piloting if we need to move?"

Isyarhi's eyes widen, but he nods determinedly. "I can do it, Aunt Nessa. What's the plan?"

I take a deep breath, steeling myself. "I'm going to attempt to shapeshift into one of those Aetherian ships. If I can mimic their energy signature, maybe I can lead the searchers away from us."

Isyarhi's antennae twitch with excitement and concern. "But Aunt Nessa, that's so dangerous! What if they detect you?"

"That's the point. I want them to follow me as I draw them away from here, giving Frakyss and Pearla more time to finish the cloaking modifications. This is our best shot."

I stop in the med bay and grab one of the Lunarite crystals, holding it tight in my hand as I enter the shuttle bay and stand in the open space next to the Shadowstrike.

Closing my eyes, I focus on the memory of the smaller Aetherian shuttles I saw in their docking bay. Their sleek, avian design, the shimmering hull, the exotic energy signature.

I've never attempted to shapeshift into an inanimate object, let alone something so large and complex before. But bioships are real and I will my body to transform.

I feel myself growing, expanding. My skin hardens and takes on a metallic sheen. Wings sprout from my sides, unfurling into graceful arcs.

Internal systems form... propulsion, weapons, sensors. It's exhilarating and terrifying all at once.

When the transformation is complete, I activate my new sensor arrays. The shuttle bay around me looks tiny now, my massive form barely fitting in the space. I glide through the atmos shield, growing larger once I'm not restricted by the cramped space.

I focus on generating the unique energy signature I detected from the Aetherian ships. "How do I look on sensors?" I ask over the *Vortex's* communication system, my voice now a mechanical approximation of my usual tone.

"It's working! You're emitting an energy signature almost identical to theirs," comes Isyarhi's excited response.

"Good," I reply. "I'm going out there to lead them away."

I engage my new propulsion systems, gliding out into the asteroid field. It feels surreal, navigating this massive form through space. But there's no time to marvel over the experience. I have a job to do.

I accelerate away from our hiding spot, making sure to generate enough of an energy signature to be detected. Sure enough, within moments, I pick up the scanning ship changing course to investigate.

"It's working," I transmit back to the *Vortex*. "They're following me. Frakyss, how much longer?"

His voice comes through, tinged with awe and concern. "Nerrisa, what you're doing is incredible. We're almost done here. Just a few more minutes."

I accelerate deeper into the asteroid field, weaving between massive chunks of debris. The pursuing ship follows, its energy signature growing stronger as it closes the distance. My new form responds instantly to my thoughts, banking and rolling with a grace that would be impossible in the *Vortex*.

"They're gaining on me," I report back to the ship. "Frakyss, please tell me you're ready."

"Almost there," he responds, his voice tight with tension. "Just hold on a little longer."

I push my new engines harder, diving into a particularly dense cluster of asteroids. The pursuing ship is fast but less maneuverable in tight spaces. I use this to my advantage, executing a series of tight turns that force them to slow down.

Suddenly, my sensors light up with multiple new contacts. More Aetherian ships converge on my position from different directions. My heart races as I realize I'm being boxed in.

"Frakyss, I'm running out of options here," I say urgently. "They're trying to trap me."

"We're ready!" his voice comes back. "Get back here now. We'll make a run for it as soon as you're on board."

I bank hard, plotting a course back to the *Vortex's* hiding spot. The pursuing ships are closing in fast, their weapons systems powering up. I push my borrowed form to its limits, dodging energy blasts that light up the void around me.

As I approach the massive asteroid concealing the *Vortex*, I shrink, shooting into a small crevasse. The size transition is disorienting, and for a moment, I'm tumbling before finding my equilibrium and racing through the maze of tunnels to the open central cavern where the *Vortex* awaits.

The docking bay opens, and I use the last of my momentum to propel myself inside. As soon as I cross the threshold, artificial gravity takes hold, and I crash to the floor.

I feel the ship lurch as Isyarhi engages the engines. Racing to the bridge, I find him at the helm, his face a mask of concentration as he guides us out of our hiding place.

"Activating enhanced cloaking now," Frakyss's voice comes over the comms. The ship shudders slightly as the new systems engage.

On the viewscreen, I watch as the asteroid field falls away behind us. The sensors show multiple Aetherian ships converging on our previous location, but none seem to have detected our escape.

"It's working," I breathe, hardly daring to believe it. "They can't see us."

Isyarhi grins. "Where to now, Aunt Nessa?"

I take the helm, plotting a course that will take us far from this sector. "First, we put some distance between us and them. Then, we've got some humans to deliver to Abrauxia.

Chapter 21 - Frakyss

Pulse of Aether

I watch the sensor readouts intently as Nerrisa guides us away from the asteroid field and our Aetherian pursuers. So far, there's no sign that we've been detected. The enhanced cloaking device, powered by the mysterious lunarite, seems to be working perfectly.

"We're clear," Nerrisa announces after several tense minutes. "No signs of pursuit."

My fingers ache from gripping the console too tightly. Next to me, Nerrisa leans back in her chair with a long breath, the tension draining from her body like air from a punctured hull. A shaky laugh escapes her, and I realize I have not heard her laugh since before Echo Station.

I let out a breath I didn't realize I'd been holding. "Good work, everyone. Especially you, Nerrisa. That was some incredible shapeshifting."

She turns to me, a tired smile on her face. "Thanks. I've never shifted into an inanimate object before. I'm just glad it worked."

"So, what now?" Isyarhi asks, looking between us expectantly.

I exchange a glance with Nerrisa before answering. "We need answers. About the Aetherians, the lunarite, all of it. And I think I know where we might find them."

She lifts an eyebrow, wary but curious. "Where?"

"Silvergate Cay," I say. "There is an ancient library hidden near the city. I stumbled across it years ago while roaming the countryside. It was half-swallowed by the cliffs overlooking the southern sea, the entrance buried behind crumbling vines."

I pause, remembering the heavy silence of that place. "The texts and artifacts inside were untouched by time. Very few Abrauxians even know it exists. It felt sacred... and dangerous. Not a place meant for casual visitors."

Nerrisa leans forward, the light in her eyes sharpening. "Then that's where we go."

Nerrisa nods slowly. "Alright. Set a course for Abrauxia."

As she begins plotting our route, I turn to Isyarhi. "Go let the others know what's happening. And check on Lira and Elora. Make sure they're holding up okay."

The young Nagorian nods and hurries off. I watch him go, marveling at how much he's grown in such a short time.

"He's becoming quite the young man," Nerrisa comments, following my gaze.

I nod, feeling a swell of pride. "He is. He's been through so much, but he's handling it all with remarkable strength."

Nerrisa's hand finds mine, giving it a gentle squeeze. "He's got good role models."

I turn to her, struck once again by her beauty and strength. Without thinking, I lean in.

For a heartbeat, I hesitate. We are bruised and tired and full of too many unanswered questions. But when I look into her eyes, I see trust, shining and fragile. I lean in slowly, giving her time to pull away. She does not.

I press my lips to hers in a soft kiss. She responds immediately, her free hand coming up to cup my cheek

When we part, her eyes are shining. "What was that for?"

"For being you," I reply simply. "For everything you've done for us - for me."

She smiles, a faint blush coloring her cheeks. "Well, in that case..." She pulls me in for another kiss, this one deeper and more passionate.

We're interrupted by a soft cough from the doorway. We spring apart to see Pearla standing there, an amused smirk on her face.

"Sorry to interrupt," she says, not sounding sorry at all. "But I thought you'd want to know - I've been analyzing that lunarite crystal and I've discovered something interesting."

I clear my throat, trying to regain my composure. "What is it?"

Pearla holds up a data pad. "The crystal seems to resonate at a specific frequency...one that matches the energy signature we detected from the Aetherian ships. I think this lunarite might be the key to their advanced technology."

Her voice hums with suppressed excitement. The data pad glows faintly in her hands, the schematics scrolling in alien patterns I can barely comprehend. I feel a cold thrill in my chest. If we can harness even a fraction of this power, we might stand a chance. But if the Aetherians have already mastered it, what horrors might they unleash?

Nerrisa leans forward, her eyes bright with interest. "So, if we can harness that energy..."

"We might be able to replicate some of their capabilities," I finish, my mind racing with the possibilities.

"Exactly," Pearla nods. "I've already started working on some modifications to our systems. With a little more time, I think we could significantly upgrade our defenses and propulsion."

"Good work, Pearla," I say, impressed by her initiative. "Keep at it. Let us know if you need anything."

She nods and turns to leave but pauses in the doorway. "Oh, and by the way, you two might want to be more discreet next time. The kids are starting to ask questions." With a wink, she's gone.

I feel my face heat up as Nerrisa chuckles beside me. "I don't know why anyone would be concerned. After all, we are mates," she says.

"I guess so. Does it bother you?"

She shakes her head, her eyes meeting mine. "Not at all. Does it bother you?"

"No," I say softly, taking her hand again. "In fact, I'm glad. I've never hidden how I feel about you, Nerrisa."

Her smile widens, and she leans in to press a quick kiss to my cheek. "No, you haven't. Thank you for giving me time to get to know you."

We sit in comfortable silence, hands intertwined, before Nerrisa turns back to the navigation console. "We should be approaching Abrauxian space in about twenty-two hours," she reports. "I suggest we all get some rest while we can. Something tells me things will get interesting once we reach Silvergate City."

I nod in agreement. "Good idea. I'll take the first watch. You go get some sleep."

She stands, stretching. "Alright. Wake me when you're ready for me to take over."

As she leaves the bridge, I settle into the pilot's chair, but sleep feels a lifetime away. Out there, beyond the black, old enemies are stirring. Powers we barely understand are watching. And inside this ship, I carry the fragile beginnings of something too rare to risk. Family, loyalty, and love. I will protect them, even if it costs me everything.

I've faced my greatest fear, the Cegnu, and conquered it. My winged savior wasn't the product of a hurt child's imagination but an Aetherian. But best of all, is the growing mate bond between Nerrisa and me.

Chapter 22 - Nerrisa

Welcome to the Family

I wake feeling refreshed after hours of deep sleep. Stretching out the stiffness from my muscles, I step into the quiet corridor and make my way to the bridge. The soft thrum of the engines vibrates gently beneath my bare feet, a comforting, steady rhythm that fills the ship.

The lights are dimmed to a muted blue, casting long, soft-edged shadows across the walls, the standard setting during night cycle.

Frakyss sits at the helm, a silent figure framed by the faint glow of the viewscreens. His posture is relaxed but alert, his eyes focused intently on the stars sliding past. The bridge feels almost sacred in its stillness, a quiet space between worlds. For a moment, I simply watch him, grateful for the calm after everything we have endured.

"Any sign of pursuit?" I ask, sliding into the co-pilot's seat beside him.

He shakes his head. "Nothing. It seems our enhanced cloaking is still holding."

I nod, relieved. "Good. How long until we reach Abrauxian space?"

"About twelve hours," he replies. "We should be approaching Silvergate City shortly after that."

I lean back in my seat, staring out at the endless stars as I gather my thoughts. The words form slowly, heavier than I expect.

"I'm sure Kishi will be glad to get her son back," I say quietly. "But... what would you think of us becoming Lira and Elora's guardians? Maybe even their parents?"

The moment the words leave my mouth, my heart kicks harder against my ribs. I risk a glance at Frakyss, searching for strength in his steady presence. Doubts swarm fast and unbidden. What if the girls see us as nothing more than another set of faces passing through their broken lives? What if we are asking too much of children who have already lost too much?

I force the fear down, swallowing it like bitter medicine. They deserve to know they are wanted, not as a duty but as family.

Frakyss turns toward me, his dark brows lifting slightly, a flicker of surprise crossing his face. "Really?" His voice is quieter than I expect, almost reverent, as if he is afraid to hope too much. "I would like that. I already feel a bond with them... after everything we faced together against the Cegnu."

The tight knot of fear in my chest loosens, but not completely. Hope is a fragile thing, easily shattered. I grip it tightly anyway, unwilling to let it slip through my fingers.

"We can talk with them when they are awake," I say, forcing my voice to steady. "First, we need to find a safe place for the human women. After that, we focus on the ancient library. If there are answers to what is happening with the Aetherians, they have to be hidden there."

Frakyss nods, but his gaze grows distant, his jaw tightening slightly. "Yes. It is hidden deep within the island, protected by technology so old and strange it barely feels real. Gaining access will not be easy."

"But you have been there before, right?" I press, needing to anchor the rising uncertainty between us.

He hesitates, his eyes shadowed with memory. "Yes," he says finally. "Years ago. After my rescue from the Cegnu, when I first set foot on Silvergate Cay. I was broken then. Lost." His voice thins, rough around the edges. "The island's guardian, an ancient AI called the Keeper, allowed me entry. I still don't understand why."

Seeing the strain in his face, I reach across the small space between us and place my hand on his arm.

"Maybe it sensed something in you," I say quietly. "Something worth protecting. A connection to the knowledge it guards."

Frakyss looks at me for a long moment, as if weighing the truth of my words. Beneath my palm, I feel the faint tremor of tension still running through him, the battle he wages against the past he never truly left behind.

Frakyss shrugs, but I can see the tension in his shoulders. "Maybe. In any case, we'll need to convince the Keeper to let us in again. And even then, finding the information we need won't be easy. The library is vast, and much of its knowledge is encoded or written in ancient languages."

"We'll figure it out," I assure him. "Between all of us, we have a pretty diverse set of skills and knowledge."

He nods, a small smile tugging at his lips. "True. And we have you... the most adaptable being I've ever met."

Warmth spreads through me. "Flatterer," I tease, but I smile, pleased by his words.

We sit in comfortable silence for a while, watching the stars streak by on the viewscreen. Finally, Frakyss speaks again, his voice low and serious.

"Nerrisa... there's something I need to tell you. About my early time on Silvergate Cay."

I turn to him. "What is it?"

He takes a deep breath before continuing. "When I first arrived there, I was broken. Physically, mentally, and emotionally. The things the Cegnu did to me..." Frakyss pauses, his eyes distant as he recalls painful memories. I squeeze his hand gently, encouraging him to continue.

"The Keeper used some kind of advanced technology, maybe Aetherian in origin, to help repair the damage," he says softly. "It was a long, difficult process. There were times I wanted to give up, to let the darkness consume me. But the Keeper wouldn't let me."

I listen intently, my heart aching for the pain he endured. "That must have been incredibly difficult," I murmur.

He nods. "It was. But it also gave me purpose. As I healed, the Keeper began teaching me, showing me knowledge from the vast archives. I learned about ancient civilizations, advanced technologies, cosmic mysteries. It was overwhelming at times, but it helped me focus on something beyond my own trauma."

"Is that how you became so knowledgeable about so many subjects?" I ask.

A small smile tugs at his lips. "Partly. The Keeper awakened a thirst for knowledge in me. Even after I left the care of the Keeper, I continued studying, learning everything I could."

I'm struck by his resilience, his ability to transform such pain into a force for growth. "You're remarkable, Frakyss," I tell him sincerely.

He meets my gaze, his red eyes intense. "I'm telling you this because... well, because I trust you. And because I want you to understand why returning to the library is significant for me. It's not just about finding answers about the Aetherians. It's also about confronting my past."

I lean in, pressing a gentle kiss to his cheek. "Thank you for sharing this with me. I'm honored by your trust. And I want you to know, whatever we face in that library, you won't face it alone."

He pulls me into a tight embrace, burying his face in my hair. We stay like that for a long moment, drawing strength and comfort from each other.

Finally, Frakyss pulls back slightly, his expression determined. "We should brief the others. They need to know what to expect when we reach Silvergate City."

I nod in agreement. "I'll gather everyone in the galley."

Soon, our entire group is assembled around the table. Frakyss explains about the hidden library and the Keeper, though he leaves out the personal details of his healing process.

"So how do we convince this Keeper to let us in?" Pearla asks, her brow furrowed in thought.

"I'm not entirely sure," Frakyss admits. "Last time, it seemed to sense my need. We may need to appeal to its purpose as a guardian of knowledge."

"Perhaps we could explain the threat posed by the Zugunu and Cegnu," Elarin suggests. "If the Keeper truly wants to protect important information, it might see the value in helping us understand these advanced beings who could potentially stop them."

Frakyss nods thoughtfully. "That's a good idea. We'll need to be careful how we present it though. The Keeper is ancient and may not view current galactic politics the same way we do."

"What about the lunarite?" Isyarhi pipes up. "Could we use that to somehow prove we've encountered the Aetherians?"

"Possibly," I say. "At the very least, it shows we've come into contact with advanced technology the Keeper might be familiar with."

Lira, who has been quiet until now, speaks up hesitantly. "Um, I'm not sure if this is relevant, but... when the Cegnu held us captive, they were very interested in some kind of psychic abilities they thought Elora and I might have. They kept talking about 'unlocking our potential' or something."

Frakyss and I exchange a look. "That could be significant," he says. "The Cegnu have long been obsessed with enhancing beings to have special abilities. If they thought you two had latent psychic powers..."

"It might be connected to why they targeted you specifically," I finish. "And it might be of interest to the Keeper."

Elora, who's been clinging to her sister's side, looks up with wide eyes. "Do you really think we might have special powers?"

I give her a gentle smile. "It's possible, sweetie. But even if you do, you don't have to use them if you don't want to. No one will force you to do anything you're not comfortable with."

She nods, seeming relieved.

"Alright," Frakyss says, addressing the group. "When we reach Silvergate City, Nerrisa and I will awaken the human females and make arrangements for them to have a safe place to stay. Once they're set up, we'll attempt to contact the Keeper."

"Pearla, are you available to keep working on integrating the lunarite into our systems? If we need to make another trip to Aetherian space, every advantage will help."

Everyone nods in agreement. As the meeting breaks up, I pull Lira and Elora aside.

"Girls, there's something Frakyss and I wanted to ask you," I begin gently. "We've grown quite fond of you both already, and we were wondering... how would you feel about us becoming your guardians or adoptive parents?"

Lira's eyes widen in surprise, while Elora's face lights up. "Really?" the younger girl asks excitedly.

I nod, smiling. "Really. But only if you're both comfortable with it. We understand if you need time to think about it."

Lira looks thoughtful for a moment before speaking. "You've both been so kind to us and saved our lives. I think we'd like that very much. Right, Elora?"

The younger girl nods enthusiastically, throwing her arms around my waist in a tight hug. I feel a warmth spread through my chest as I return the embrace, looking up to see Frakyss watching us with a soft smile.

"Welcome to the family, girls," he says, his deep voice gentle. Lira hesitates only a moment before hugging him as well, and soon we're all wrapped in a group embrace.

As we break apart, I notice tears glistening in Lira's eyes. "Thank you," she whispers. "For everything."

I cup her cheek gently. "You're very welcome, sweetheart. We'll do our best to give you both a good home and a bright future."

Over the next several hours, we prepare for our arrival. Pearla continues her work with the lunarite, occasionally calling Frakyss or me to the lab to consult on a new discovery. Isyarhi spends time with Lira and Elora, telling them about life on Abrauxia and answering their excited questions about their new home.

"Entering Abrauxian space," Frakyss announces from the helm. "Silvergate City, in another hour."

Chapter 23 - Frakyss

Wraith Season Whiteout

As we descend through Abrauxia's atmosphere, the familiar sight of Silvergate Cay comes into view. The island is cloaked in white, an end of wraith season storm causing whiteout conditions.

"Silvergate Spaceport, this is *LWB05 Vortex*, requesting instrument landing at the Galactic Freight pad."

"*LWB05 Vortex*, hold position for clearing of the requested pad."

"Affirmative, Silvergate Spaceport."

"Wow, it's so beautiful," Lira breathes, her silver face peeking between Isyarhi's seat and mine.

Elora nods in agreement, her fathomless black eyes wide with wonder. "Is that snow?"

"Yes. Remember the story of Wraith, the ice dragon? Five months out of ten on Abrauxia, he brings snow and ice to Silvergate Cay, holding the island captive in his clawed grasp."

"Can we see him? In the storm?" Elora gasps.

"He hasn't been seen for centuries, but his children still fly the skies of Abrauxia. There is a blue Ryze near our house on the island's north shore. I feel a twinge of nostalgia, remembering the dragon's tale from my father and Volenne, our estate manager, so long ago.

"Elora, come sit with me. It's going to be bumpy when we get closer to the island." Nerrisa calls our youngest daughter to her. The Abrauxian-sized chair has ample room to hold them both belted in. Lira climbs up next to Isyarhi and buckles the lap strap over them both.

"*LWB05 Vortex* cleared to land at requested Galactic Freight coordinates."

Snow and high winds pound the exterior of the *Vortex* shaking the ship aggressively as I concentrate on bringing us down safely. After fifteen minutes of white-knuckle flying, we're finally on my private pad at the Silvergate City spaceport. A large drone pulls the ship into the hangar, and the exterior door rolls closed, cutting off the sound of the howling wind.

"The last week of winter is certainly trying to leave its mark," I comment as I wait for the ship's exterior to de-ice so the bay door will open. The small room is crowded with the seven of us and the six stasis pods. A metallic clank at the door lets me know Evruik has attached the requested gangplank. I release the safety mechanism, and the door opens to the outside.

"Frakyss, Nerrisa, I'm glad to see the two of you. This storm is really ramping up to be one for the ages. Oh, hey Pearla and Isyarhi."

Eri patiently waits behind him to escort the Hosliens and Uncle Elarin to the security office, where they will be added to the Alien Visitor System.

"Hey Evruik," Nerrisa responds, squeezing past him and pulling Elora with her. Isyarhi follows leading Lira. Elarin is behind them, and Pearla brings up the rear.

Evruik enters and inspects the stacked pods. "The transport to take the stasis pods to the medical center is delayed due to the storm. I had the furniture removed from Conference Room Four so we can put them in there."

I nod and return the pods to their horizontal positions so he can hover them onto the lift to be lowered to floor level. I follow the final unit out and stand next to it, and he follows, tapping the controls and taking us down. Four cargo handlers help us move them to the large conference room.

Evruik peers inside the pod closest to him. "Are these Aquar'thyn females like Nerrisa?"

"No, she said they are from the same planet, but these are humans." I glance inside, where the female lies suspended in a tranquil state. Her rich, warm chestnut skin glistens softly in the ambient glow of the pod's internal lights, creating a serene halo effect around her. Her hair is a cascade of deep dark curls.

"She is stunning," he gazes down at the female.

I narrow my eyes at him. "Don't get any ideas. If these humans are anything like the Aquar'thyn females, they have very strong feelings about being a mate."

"Our strong feelings have more to do with being kidnapped off our planet and waking up to giant aliens with horns and glowing eyes claiming to be our mates," Nerrisa retorts as she enters the room behind me.

Evruik snorts and struggles not to laugh.

I fix him with a baleful glare that would strike terror in most of the Universe's beings. But not my faithful and annoying friend.

"I just spoke with Queen Astrid. She agrees with me that we should wake these women right away. It's wrong to keep them in this frozen state."

I nod my agreement, but I'm nervous about how they will react to finding themselves on an alien planet, 'waking up to giant aliens with horns and glowing eyes,' as my mate so eloquently pointed out.

"Frakyss and Evruik, please bring the replicator into the conference room. Do we know where they will be housed until they decide what to do?"

"The floor two levels below yours has eight unoccupied apartments," I tell her, nervous about her reaction.

"And how would you know that?" She puts her hands on her hips and glares at me.

"Because I own the building?" I grimace, expecting her ire.

Instead, she shakes her head and mutters, "Of course you do," waving her hand toward the door. "Go, get the replicator."

Evruik and I bolt from the room before she yells at us for not telling her. It takes me a few minutes to maneuver the large replicator out of the supply room with a two-wheeled dolly.

Evruik carries the wall-mounted scanner we normally use to measure new hires for uniforms, and we arrange everything at one end of the conference room. Grikrex follows behind us, carrying the privacy screen under my mate's watchful eyes.

"Can you bring in enough chairs and a table for the ladies? We'll also need six sets of nano injections and some of the 'Welcome to Abrauxia' tourist materials from the travel terminal." After a half hour, everything is arranged just as Nerrisa wants, and she shoos us out of the room.

I tap my wrist communicator for the Celestial Spire.

"Frakyss, how can I help you?" Stel'Xon answers immediately.

"Please prepare the apartments on the 105th level for habitation by one Aquar'thyn female, six human females, and one elderly Nagorian male, with furniture, replicators, food synthesizers, and cleaning drones. I need them ready within the next three hours, if possible, with this dismal weather event."

"I'll do my best and send you confirmation when everything is complete."

"Thanks." I tap the disconnect and head to my office.

Chapter 24 - Nerrisa

Stasis Pod Squad

I press the button on the side of the stasis pod on the first unit, and the top swings upward. I press a nano injector to the woman's neck and pull it away after the dispenser hisses. I work my way down the row until all six women have been injected. By the time I reach the last one, the first two are already sitting up in their pods, glancing around the room, confused.

"Welcome, ladies. I'm Nerrisa Byrne, a former US Air Force Major." I help the first woman out of the pod and into a chair, then move on to the next until everyone is seated.

"Help yourselves to tea, coffee, and biscuits," I encourage them, eyeing the disparate group as they fill their cups and nibble the snacks while glancing at each other.

"Do any of you know each other?"

They shake their heads while glancing around.

"Please pass this tablet down, adding your name, age, and where you lived." I hand a datapad to the woman next to me and wait until it makes its way around the table and back to me. I glance at the information they listed.

The women are aged eighteen to forty-nine. Three are from Texas, one from Georgia, one from South Carolina, and one from Missouri.

"I'm sure you have many questions, but I hope you'll let me explain a few things first." They all nod.

"Again, my name is Nerrisa Byrne. I was a US Air Force Major in the Mars Mission until about seven months ago. Like you, I woke in a similar stasis pod." I nod my head toward the empty units against the wall.

"My experience was a little different than yours, but like you, I was kidnapped from Earth by aliens and found myself on planet Abrauxia."

Every single one of them looks at me as if I've sprouted a second head. The older woman laughs and shakes her head. I wait for them to get quiet before I walk to the closed draperies over the large floor-to-ceiling windows and hit the button to open them.

All six women come to stand and stare out at the wild snowstorm that doesn't quite hide the towering silver skyscrapers or lilac-tinged sky. I return to the table, pour myself a cup of tea, and give them time to absorb the information and accept that they aren't on Earth anymore.

One by one, they return to the table and sit looking shell-shocked.

"My mate and I were on a rescue mission in the Zyphora Galaxy, Nerath System, where two young girls were being held captive on the derelict Echo Station. While there, we discovered your stasis pods, evacuated you along with the subjects of our rescue, and brought you back to Silvergate City on planet Abrauxia. We just arrived about an hour ago."

A dark-haired woman with brown eyes glances from the window to me. "This is a lot to take in."

"Believe me, I know."

"Can we see an alien? Maybe it will be easier to believe. That..." she waves her hand at the windows. "That could be video screens."

I tap my communicator. "Frakyss, could you please send Isyarhi into the conference room?"

"Of course," he responds promptly.

My handsome nephew enters the room and shuts the door behind him. "Hello, I'm Isyarhi. I'm pleased to meet you."

The women ogle him. "Ladies, this is my nephew. He is a Nagorian from the planet Nagoria, who now lives on Abrauxia."

He gives a slight bow, his antennas bobbing with the movement.

"Thank you, sweetheart. You can go back to Lira now. I don't want to keep you." He nods and leaves the room.

"Do all the aliens look like him?" the eighteen year old asks.

"No. Would you like to meet my mate or get dressed and read some information about Abrauxia first?"

The older woman shrugs. "In for a dollar... let's meet your mate."

I nod and open the door again. "Frakyss, would you like to come in and meet the ladies?" He looks surprised at my request but nods and enters, standing just inside the door that I leave open. I don't want anyone to feel trapped, as I did on my first day on the planet.

There are the expected gasps all around and gaping mouths as every woman arches their neck to look up at my towering mate. To demonstrate he's not dangerous despite his appearance, I wrap my arm around his waist and give him a playful bump with my shoulder, glancing up and winking.

"Do you have any questions you'd like to ask Frakyss while he's here?"

One of the thirty-something females gingerly raises her hand.

"Yes?" Frakyss asks her.

"Do you have a brother?" She gives him a flirty smile, and I roll my eyes while the other women titter.

"No?" He responds, obviously unsure why she's asking such a thing.

"It's okay, sweetheart. That's not a real question. I'll let you get back to work. I'll ping you when we're ready to head to the Celestial Spire." He nods and gives the woman a curious glance before leaving, and I shut the door behind him.

"Trust me, there are a whole lot of single Abrauxian males on this planet. All their women were killed in a plague about seventy-five years ago. But don't even think about harmless flirting because these guys mate for life, and they don't cheat."

"Do they all look like him?"

"With slight variations, yes. Okay, who wants real clothes first?" I walk to the scanning unit propped against the wall. "We need to get you outfitted in something warmer than those flimsy shifts so we can go to the apartment building where you'll be staying for now."

The Texan in her late forties is the first to get up and join me. "Hi, I'm Michelle, from Austin, Texas. I'll definitely want something warm because I've never been in weather like that!" She glances at the blizzard raging outside.

"Nice to meet you, Michelle. Stand right here so it can scan you. When it beeps, turn and face the opposite way." She gets into position and stands facing the machine while the scan sequence starts. "What did you do on Earth, Michelle?"

"I'm a pediatric surgeon." She turns when the unit beeps. "I had just left the hospital from my evening rounds when I heard something in the parking garage." She frowns as she tries to remember. "That's the last thing I recall before waking up here."

The scanner beeps to indicate the cycle is complete, so I stand at the replicator and set up the clothing request. "Is there a particular color you'd like?"

"Red, please."

A tray slides out, and I hand her the bundle of red clothes. "Here you go. You can get dressed in the restroom through that door. She takes the armload of clothing and enters the restroom, shutting the door behind her.

"Next?"

"Hi, I'm Lily, a barista from Austin," says the curly-haired young woman with dark, soulful eyes.

Outfitting everyone and getting them into their warm clothes takes a few hours. When I message Frakyss to let him know we're ready, he has already arranged for transport at the spaceport's passenger terminal exit. Frakyss and I lead the way, followed by Isyarhi, Lira, Elora, and Uncle Elarin. The six pod women trail behind, with Pearla, Evruik, and Eri at the back.

Frakyss leans close to me. "I didn't invite Evruik, but I couldn't keep the male away."

I glance back to see the subject of our conversation glued to Lily's flank.

The portico does little to keep us from being blasted by the thick snow and wind when we step outside. We hurry to climb into the van and settle in so the doors can be shut. The vehicle has a great heater with comfortable seats.

"Sorry, we cannot fly today because of the high winds. I am taking you to the underground garage entrance of your building," the lanky orange driver calls over the chattering voices.

"Thank you for that!" gasps Michelle from the window seat behind the driver. "Lawdy, this weather!"

The trip that normally takes me fifteen minutes to walk becomes a forty-five-minute drive on the perilously drifted surface streets. Finally, we're under the building and piled into the elevator.

"One-hundred and fifth floor," Frakyss states over the chattering voices.

"One-hundred and seventh floor," I add, glancing up at him. "I'm sure Kishi wants her son back, and the girls will be more comfortable with her fussing over them while we get the pod ladies situated.

"Who are you calling a pod lady? You make me feel like I'm out of an eighties sci-fi movie!" Michelle grins and winks at me.

I usher everyone out when the doors slide open except for Isyarhi, Lira, and Elora. "Go on up, you three. Kishi is waiting for you."

As we exit, Stel'Xon, the horned blue realtor who showed me apartments upon my arrival to Silvergate City, stands waiting in the hallway. "Uncle Elarin, consider this apartment," I say, gesturing to the door right across from the elevator. "You shouldn't have to walk any farther than necessary. You'll be able to come up to the top floor when you want to see us."

He nods, his long antennas bobbing behind him. "Thank you for thinking of an old male's immobility." He opens the apartment door, and I glance in to see a beautifully furnished space.

"Let's divide and conquer," I order the group. "Locals, pair up with a human lady and choose an apartment. Please show them how to use the replicators, food synthesizers, and communications." Before I've finished speaking, Evruik has glued himself to Lily's side.

Michelle stares at him and leans toward me, whispering conspiratorially, "That boy is stuck to her like a tick on a cattle dog. I think someone has a crush."

I snort and shake my head. "Just what we need, the beginnings of the Real Housewives of Silvergate City." We walk to the last apartment on the right, and Michelle opens the door, leading the way inside. It's a corner unit with a dazzling city view through the swirling snow.

It's a beautiful single bedroom tastefully furnished in neutral gray and crisp white. Once I've shown her how everything works, she walks me to the door.

"Thank you for rescuing us and bringing us here. I don't think it's quite sunk in that this is all real, and I won't wake up in the Texas Hill Country tomorrow morning."

"I'm sorry you were taken. If it's any consolation, Abrauxia is an amazing place, and the technology will blow your mind. I'm thankful every day that I didn't end up in some primitive hell hole where the aliens think we're dinner." Her eyes widen as that thought sinks in.

"I'm just upstairs, so if you need anything, start feeling overwhelmed, or just need a friend to share a cup of tea with, I'm there. I travel often, but my best friend and roommate, Kishi, is usually around."

"Thanks for that. Having a new friend will help."

I hear her door click shut as I walk down the hall toward the elevator where Frakyss waits with Pearla.

"Nerrisa, I was just telling Pearla to take this last apartment." He points at the apartment door just past the elevator. "She's not going to be able to go anywhere in this weather."

"I don't want to be an inconvenience," Pearla adds, her pale eyes concerned.

"You could never be an inconvenience, Pearla. Please, take the apartment for as long as you need it. We're right upstairs. I'd invite you to stay with us up there, but it will be a little crowded with me, Kishi, a huge Abrauxian, a toddler, a juvenile, and two teens in love." I wink, and she grins back.

"Okay, thank you. Please let me know when we're ready to visit the ancient library. You know I love a good mystery, and this is one we need to solve. Since your girls were the last of the missing orphanage children, I suddenly find myself without a purpose."

"Aren't you mated to Emeric?" Frakyss asks with a surprised tone. "I am sure there are lots of cases across this galaxy alone that you would be well suited to investigate."

Pearla narrows her eyes and wrinkles her nose. "That patronizing blow hard? He thinks he's god's gift to the universe, and I'm supposed to recline at his feet and worship him. I detest the male. When the Ulae'Zep return, I will have them break the bond."

"I'm sorry to hear that. I didn't realize things weren't going well." I respond, putting a gentle hand on her shoulder.

She pats my hand before stepping away. "Don't worry about it. Thank you for the apartment." She goes in and closes the door.

Frakyss and I exchange a concerned look before getting in the waiting elevator.

"What do you do with my rent payment every month?" I ask him as the door slides shut.

He flashes me a wide grin. "I deposit it right back into your account."

Chapter 25 - Frakyss

The Keeper's Library

"Of course you do," she responds, shaking her head and rolling her eyes.

The elevator opens to utter chaos. Brier races across the expansive living room completely naked, giggling and screeching, with Elora laughing and catching up to him with each stride.

"I'm so sorry," Kishi shouts as she hurries after them with a pair of small fleece pants dangling from her hand.

"I don't know why she bothers," I whisper to Nerrisa. "If the boy doesn't want clothes, he'll just take them off again."

"Brier!" Nerrisa calls. "Uncle Frakyss is here to see you!" She elbows me, and I take the hint.

"Brier, where is my favorite little Omatu nephew?" I hear the slapping of bare feet on the marble floor as the child races from the direction of the kitchen. Within seconds, he stands staring up at me, his big dark eyes gleaming with mischief. I lift him up, balancing him on one palm.

"It's too bad you don't like clothes. You would look very handsome in leather trousers and a warm vest like I wear."

His eyes travel down, inspecting my clothing, right down to my boots. His little head is bobbing up and down. "Brier a warrior," he declares solemnly.

"Then let's see what we can do." I carry him to the replicator and tap in my request. The machine hums softly, then beeps, and a tray slides out. In it is a tiny exact replica of my clothing, including the boots.

When Brier peers into the tray, I can feel him start to tremble with excitement, so I put him down and start handing him each piece in the order he needs to put it on.

He dresses with infinite care, and when he's done, he stands with his fists on his hips, puffing out his chest and scowling. He reaches up and pats the top of his head, pressing his white fluffy hair flat.

"I think he wants horns too." Nerrisa comments from the doorway, where she leans, watching us.

After a few commands to the replicator and a short wait, I have a small hat with soft ridged horns that are identical to mine. I place it on his head and stand back, inspecting him from head to toe. I strike my chest once and bow to him in the traditional Abrauxian sign of respect. He repeats the gesture before focusing on my arms and then eyeing his.

"Someday, when you are older, you will have a beautiful mate who means more than anything in the universe, and you will have mate marks to show everyone that she makes you better than you were before, bringing beauty even to a hideous scarred warrior."

Brier nods solemnly and marches from the room. I follow him to the doorway and look into the eyes of the most exquisite female I've ever seen.

"You were beautiful before I came along, Frakyss. The fire in your survivor's soul shines bright through your eyes, a beacon that calls to me and anchors my very existence," Nerrisa says softly, her voice like a warm breeze across the room's chill.

I can barely find my voice as her words settle over me. "Nerrisa, you know it's not my scars you should admire. They are reminders of a childhood lost."

"Yet those scars have shaped your heart and spirit, and I see them as part of who you are, stronger, kinder, and wiser." Her gaze flickers past me to where Brier stands, examining his reflection in the floor-to-ceiling mirror next to the entry door.

"See? Even he knows you're worth celebrating," she adds with a playful tilt of her head. "You've given him an identity to grow into... a warrior's heart within a child's small frame."

I reach for Nerrisa's hand, threading my fingers through hers as we watch Brier parade around the living room. He giggles at his reflection in the windows and stretches his arms wide, pretending to swoop in to defeat invisible foes.

"Brier the Brave! Mighty protector of the realm!" he shouts, his voice high and ringing with joy.

"Now, doesn't that remind you of someone?" I ask, a chuckle escaping my lips as I watch him spin in circles. The light catches the small horns on his head, making him look even more like the warrior he intends to be.

Nerrisa laughs softly, her eyes sparkling. "You mean me or you? Because I'm not sure either of us can match that level of fearless enthusiasm."

"I definitely don't recall any overwhelming bravery as a child. More like flailing about, almost dying until a glowing Aetherian rescued me and dumped me back on Abrauxia," I say, shaking my head in mock reflection.

Just then, Brier trips and tumbles to the floor, but instead of crying out, he bursts into laughter, rolling onto his back and kicking his booted feet into the air.

"On the contrary, you survived a horrific, life-altering event. I'm still pissed at the Aetherians for not taking care of the Cegnu issue when you were rescued."

"Who do we want to take with us to the ancient library?" I change the subject

Nerrisa considers for a moment before responding. "I think we should keep the group small. You and me, of course. Pearla would be helpful with her investigative skills. And maybe Isyarhi, Lira, and Elora... their youthful perspectives could be valuable."

I nod in agreement. "That sounds like a good team. We don't want to overwhelm the Keeper with too many people."

"Should we go now or wait until the storm passes?" Nerrisa asks, glancing out the window at the still-raging blizzard.

"I think we should go as soon as possible. The storm provides good cover, and I'm anxious to unravel this mystery."

Nerrisa nods. "Alright then. Let's gather the others and head out."

We round up Pearla, Isyarhi, Lira, and Elora and explain our plan, and they are excited to join us. After bundling up in warm clothing, we make our way down to the underground garage, where my personal vehicle waits.

The transport glides silently through the storm-swept streets of Silvergate City, snow streaking across the windshield in glittering streaks. Lightning dances on the horizon, flashing like a warning no one will heed. Most citizens have the sense to stay inside. The roads are slick and empty, drifted full under the fury of Abrauxia's relentless winter onslaught.

I activate the cloaking system as we near the outskirts. The vehicle shimmers and disappears from view.

"We're getting close," I say, my voice quiet but steady. "Everyone, prepare yourselves. Meeting the Keeper can be a bit unsettling."

No one speaks. They feel it too. The shift in the air. The weight of what we're approaching.

The terrain grows wilder, less touched by civilization. Wind howls across the rocky cliffs as we reach what appears to be an unremarkable wall of stone, jagged and frozen by the sweeping snow. But I know the path.

I guide the transport into a narrow gap nearly invisible to the eye. The walls close around us as the passage twists deeper underground, the sound of the storm fading until only silence remains. Ancient silence.

Then, we emerge.

The chamber opens like the inside of a giant geode, vast and shadowed, lit only by the ambient glow of the structure at its heart.

The ancient library.

It rises from the cavern floor in jagged crystalline spires, violet and silver, as if the mountain itself birthed it. The walls shimmer with unreadable glyphs. Thin waterfalls trickle down the stone around it, pooling into still, mirror-like basins at its base. The air here is different, charged and reverent.

Someone behind me finally speaks, their voice hushed.

"What is this place? Who built it?"

I don't turn around. I don't need to.

"I asked the Keeper that once," I say. My voice echoes strangely in this space, muted and deep. "It answered, but not in a way that made sense."

I glance up at the tallest spire, vanishing into the blackness above.

"It said the library has been here since the planet was born. That it remembers the sky before the moons."

A beat of silence follows.

"It might be a metaphor," I add, though even as I say it, I don't believe it.

Because the Keeper doesn't speak in metaphors.

It speaks in truths too old for our kind to grasp.

I step from the transport, boots echoing against the stone.

And the library waits.

As we exit the vehicle, a shimmering hologram materializes before us... the Keeper. Its form constantly shifts, never settling on a single appearance for more than a moment.

"Frakyss," the Keeper's voice echoes around us, neither male nor female, young nor old. "You have returned and you have brought others."

I step forward, bowing my head slightly in respect. "Yes, Keeper. We seek your wisdom and guidance. The fate of many worlds may depend on what we learn here today."

The Keeper's form ripples, and I sense its intense scrutiny falling upon each member of our group. "Very well," it says after a long moment. "Enter, seekers of knowledge. But be warned, the truths you uncover here may change everything you thought you knew about the universe."

With those ominous words hanging in the air, the massive doors of the ancient library slowly swing open, revealing a chamber filled with towering shelves of books, scrolls, and holographic displays. The air is thick with the scent of ancient paper and a faint electrical hum.

As we step inside, lights flicker to life around us, illuminating the space in a soft, ethereal glow. The Keeper's form shimmers and reappears before us, gesturing toward a central area with several ornate chairs arranged in a circle.

"Be seated," the Keeper instructs. "And tell me what knowledge you seek."

We take our places, and I feel the nervous energy radiating from my companions. Nerrisa reaches over and squeezes my hand reassuringly before addressing the Keeper.

"We seek information about the Aetherian Guardians," she begins. "And their connection to a substance called lunarite."

The Keeper's form flickers, and for a moment, I catch a glimpse of what might be surprise in its ever-changing features.

"The Aetherians," it muses. "It has been many ages since anyone has inquired about them. And lunarite... a most intriguing substance. What has led you to pursue this knowledge?"

I lean forward, my voice low and urgent. "We've encountered them, Keeper. The Aetherians. They rescued us from a derelict space station and repaired our ship but then tried to erase all evidence of their existence. We need to understand why they're hiding, and what threat they might be protecting the universe from."

The Keeper is silent for a long moment, its form shifting rapidly through a series of complex patterns. Finally, it speaks. "The story of the Aetherians is long and complex, stretching back to the very dawn of our universe. They were among the first sentient beings to evolve, achieving a level of technological and spiritual advancement that borders on the divine."

Holographic images spring to life around us, showing beings of pure light and energy, manipulating the very fabric of reality.

"For eons, they served as guardians of the cosmic balance, nurturing young civilizations and defending against threats from beyond our realm of existence. But their power and knowledge came at a great cost."

The images shift, showing scenes of devastation and cosmic horror that make my blood run cold.

"They discovered that their very presence in our universe was causing instabilities, tears in the fabric of space-time that allowed things to slip through from other dimensions. Monstrous entities beyond mortal comprehension."

Pearla gasps, her eyes wide. "The Cegnu," she whispers. "Could they be one of these entities?"

The Keeper nods, its form briefly taking on a more solid appearance. "Indeed. The Cegnu are but one of many such horrors that the Aetherians inadvertently unleashed upon our reality. In their guilt and desperation to contain the threat, the Aetherians withdrew to a pocket dimension of their own creation, a place beyond the reach of mortal beings. From there, they could continue to monitor and subtly influence events in our universe without risking further damage to the cosmic fabric."

"But if they're so powerful, why don't they just destroy threats like the Cegnu?" Isyarhi asks, his antennae twitching with curiosity.

The Keeper turns its attention to the young Nagorian. "A valid question, young one. The answer lies in the delicate balance of cosmic forces. Direct intervention by the Aetherians could cause more harm than good, potentially tearing open new rifts in reality. Instead, they chose a path of subtle guidance, nurturing civilizations that might one day be capable of facing these threats on their own."

"And the lunarite?" Nerrisa prompts. "How does it fit into all of this?"

The air around us shimmers and a holographic representation of a glowing crystal appears. "Lunarite is a byproduct of Aetherian technology," the Keeper explains. "It is infused with a fraction of their power, capable of enhancing the natural abilities of other beings. In the right hands, it can be a powerful tool against the threats that plague our universe."

I lean forward, my mind racing. "Why was it just lying around on the surface of asteroids where anyone can find it?"

The Keeper's form flickers, and for a moment, I glimpse what might be approval in its ever-changing features. "Lunarite is left in the path of those who the Aetherians believe have the potential to become guardians."

"But why erase their involvement?" Pearla asks. "Why not just tell us directly?"

"Direct knowledge of the Aetherians' existence can be dangerous," the Keeper replies. "It draws the attention of the very entities they seek to keep at bay. By maintaining their secrecy, they protect not only themselves but all of our reality."

A heavy silence falls over our group as we absorb this information. The implications are staggering. We're not just dealing with interstellar politics or the machinations of advanced alien races. We're caught in the middle of a cosmic struggle for the very fabric of our universe.

"So, what do we do now?" Nerrisa asks, her voice barely above a whisper. "How do we fight something like the Cegnu without risking further damage to reality?"

The Keeper's form solidifies slightly, taking on an almost humanoid appearance. "You must learn to harness the power of the lunarite, to become the guardians that this universe needs. The Aetherians cannot fight this battle directly, but through you and others like you, they can guide the forces of light against the encroaching darkness."

I feel a weight settle on my shoulders, a mix of responsibility and purpose. "How do we begin?" I ask.

The Keeper gestures, and a section of the library's wall shimmers and parts, revealing a hidden chamber. Inside, we see a pedestal upon which rests a glowing crystal, larger and more brilliant than any lunarite we've encountered before.

"This is the Heart of Aether," the Keeper explains. "A fragment of pure Aetherian energy, left here eons ago by the Aetherians for safekeeping. It has the power to awaken and amplify the latent abilities within you all."

We approach the pedestal cautiously. The crystal pulses with an inner light, sending waves of energy washing over us. I reach out, my hand hovering just above its surface.

"But be warned," the Keeper's voice echoes around us. "Touching the Heart of Aether will irrevocably change you. Your potential will be unlocked, but with it comes great responsibility. Are you prepared to bear this burden?"

I look to my companions. Nerrisa nods, her eyes shining with determination. Pearla squares her shoulders, a fierce resolve in her gaze. The three youngsters, though clearly nervous, step forward bravely.

"We are," I say, speaking for us all.

As one, we reach out and place our hands on the crystal. The world explodes into light and sensation. I feel power coursing through me, awakening parts of myself I never knew existed. Memories flood my mind... not just my own, but glimpses of ancient battles, cosmic wonders, and the very birth of stars.

When the light fades, we stumble back, gasping. I look down at my hands to see intricate patterns of light dancing beneath my skin. Nerrisa's eyes glow with an otherworldly radiance, while Pearla seems to flicker in and out of existence. Isyarhi's antennae crackle with energy. Lira and Elora have become mirror-like, even their eyes. Their silver hair floats around them with a life of its own.

"It is done," the Keeper intones.

"You have taken your first steps on a long and challenging journey. Remember, the power of the lunarite is a tool, not a solution in itself. Your greatest strength will always be your compassion, determination, and willingness to stand against the darkness."

We thank the Keeper and return to the transport, each of us lost in thought. As we emerge from the hidden cavern and rejoin the storm-swept streets of Silvergate City, I am both exhilarated and overwhelmed by the magnitude of what we've learned.

"So," Nerrisa says, breaking the silence as we near home. "Cosmic guardians fighting interdimensional horrors. Just another day in the life, right?"

I chuckle, some of the tension easing from my shoulders. "Well, when you put it that way, who wants pancakes?"

Chapter 26 - Nerrisa

Power and Pancakes

As we ride back to the Celestial Spire in silence, I feel the energy from the Heart of Aether still thrumming through my body. My skin tingles, and when I look down at my hands, I see faint patterns of light shifting beneath the surface.

I turn them palms up, and see designs flicker. I shift them through a series of mutations and stop, remembering the touch of the Aetherian's wing as I hid under the cabinet's edge in the life pod chamber of the *Vortex*.

A bright flash fills the transport, and Frakyss nearly loses control before sliding to a stop. Huge, feathered wings fill the front of the transport, shoving Frakyss against his door, and I'm pressed against the dashboard. The only sound is the quiet whisper of heavy snow against the windshield.

"Uhm, Mom?" Elora's voice giggles from the back seat.

"Oh, for crying out loud," I mutter as I struggle to shift.

Then, they are all laughing, and I snicker. As soon as I stop concentrating, I'm suddenly back to myself again, amused tears running unchecked down my face at Frakyss's relieved expression.

When I glance at everyone, Frakyss's eyes seem to glow even brighter, his scars now traced with delicate lines of luminescence. Pearla keeps flickering in and out of visibility as if she can't entirely control her newfound abilities, either. Isyarhi's antennae crackle with small arcs of electricity. My adorable polished chrome daughters are sitting beside him with beatific smiles on their faces.

"So," I say, breaking the heavy silence. "I guess we're cosmic guardians now. Any idea how we're supposed to control these new powers?"

Frakyss shakes his head, a wry smile on his face as he starts driving again. "I think we'll be figuring that out as we go along. The Keeper wasn't exactly forthcoming with an instruction manual."

"Maybe that's part of the test," Pearla muses. "Learning to control and harness these abilities on our own."

Isyarhi nods enthusiastically, his antennae sending off a shower of sparks. "Oops," he mutters, trying to pat them down.

As we pull into the underground garage of the Celestial Spire, I wonder how we're going to explain all of this to the others. How do you tell someone that you've basically become a superhero overnight?

When the elevator doors open on our floor, we're greeted by the chaos that seems to follow Brier wherever he goes. The little boy is running through the living room, still dressed in his mini-Frakyss outfit, only now he has a wooden sword.

"Uncle Frakyss!" Brier shouts, barreling toward us. He stops short, his eyes widening as he takes in our glowing appearances. "Whoa..."

Kishi emerges from the kitchen, a towel in her hands. "Oh good, you're back. I was starting to worry with this storm and..." She trails off, her eyes wide in confusion. "What happened to you all?"

I exchange a look with Frakyss. "It's a long story," I say. "Maybe we should sit down."

Over the next hour, we recount our experience at the ancient library, explaining the Aetherians, the cosmic threats, and our newfound abilities. By the time we finish, Kishi looks shell-shocked, while Brier stares at us with awe and excitement.

"So, you're like superheroes now?" Kishi asks, her eyes shining.

I laugh softly. "I'm not sure I'd go that far. We have some new abilities, but we're still figuring out what they mean and how to use them."

"Can you show me?" Kishi asks eagerly.

I glance at Frakyss, unsure. He shrugs, a small smile playing at his lips. "I suppose a small demonstration couldn't hurt."

I stand and walk to the open center of the two-story living room. Focusing inward, I remember the touch of the Aetherian's wing, and in a bright flash, I've transformed into a pale, glowing female warrior wearing silver and gold engraved armor with glorious majestic wings. I catch my glowing reflection in the night-darkened windows. Tapping into the strange new energy flowing through me, I flap my wings. To my surprise, I rise high above the floor as if weightless.

Pearla flickers in and out of visibility while Isyarhi creates small arcs of electricity between his fingertips. Frakyss stands there, his entire body glowing with an otherworldly light. Lira stands facing her sister, and as the two reach out to touch, their hands become liquid metal, twisting around each other before reshaping.

"Incredible," Kishi breathes.

Brier claps his hands excitedly. "Me too! Me too!" he shouts, jumping up and down.

I cup my wings and drift to the floor. "I'm sorry, little one. This isn't something we can share. When you're older, you'll have amazing powers of your own."

Frakyss clears his throat. "We need to be careful with these abilities. The Keeper warned us that they come with great responsibility."

I nod in agreement. "And we still don't know the full extent of what we can do or how it might affect us or those around us."

"So, what's our next move?" Pearla asks, finally managing to stabilize her visibility.

"We need to train," Frakyss says firmly. "Learn to control ourselves and understand our limitations. And then we need to figure out how to use them against the Cegnu, Zugunu, Ven'aens, and any other threats out there from the rift."

"Don't forget about the human women," I remind him. "We still need to help them adjust to life here on Abrauxia."

Kishi steps forward. "I can help with them. You focus on your training and saving the universe. I'll make sure our new arrivals are well taken care of."

I smile gratefully at my friend. "Thank you, Kishi. We couldn't do this without you."

We discuss training plans and next steps. We've been thrust into a cosmic conflict beyond anything I could have imagined when I first awoke on this alien world. I study my makeshift family... Frakyss at my side, our daughters playing with Brier on the floor, Isyarhi smiling as he juggles crackling energy balls between his hands, and Pearla fading in and out of view.

Chapter 27 - Frakyss

Freighters, Family, and Freedom

I sit in my home office with Bruud, who is trying his best to pounce on the floating holographic image of a new tanker vessel I am considering for the fleet. The Nostronix hovers above my desk, its projection rotating slowly. It is approximately eight hundred twenty feet long, built with an industrial aesthetic and a rugged, utilitarian design that reflects its sole purpose as a cargo vessel. She is designed to carry thousands of liters of liquid payload, something our fleet has needed for a while.

Nerrisa walks in, catching sight of the hologram. She wrinkles her nose in amusement. "That is an ugly monster. Are you thinking of getting one?"

"Maybe," I say, rubbing my beard thoughtfully. "We get requests to transport liquids daily, but none of our current ships can accommodate more than a thousand liters. A tanker this size would open us up to new areas of business."

"Not to mention," she adds, "if the Ulae'Zep ever find King Zaphre Kragmals' mate, Jakvar assigned me with her transport to Abrauxia."

"True," I say, picturing the logistics. "I cannot even imagine the size of the stasis pod needed to move a troqel."

Nerrisa laughs and scoops up Bruud from the corner of my desk, cuddling him against her chest and peppering his fluffy head with kissy noises. "I do not even want to think about the physics and logistics it is going to take to move a creature that huge. Hopefully Makena and Dyebarth are the ones solving that particular headache. My brain hurts just thinking about it."

"The lunarite did not gift you with the knowledge of mechanical physics?" I tease her.

"Not even close. Apparently, I can only fly. Without a ship."

"Starfire, you turned into an Aetherian ship and flew through outer space," I remind her with a grin. "That was before the lunarite infusion." I wink at her.

Before she can respond, my communicator buzzes. I glance at the display and straighten slightly when I see the name.

"King Jakvar, how are you?" I answer.

"Frakyss, where have you been? I have tried reaching you for a few days," Jakvar says, his voice carrying a hint of impatience.

"We were on a mission to recover the missing Hosliens girls from the Coprinus-LV3 orphanage," I explain. "Nerrisa and I are now the proud parents of Lira and Elora, who were being held by Cegnu on the abandoned Echo Station in the Zyphora Galaxy."

I hear the words leave my mouth, proud parents of Lira and Elora, and for a moment something tight and fierce tugs deep in my chest. Nerrisa's hand brushes lightly over mine, her touch grounding me, her eyes shining with a pride that mirrors my own.

"Congratulations," Jakvar says warmly. "You deserve this, Frakyss. After everything you have endured, you deserve a family of your own."

"Thank you, Your Majesty," I say, the weight of his words lingering in my chest.

"I need to update you as well," he continues. "General Grizlor and his team have just executed a secret mission, defeating the Ven'aens. They found the second underwater facility where the new plague was being created."

"Is there a threat to humans?" I ask immediately. "We recovered six of them in stasis pods on Echo Station. They are currently awake and staying here at the Celestial Spire in Silvergate City."

"No threat," Jakvar assures me. "The pathogens were neutralized before they could spread. I also got a panicked call from Emeric. His mate marks disappeared late yesterday. I have never heard of that happening before."

I feel the blood drain from my face. Beside me, Nerrisa stiffens, her hand going still on Bruud's soft fur.

A bond, broken naturally? Without death? Without violence? It shakes the foundation of everything we thought we understood about the Heart of Aether and the ancient forces binding our people.

"Is he not aware of Pearla's location?" I ask carefully.

"No, he has not seen her in months," Jakvar says. "That is one situation where I think the Ulae'Zep got it wrong. You know what an insufferable zorblax Emeric can be."

"Then it is a good thing the bond somehow broke naturally," I mutter.

"I hope any new females will be able to choose their own mates, and only if they want them," Jakvar says firmly. "No one has the right to choose for someone else. While I am glad things worked out for a few of us, there will be no more in absentia bondings."

"Good to hear," I say. I hesitate, then add with a faint smile, "I do not suppose you will be visiting Silvergate City anytime soon, Your Majesty?"

"Not until the wraith season is over," he chuckles. "General Grizlor told me about the blizzard you are having. I would rather visit Whitevale Citadel."

I end the call, setting the communicator down with a heavy hand. Silence settles between Nerrisa and me, thick and full of unspoken thoughts.

"Do you think the Heart of Aether dissolved the bond and set Pearla free?" I ask, my voice quieter than before, as if speaking too loudly might break the fragile hope forming between us.

"I hope so," she says, her tone soft and full of wonder. She strokes Bruud absently, her fingers gentle against his fur, but I can see the thoughts racing behind her bright eyes.

"So why did mine not disappear?" I ask, the words escaping before I can stop them. Some deep part of me still fears the answer.

Nerrisa smiles, the kind of smile that makes my chest ache with how much I love her. "Because I love you. I already decided to keep you a while ago," she says, her laughter like sunlight after a long winter.

I look at her, really look, at the way her eyes shine and her spirit burns so brightly it could outshine stars. The bond between us thrums, steady and strong, chosen freely by the only heart that has ever truly mattered to me.

"I will never stop being grateful you chose me," I say, my voice thick with emotion. I reach out and tuck a stray piece of hair behind her ear, needing to touch her, to anchor this moment as something real and lasting.

She leans into my touch without hesitation, her smile softening even further, and in that breath, I know. No matter what storms come for us, no matter what battles lie ahead, this bond will hold.

Because we chose it.

We chose each other.

Chapter 28 - Nerrisa

The Blooming Season

"Speaking of keeping me," Frakyss says, his red eyes glinting with mischief, "how about we take advantage of this blizzard and have a quiet evening in?"

For a moment, the suggestion catches me off guard. A quiet evening. The words settle over me like a balm. After everything we have faced, battles, fear, constant vigilance, the thought of peace, of simply being together without the weight of survival pressing on us, feels like a rare and precious thing. I want that. More than I can easily say.

"That sounds perfect," I agree softly. Then a thought tugs at me. "But first, we should check on Pearla. I wonder if she knows her bond with Emeric is gone?"

Frakyss nods, and we take the elevator down to her floor. When she opens the door, I have to blink. For a second, I barely recognize her.

Pearla practically glows. Her pale skin seems to shimmer from within, and there is a lightness to her movements I have never seen before. Her lush dark hair falls loose to her waist in soft waves, a picture of effortless grace. She looks free. And the sight of it steals the breath right out of my chest.

"Nerrisa, Frakyss," she says warmly, her voice bright. "Come in. I was just about to call you. My bond with Emeric is gone."

Relief crashes into me so hard my knees nearly buckle. I step forward and pull her into a tight hug, feeling the strength and vitality humming through her now.

"That's wonderful news," I murmur against her shoulder. "How are you feeling?"

She hugs me back fiercely, her fingers digging into my back. When she pulls away, her eyes shine. "Better than I have felt in my entire life," she says, voice trembling with emotion. "And relieved, of course. Thinking I would be chained to him forever..." She shudders visibly, wrapping her arms around herself. "It was too horrible to even contemplate. But now I'm free."

There is something raw and beautiful in her expression, like someone who has clawed her way out of the dark and found herself blinking in the sun.

"Have you thought about what you want to do now?" I ask gently as I release her.

Pearla's smile wavers, thoughtful. "I am not sure yet. I loved being an investigator on Earth. That was what I was good at. My intuition helped me excel. And now, with the lunarite," she trails off, wonder flickering across her face. "I can only imagine how much stronger those instincts will be."

"There's no rush to figure it out," I assure her, giving her arm a gentle squeeze. "You'll find your place again. I have no doubt."

She nods, and for the first time in a long time, her entire posture radiates hope.

We stay only a few minutes longer before Frakyss and I say our goodbyes and head back upstairs. As we step into the apartment, a wave of warmth and noise hits me.

Laughter bubbles up from the living room. The girls and Isyarhi are deep into a holographic game, the air alive with bursts of color and playful shrieks. Brier is practicing his sword work against the edge of the sofa, his brow furrowed in fierce concentration. Kishi stands in the kitchen, working with our house droid to prepare dinner, the scent of fresh bread and roasted vegetables filling the air.

For a moment, I just stand there, taking it all in. The normalcy, safety, and the life we have fought so hard to reclaim.

This, I think, is what healing looks like.

"Is everything okay?" Kishi calls from the kitchen, glancing over her shoulder.

I nod, smiling as I step further inside. "We got some interesting news from King Jakvar."

As we fill her in on the latest updates about Pearla's broken bond, the defeated Ven'aens, and the safety of the human survivors from the new pathogens, she listens carefully.

"So," she says when we finish, "what's our next move?"

I glance at Frakyss, feeling the weight of everything still ahead of us, and then back at the home we have built, fragile but real.

"For now," I say, my voice steady, "we rest. And when the time comes, we rise."

***

As the cold grip of Wraith Season loosens its hold, Searfang creeps slowly across Abrauxia. Life stirs again.

The ground, once frozen and brittle, now breathes with new color. Pale green shoots push bravely through the thawed soil, and flowers unfurl bright petals toward Xonus hanging high in the sky.

The air smells different, sweeter, carrying the scent of damp earth and something almost electric, like the world itself is waking after too long asleep.

I feel it too. A loosening inside me. A soft, tentative hope taking root.

Life settles into a new rhythm. I spend my days running cargo shipments through the galaxy, slipping between star systems like the seasoned pilot I always wanted to become. The girls start school with Isyarhi, their days filled with laughter, study, and regular video calls with Queen Astrid, working through the trauma they endured at the hands of the Cegnu.

Some mornings, I find Lira doubled over in laughter at one of Isyarhi's bad jokes, her silver hair flashing in the sun. Other times, I see Elora bent seriously over her datapad, her little brow furrowed in concentration, stubbornly solving complex equations like a warrior. Healing is messy, fierce, and beautiful.

We expand the Celestial Spire's 106th level, converting it into a sprawling third floor to accommodate our growing family. A wide, sweeping staircase curves elegantly between the levels now, open and light filled.

Frakyss and I worried at first about how Lira and Elora, born on sunless Nocturnia, would handle the intense Abrauxian sun. But their gifts, whatever the Heart of Aether unlocked in them, seem to protect them. They do not burn in the light. They thrive in it.

One thing remains steady through all the changes and challenges. My love for Frakyss grows, deepening like roots digging into rich, dark soil.

We respect each other's need for space and time, never rushing what feels sacred. But the pull between us, the bond, hums stronger with every passing day.

Late one evening, long after the stars have risen, I find myself standing on my bedroom balcony, watching the ringed moon climb above the distant cliffs. Its light casts a silver sheen across the ocean, turning the waves into a river of molten metal.

Frakyss joins me, the comforting heat of his presence easing into the space beside me. He does not speak at first. Just stands there, hands braced lightly on the railing, his gaze soft.

"Beautiful night," he murmurs, voice roughened by the cool evening air.

I nod but keep my eyes on him instead of the sky. The moonlight bathes his strong profile, catching the faint patterns of light that now shimmer beneath his skin, a mark of the Aether's touch.

Looking at him, something fierce and trembling rises inside me. I cannot hold it back.

"Frakyss," I say, my voice barely above a whisper. "Can we talk?"

He turns to me fully, his eyes luminous against the darkness. "About what?"

I take a breath, deeper than any I have ever taken, gathering all the fragile, terrifying hope I carry. How easy it would be to stay silent. How much harder it is to open my heart.

"I have been thinking," I say, my voice steadier now. "About us. About how much you mean to me. I know we have been taking things slow, and I respect that, I do. But I need you to know I love you, Frakyss. More than I ever thought possible."

For a heartbeat, he just stares at me.

Then his face softens, and he steps closer, cupping my cheek with a hand that feels both reverent and sure.

"Oh, Nerrisa," he whispers. "I love you too. I have for a long time now."

I lean into his touch, feeling the roughness of his calloused fingers against my skin, the tenderness hidden behind them.

"I do not want to pressure you," I say softly. "I just want you to know that I am ready for everything. Whenever you are."

Frakyss's smile curves into something darker, more dangerous, his voice a low murmur that slides over my skin like velvet. "Who says I'm not ready now?" he asks, and the daring in his tone makes my breath catch.

Then his lips are on mine, claiming me with a heat that steals all thought. His kiss is not gentle. It's fierce and consuming, a blaze that ignites everything inside me. The world around us vanishes, and all that remains is his mouth moving against mine with purpose, his hands pulling me closer like he never intends to let go.

Behind the fire, though, there is something deeper. His touch, even as it demands, still reveres. His strength surrounds me, lifts me, holds me like I'm precious. Like I'm his beginning and his end. And I realize, even as I burn, that I have never felt so safe.

Without breaking the kiss, Frakyss gathers me into his arms. The movement is effortless, but the way he holds me feels anything but casual. His grip is firm, possessive, and full of intent. My heart hammers in my chest as he carries me through the doors, each step resonating with a quiet urgency that coils heat low in my belly.

When he reaches the bed, he lowers me onto the soft sheets like I'm something sacred. His eyes never leave mine. The hunger is still there, fierce and undeniable, but layered beneath it is reverence. A quiet question in the way his fingers brush my jaw. A promise in the way his body surrounds mine.

Each breath between us grows heavier, thick with unspoken promises and everything we've kept locked behind fear and caution. The space between what we were and what we're about to become disappears, drawn tight by the gravity of the moment. I feel it break, like a tide cresting and finally crashing. There's no turning back. Not from this and not from him.

The night rises around us like a wave, and I let it carry me, let it drown every wall I ever built.

His hands find me with a reverence that shakes me to my core. Every stroke is slow, deliberate, as if he is discovering a language only my body can speak. His touch is grounding, electric, impossibly gentle and impossibly sure. It isn't just want. It's worship.

When his mouth finds my skin, the heat of him seeps into me. He moves slowly, tasting, learning, each kiss a vow pressed into my flesh. I feel the way he memorizes me, how every freckle, every scar, is touched like a secret. Like a constellation only he can read.

"You are not what I expected," he murmurs against the curve of my collarbone, his breath making my entire body clench with anticipation.

"Good," I whisper, curling my fingers into his hair. "I want to ruin every expectation you ever had."

His low laugh vibrates against my skin, rough and full of hunger. Then his mouth trails lower, following the line of freckles down my sternum like a pilgrim tracing the path to something holy.

The air around us shifts, saturated with his wild and clean scent, like rain striking hot stone. I inhale him, greedy for it, dizzy from it. Every sense sharpens, and I realize with startling clarity that no one has ever touched me like this. Not just with his hands.

But with awe.

The sound of my name, broken and raw on his lips, shatters something inside me, replacing it with a deeper need.

When his mouth finds the aching bundle of nerves between my thighs, I cry out, stars spinning wildly behind my closed eyes.

The Aether floods my blood with unnatural heat. My body responds to his searing touch like a live wire, every nerve ablaze. Jolts of electric pleasure make me buck beneath him as dual sensations overwhelm me, the rasp of his teeth and tug of his tongue on my aching nub.

Oh stars... My hips jerk against his mouth, thighs clamping around his head as I crave more friction from that wicked Abrauxian tongue.

"Yes," I hiss through clenched teeth, "Right there! Don't you dare stop!" His split tongue flicks and teases, coaxing pleasure from me. He nibbles and scrapes his sharp fangs on my sensitive pearl repeatedly while he seeks that pleasure spot deep inside with his long, curled tongue. When release finally tears through me, all I can do is shriek his name.

When he finally pulls away, his mouth and chin gleaming with the raw evidence of our insatiable desire, his gaze sears into mine with a fiery intensity. "Are you truly ready for everything, Starfire?" he hisses, his voice charged with an urgent intimacy that electrifies the air.

"I need you," I respond, my voice breaking with a primal hunger, "in every way imaginable." As he positions himself against my slick entrance, I wrap my legs around his waist with a desperate fervor, pulling him toward me, yearning to envelop him completely.

Each ringed section of his shaft forces its way inside, stretching me to my utmost limits with a searing burn that teeters on the brink of pain, yet craved with every fiber of my being. At last, he is fully seated within me, filling every hidden void I never knew was aching to be complete.

He thrusts with a deep, unyielding certainty, his movements slow and deliberate, each one a powerful, possessive claim that leaves no part of me untouched. His large hands grip my hips, lifting me for a better angle.

The friction, the heat, the relentless pressure builds and builds until my entire body is a live wire sparking wildly beneath him.

"You are mine," he snarls against my mouth, and when I cry out, it is not in fear. It is in recognition and surrender.

My climax tears through me like a supernova, exploding outward and drawing him with me into a vortex of pleasure so deep it feels endless.

Frakyss groans my name against my skin, his body shuddering violently as he pours himself into me, the rings of his shaft swelling impossibly, sealing us together.

For a long time, we cling to each other, gasping and trembling, our bodies fused by more than just passion.

When he lifts his head to look at me, his eyes catch the faint light and glow with something that humbles me.

Not possession or victory. Worship.

He holds me as if I am something sacred, something fragile and powerful all at once.

And for the first time in my life, I believe I am worth holding. Worth choosing.

I press my face against his chest, feeling his hearts beating strong and steady beneath my cheek.

The faint light of morning spills across the bed, casting a warm glow over everything it touches. Frakyss is still wrapped around me, his arm heavy across my waist, his breath slow and steady against the back of my neck. His warmth seeps into me, grounding me in a way nothing else ever has.

For a long moment, I simply lie there, listening to the steady rhythm of his heartbeats, feeling the rise and fall of his chest against my back.

This is what it means to belong, I realize. Not to be claimed or trapped, but to be chosen and cherished.

I press a soft kiss to the back of his hand where it rests against me and close my eyes again, letting myself drift in the rare, precious peace of being exactly where I want to be.

Chapter 29 - Frakyss

Trips and Troqels

I wake slowly, savoring the warm weight of Nerrisa curled against my side. Last night was transcendent. Our lovemaking unlocked something within us, a deeper connection beyond the physical. I feel her presence in my mind now, a comforting glow of love and contentment.

Taking care not to disturb her, I slip out of bed, pull on my trousers, and stand on the balcony. Xonus is just peeking over the horizon, painting the sky in brilliant hues of purple and gold. I take a deep breath, feeling more at peace than I have in years.

"Good morning, handsome," Nerrisa's sleepy voice comes from behind me. I turn to see her standing in the doorway, wrapped in a silken robe, her hair delightfully mussed from sleep.

"Good morning, Starfire," I reply, holding out my arm in invitation. She comes to me willingly, fitting herself against my side as if she was made to be there. "Sleep well?"

She hums contentedly. "Better than I have in ages. You?"

"Same," I murmur, pressing a kiss to the top of her head. We stand in comfortable silence for a while, watching the city below come to life.

"So," Nerrisa says eventually, a hint of mischief in her voice. "What's on the agenda for today? Saving the universe? Battling interdimensional horrors?"

I chuckle. "How about breakfast first? Then we can tackle the cosmic threats."

As if on cue, there's a knock at the door. "Come in," I call out.

Elora bounds into the room, her bright silver hair flying behind her. "Mom, Dad! It's pancake day!" She wraps her arms around us and squeezes.

Nerrisa laughs. "I thought every day was pancake day."

As we settle in around our large dining table, with Lira and Isyarhi already enjoying their breakfast, Nerrisa's communicator buzzes.

"Huh, it's a message from an unknown source."

Mission Leader Nerrisa Byrne:
Female troqel located.
Mating contract negotiated.
Transport required.
Gilles XPM.
Coordinates: Tidehaven Reef G-7.23, QX-4.56, ZR-9.81.

"It's a good thing the Nostronix is available, along with the water tank King Jakvar commissioned."

"I wondered when they'd get around to finding the troqel."

"What's a troqel?" Lira asks, curiosity shining in her large mirror eyes.

"A very large aquatic species," I explain. "We've been asked to help bring one to Abrauxia as a mate for King Zaphre Kragmals."

Isyarhi's antennae perk up with interest. "Can we come? Please?"

Nerrisa and I exchange a look. After our experience with the Heart of Aether and our newfound abilities, the idea of leaving the children behind makes me uneasy. But bringing them into a potentially dangerous situation isn't ideal either.

"Let's discuss it after breakfast," I suggest diplomatically. "This mission will require careful planning."

As we finish our meal, I see the wheels turning in Nerrisa's mind. "What are you thinking?" I ask.

She sets down her fork, her expression thoughtful. "We'll use the Nostronix and the new water tank. But transporting a creature that large... it's going to be tricky."

"Not to mention potentially dangerous," I add. "We don't know much about troqel behavior or biology."

I nod. "True. We should contact Dyebarth and Dr. Makena. His expertise could be invaluable."

After breakfast, we gather in the living room for an impromptu family meeting. Lira and Isyarhi sit cross-legged on the floor while Elora perches on the arm of the couch next to me.

"Alright," I begin, "here's the situation. We've been tasked with transporting a female troqel from Gilles XPM to Abrauxia. It's going to be a challenging mission and potentially dangerous."

"Which is why," Nerrisa continues, "we need to decide if I do this haul with my normal crew and Frakyss stays here with you kids, or if all of us should go."

Lira's face falls. "But we want to help! We're part of this family too."

"And we've been training with our new abilities," Isyarhi adds eagerly. "We could be useful!"

I feel a swell of pride at their enthusiasm and bravery, but the protective part of me is still hesitant. "It's true; you've made incredible progress with your training. But King Jakvar has assigned this job to Nerrisa. Her crew is trained to operate the Nostronix, and since the ship is a freighter, it's not comfortable for pleasure travel."

Elora's eyes widen. "But we want to see the troqel! Please, can't we come?"

I exchange a look with Nerrisa, seeing my own hesitation mirrored in her eyes. But there's also understanding there. We both know how important it is for the children to feel included, especially after everything they've been through.

"What if we compromise?" Nerrisa suggests. "I'll take the Nostronix with my regular crew to transport the troqel. Frakyss, you could take the kids to Romrey Island and show them your ancestral home while I'm on the mission."

"Really?" Isyarhi asks excitedly. "I've always wanted to see where Uncle Frakyss came from!"

I feel a mix of emotions at the thought of returning to Romrey. It's been years since I've visited Starlight Hall. But seeing it through the eyes of these children I've come to love... perhaps it's time to make some new, happier memories there.

"That's a great idea," I say, smiling at Nerrisa. "What do you think, girls? Would you like to see where I grew up?"

Elora nods enthusiastically while Lira asks, "Will there be other Abrauxians there? I'd love to learn more about your culture."

"There's a small village near the estate," I explain. "And yes, mostly Abrauxians. It would be a good opportunity to experience a more rural culture."

"Then it's settled," Nerrisa says with a grin. "Isyarhi, talk to your mom about going on holiday and tell her she and Brier are invited. I'll take the

Nostronix to pick up our oversized passenger, and you'll all have a lovely family vacation."

As the kids chatter excitedly about the upcoming trip, I pull Nerrisa aside. "Are you sure about this? I know how dangerous this transport could be."

She cups my cheek gently. "I'll be fine, love. My crew is the finest, hand-picked by my boss. And don't forget, I have some new tricks up my sleeve now." Her eyes glow briefly, reminding me of the power we now possess.

I nod, leaning into her touch. "Just be careful, Starfire. And come back to me."

"Always," she promises, sealing it with a kiss.

The kids are already chattering about what they might see on Romrey Island.

"Alright then," I say, clapping my hands together. "Let's start preparing. We'll need to pack for the warm climate and bright sunshine."

As the kids rush off to start packing, Nerrisa turns to me with a soft smile. "Thank you for being flexible," she says. "I know you're worried about their safety."

I pull her into a gentle embrace. "They're resilient kids, and they have us to protect them.

Plus, I think this experience will be good for them. And for me... I haven't been back to Romrey Island in years."

She looks up at me, concern flickering in her eyes. "Are you okay with that? Going back?"

I take a deep breath, considering. "I think so. It's time to face those memories, to show the kids where I came from. And who knows? Maybe being there will help unlock more of my oracle abilities."

Nerrisa nods, squeezing my hand reassuringly. "Just remember, whatever happens, you're not alone anymore. You have us, your family."

I lean down to kiss her softly. "I know. And that makes all the difference. I will contact Volenne, our Thryllian estate manager at Starlight Hall, to have it readied for our stay."

The next few days are a flurry of activity as we prepare for our respective journeys. Kishi turned down the invitation due to activities already planned with the humans.

Nerrisa coordinates with her crew and arranges for the specialized equipment to transport the troqel.

Meanwhile, Isyarhi and the girls marvel over pictures of my family estate, admiring the white marble cliffs and the enormous old house. They are already planning for a lengthy family visit after Nerrisa returns.

The morning of our departure arrives all too soon. We gather at the spaceport, the kids buzzing with excitement as they board our private shuttle. Nerrisa and I hang back, savoring our last few minutes together.

"I love you," I murmur, pulling her close. "Stay safe out there."

She smiles up at me, her eyes shining. "I love you too. Have fun with the kids and try not to let the ghosts of your past overshadow who you have become."

Chapter 30 - Nerrisa

Cargo of Souls

As I watch Frakyss and the kids board our family transport, I give a final wave. I'm nervous about the challenging transport of the troqel, and sad being separated from my family. I push those feelings aside and focus on the task at hand.

The Nostronix is too massive to dock on the planet's surface, so I board my Shadowstrike and ascend from the Silvergate spaceport. Once out of the planet's atmosphere, I speed to the Qirath Drift space dock, where larger ships are moored. Within half an hour, I enter the hauler's shuttle bay through the atmos shield. My crew is already aboard, running final checks on all systems. I take the large elevator to the top of the ship.

"Captain on deck," my first officer, Zara, announces as I enter the bridge. The Talurian female gives me a sharp salute, her iridescent scales shimmering as she moves.

"At ease," I reply with a smile. "Status report?"

"All systems go, Captain," Zara responds crisply. "We're just awaiting your command to depart."

I nod, settling into the captain's chair. "Excellent work, everyone. Let's get this show on the road. Navigation, set course for Gilles XPM."

As we speed away from Abrauxia, I cast one last glance at the screen displaying an image of the planet receding behind us. Somewhere back there, my family is embarking on their own journey. I send up a silent wish for their safety before fully focusing on the mission ahead.

The journey to Gilles XPM is uneventful, giving me plenty of time to review our scant information on troqels. Massive aquatic creatures, extremely intelligent but non-verbal, capable of telepathic communication. Their biology is similar to Earth's whales so not entirely foreign to me.

As we approach Gilles XPM, we're hailed from a vast bright ship the size of a moon.

"Captain, we are being hailed by Commander Vur'thalon of the Ulaenova."

"On the screen, Fryth."

"Captain Nerrisa," the creature on the screen greets me. I'm shocked by her humanoid face, featuring flesh that resembles intricately carved ivory, made up of long, thin vining fibers that ripple and twist in elaborate, organic designs.

She shimmers softly with a bioluminescence that lights her from within. Her hair is a magnificent spectacle in itself... vines that extend from her head like the tendrils of a mythical creature, floating weightlessly in the air around her.

They sway and curl with a life of their own.

Finally, my gaze meets hers. Eyes reminiscent of large, flawless diamonds, catching and refracting light in a dazzling array of colors.

I glare at her. "I don't like working with people who think it's okay to kidnap women, so you know that upfront. The only reason I'm here is to get the troqel's mate and transport her to Abrauxia."

"I apologize for that mistake. The previous commander committed an egregious crime in matching the Aquar'thyn of Earth with Abrauxian males, believing perfect DNA matches were more important than personal choice. He has been reassigned."

"Good to know."

"Before we coordinate the loading of Kalyndra, the female troqel, we have twenty-five hundred human females from Earth in stasis pods who signed up for the Abrauxian Bride program; fifty-four Omatu; and nine Viceus who need to be transferred to your ship."

"I was not notified I would also be transporting all these people."

"We did not communicate this information to the Abrauxians. We felt it prudent to coordinate the transfer with a female from Earth to eliminate conflicts of interest."

"Understood. Send docking coordinates to attach the voidlink conveyor to transfer the pods to the Nostronix."

"Coordinates received Captain Nerrisa," Zara informs me.

With careful thruster adjustments, I maneuver into position next to the massive Ulaenova ship.

"Cargo team, extend the voidlink." The white telescoping walkway with a conveyor unfolds across the short space and anchors to the hull of the Ulaenova, creating a sealed corridor for the transfer of the stasis pods.

"Beginning transfer, Captain."

"The first batch of pods is coming through now," Zara reports.

I nod, my mind racing. Twenty-five hundred human women. The implications are staggering. How will Abrauxia handle such an influx?

"Zara, coordinate with engineering to inspect the stasis pods for power levels," I order.

Hours later, the last pod along with a dozen large crates of belongings for all the passengers, is secured in our cargo hold.

"Transfer complete, Captain," Zara announces. "All twenty-five-hundred and sixty-three pods accounted for and life support systems stable."

"Excellent work, everyone. Now for the main event. Commander Vur'thalon, we're ready to receive Kalyndra."

The Ulaenova commander nods, her crystalline eyes glinting. "Understood, Captain Nerrisa. Kalyndra is ready for boarding. Descend to Tidehaven Reef G-7.23, QX-4.56, ZR-9.81, and open your tank."

I guide the ship into the thin atmosphere of Gilles XPM, opening the clamshell-hinged water tank before sinking it into the water at the designated coordinates. Multiple screens show the sapphire blue leviathan swimming into position between the two sides of the tank.

"Close the tank, Zara."

The huge external pistons force the tank sides shut, pumping all air out before sealing. Nanos are released into the water to monitor water temperature and the troqel's vitals. The temperature modulators begin operating, adjusting the temperature based on readings.

"Please be advised, Kalyndra may become agitated during transport. We sent over a sedative with the stasis pods that can be released into her tank if needed, but we hope it won't be necessary."

I frown at this. "Has she agreed to this arrangement? To being the mate of King Zaphre?"

Vur'thalon's expression softens slightly. "She has, Captain. She was worried she might become claustrophobic. And leaving one's home world is never easy, even when it's by choice."

I nod, understanding all too well. "We'll do our best to make her comfortable."

Her massive form is awe-inspiring. Easily the size of a blue whale, her sleek body shimmers with iridescent scales of royal blue.

"Safe journey to you and your passengers. Commander Vur'thalon out."

As we rise slowly away from the surface of Gillis XPM, I make a short call to Frakyss. before addressing my crew. "Alright, people. Let's get everyone home. Set course for Abrauxia, best speed."

Chapter 31 - Frakyss

In the House of My Father

I fly our transport to Romrey Island. It's been years since I've returned to my childhood home, and I'm not sure what emotions the visit will stir up.

The kids press their faces against the windows, oohing and aahing at the green and white mountainous landscape below. Romrey Island is a jewel in Abrauxia's vast oceans, known for its pristine beaches, dense forests, and towering white marble mountains.

"It's so beautiful!" Elora exclaims, her eyes wide with wonder.

I smile, pleased by their youthful exuberance. "Wait until you see the estate," I tell them. "It's been in my family for thousands of years."

As we approach the landing pad, I catch my first glimpse of the sprawling estate. The main house, a grand structure of gleaming white marble and sweeping arches, stands proudly atop a cliff overlooking the amethyst sea. Surrounding it are lush gardens, meandering paths, and smaller outbuildings.

We touch down smoothly, and as the doors open, we're greeted by a warm, fragrant breeze. The kids tumble out excitedly, Isyarhi helping Lira and Elora with their bags.

"Welcome home, Master Frakyss," a familiar voice calls out. I turn to see Volenne, our longtime estate manager, approaching with a warm smile. Her white hair is braided in a crown over her head, and her violet eyes sparkle with genuine affection.

"Volenne," I greet her, feeling a rush of nostalgia. "It's good to see you. Thank you for preparing the house on such short notice."

She waves off my thanks. "It's my pleasure. The estate has been quiet for too long." Her gaze shifts to the children. "And who do we have here?"

I introduce each child, explaining their connection to Nerrisa and me. Volenne's smile grows wider with each introduction.

"Well, it's about time this place had some young energy again," she says, clapping her hands together. "Come along."

As we follow Volenne into the house, I'm struck by how little has changed. The grand foyer with its soaring ceilings and intricate mosaic floor, the winding staircase leading to the upper floors, the smell of polished wood and fragrant flowers... it's exactly as I remember.

"Wow," Lira breathes, taking it all in. "You grew up here?"

I feel a twinge of something. Pride? Guilt? It's hard to say. "I did."

"But you left," Isyarhi says quietly, his antennae twitching thoughtfully. "Why?"

I pause, considering how to answer. "It's complicated," I say finally. "After I was rescued from the Cegnu, I came back to find my father had died while I was gone. I needed a fresh start. But this place will always be a part of me."

Volenne gives me a sympathetic look before turning to the children with a bright smile. "Who wants to see their rooms? And then perhaps a tour of the grounds?"

The kids cheer, momentarily distracted from the heavier topics. As Volenne leads them upstairs, chattering about the estate's history, I take a moment to center myself. Being back here is stirring up more emotions than I expected.

I wander into my father's old study, running my hand along the polished desk. Everything is exactly as he left it, books neatly arranged on the shelves, star charts spread across the table, and his favorite pen still in its holder. For a moment, I can almost hear his deep, rumbling laugh, see the twinkle in his eye as he explained some cosmic phenomenon to me.

"Master Frakyss?" Volenne's voice breaks me out of my reverie. She stands in the doorway, a concerned look on her face. "Are you alright?"

I shrug, forcing a smile. "Just remembering. It's been a long time."

She comes to stand beside me, her presence comforting in its familiarity. "Your parents would be proud of you, you know. Of the male you've become and the family you've made."

I feel a lump form in my throat. "I hope so," I manage to say.

Volenne pats my arm gently. "I know so. Now, come on. Those children of yours are eager to explore, and I think a walk might do you good."

I take a deep breath and follow her onto the sun-drenched terrace where the kids are waiting. Their excitement is infectious, and I feel the heaviness lift from my shoulders.

"Alright, explorers," I say, clapping my hands together. "Who's ready for the grand tour?"

As we set off down one of the winding paths, Elora slips her small hand into mine. "Thanks for bringing us here, Dad," she says, looking up at me with those big, mirror eyes. "It means a lot that you want to share this with us."

I squeeze her hand gently, feeling a rush of love for this child who has so quickly become such an important part of my life. "Thank you for being here," I tell her softly. "All of you. You're helping me make new, happier memories in this place."

As we continue our exploration, I find myself sharing stories about my childhood... climbing the ancient trees in the orchard, sneaking down to the beach for midnight swims, and stargazing with my father on clear nights. The kids listen with rapt attention, asking questions and imagining themselves in those same adventures.

We reach a clearing overlooking the sea, where an old stone bench sits beneath a gnarled tree. I pause, memories washing over me.

"My father told me this was my mother's favorite spot," I tell them softly. "She would come here to paint or just sit and watch the waves."

Lira steps closer to the edge, her silver skin shimmering in the sunlight. "It's so peaceful here," she says. "I can see why she loved it. What was my grandmother's name?"

"Her name was Isda," I respond, a bittersweet smile tugging at my lips. "My father said her favorite saying was that the sea reminded her that there's beauty and mystery in the universe, no matter how dark things might seem."

Isyarhi's antennae twitch thoughtfully. "Is that why you started Galactic Freight? To explore those mysteries?"

His question catches me off guard, and I take a moment to consider. "I suppose that was part of it," I admit. "But mostly, I think I was running... from memories and the pain. It took me a long time to realize that you can't outrun your past. You have to face it and learn from it."

Elora wraps her arms around my waist in a tight hug. "We're glad you stopped running," she says. "Otherwise, you might not have found us."

I feel a lump form in my throat as I hug her back. "I'm glad too, little one. More than you know."

As the sun begins to set, painting the sky in brilliant hues of purple and gold, we stroll back to the main house. The kids are tired but happy, chattering excitedly about all they've seen and learned.

Volenne meets us at the door, a knowing smile on her face. "Dinner will be ready soon," she informs us. "I've prepared some of your old favorites, Master Frakyss."

The smell of roasting meat and fresh bread wafts from the kitchen, and my stomach growls in anticipation. "Thank you, Volenne. You always know just what we need."

We gather around the dining table, filling our plates with the delicious options. The kids eagerly try everything, exclaiming over the flavors and textures.

"This is amazing!" Lira declares after taking a bite of the roasted fish. "I didn't know food could taste this good."

Isyarhi nods in agreement, his mouth full of bread. "Don't tell mom and Auntie Nessa, but this is so different from what we have at home."

Elora giggles as she balances on the tall children's chair. "I don't think I've ever eaten this much before," she says with a satisfied sigh.

I watch them all with fondness, grateful for this moment of peace and contentment. We talk, laugh, and share stories, making new memories.

After dinner, we sit by the fireplace in the living room, sipping hot cocoa. Even Volenne joins us after cleaning the kitchen.

"Dad, I want to hear the story of Wraith the Ice Dragon and Starfire again."

"I've never heard this story. When did you hear it?" Lira asks.

"When I was in the healing pod after Mom and Dad rescued us from Echo Station," Elora responds.

"Volenne tells it better than me." I nod to the dear old female. "Would you tell us the story? The one you used to tell me as a child?"

Her eyes twinkle with amusement. "Very well. Settle in, young mistresses and masters. This is a tale as old as Abrauxia itself..."

"Long ago, when Abrauxia was young, the fearsome ice dragon Wraith ruled over the land. His icy breath covered the world in frost and snow, and his mighty wings brought howling blizzards wherever he flew. For ten long months each year, Wraith held Abrauxia in his frozen grip, leaving the people shivering and struggling to survive.

"But there was one who dared to stand against the dragon's tyranny...a beautiful warrior maiden named Starfire. With hair as red as flame and eyes as green as summer leaves, Starfire was as fierce as she was lovely. She vowed to free Abrauxia from Wraith's eternal winter.

"Donning her gleaming armor and armed with a sword forged in the heart of a dying star, Starfire climbed the tallest mountain to confront Wraith in his icy lair. The battle that ensued shook the very foundations of Abrauxia. Starfire's blade clashed against Wraith's diamond-hard scales, her fiery spirit a match for his icy fury.

"For days they fought, neither willing to yield. But as the battle wore on, something unexpected happened. Wraith found himself captivated by Starfire's bravery and beauty, while Starfire saw past the dragon's fearsome exterior to the lonely soul within.

"As their combat reached its peak, Starfire made a bold proposal. "Mighty Wraith," she called out, lowering her sword. "I offer you a bargain. My hand in marriage if you will grant Abrauxia five months of summer each year."

"Wraith was taken aback by her offer. "You would bind yourself to me, a creature of ice and winter, to bring warmth to your people?"

"Starfire nodded solemnly. "I would. For I see now that you are not a monster, but a being of great power and complexity. Together, we could bring balance to Abrauxia."

"Moved by her words and her sacrifice, Wraith agreed. And so, Starfire became the bride of the ice dragon. True to their bargain, Wraith loosened his hold on Abrauxia, allowing five months of glorious summer to bless the land.

"And so it was that Starfire and Wraith were wed, their union marking the end of Wraith's reign of terror and the beginning of a new era for Abrauxia.

"With Starfire by his side, Wraith's heart softened, and he became a benevolent ruler. He used his powerful ice magic to create stunning ice sculptures to decorate the land during the winter months, and together with Starfire, they brought warmth and life to the kingdom during the summer.

"The people rejoiced at the change in their climate and celebrated Starfire as their hero. She had not only defeated Wraith but had also tamed him with her love. And in return, Wraith showered her with gifts, including a magnificent palace made entirely of ice.

"Years passed, and Starfire and Wraith ruled over Abrauxia as king and queen. They were blessed with twin children…a daughter named Glaciana and a son named Draconis. The siblings possessed both their parents' powers. Glaciana could control ice, while Draconis could manipulate fire.

"The family lived happily together until one day, an evil sorcerer cast a spell on Wraith, causing him to revert to his former cruel ways. He turned on Starfire, blaming her for his changed behavior. In order to save her family and her kingdom once again, Starfire made the ultimate sacrifice. She sealed herself away in a crystal prison deep within Romrey Island.

"Heartbroken at losing his beloved wife, Wraith returned to his icy lair, where he sealed himself into a glacial prison, overcome with grief and remorse.

"Starfire's children continued her legacy of bringing balance to Abrauxia: Glaciana ruling over winter while Draconis ruled over summer. It is said that on rare occasions when the sun shines through a rainstorm or when snow falls softly on a warm spring day, it is a sign that Starfire still watches over her beloved kingdom from the island's heart."

I hear a soft sniff from Elora and when I look down at her, she quickly brushes a tear from her cheek.

"What's wrong, Elora?"

"I'm so sad that they didn't live happily forever after. Why did the evil sorcerer cast a spell on Wraith? Why did Wraith blame Starfire?" Her bottom lip trembles.

"It's a cautionary tale that teaches us not to let outsiders meddle with our feelings for those we love."

"I want to find Starfire and release her from her self-imposed exile."

"Me too," says Isyarhi, nodding his head and sending his antennas crackling with energy.

"No more stories tonight. We've had a long day. Thank Volenne for preparing the delicious meal and telling you the story, so we can head to bed."

"Thank you, Volenne!" they all chorus and surround the elderly female with hugs before trudging up the stairs with me in their wake. I tuck the soft blankets around Elora in her bed and dim the lights.

"Goodnight, little one," I say softly as I kiss her forehead. "Sleep well."

Elora yawns and smiles at me drowsily. "Goodnight, Master Frakyss," she murmurs before drifting off to sleep.

I chuckle and check on Lira, who is settled into her room, and Isyarhi in his, before heading downstairs to the grand master suite that is now mine. The bed is soft and inviting, but my mind is too restless for sleep just yet.

I walk to the balcony overlooking the sea, breathing in the crisp ocean air as I gaze up at the stars above. Memories flood back, both happy and painful ones, but I let them wash over me without resistance.

"You're still awake?" a voice asks from behind me.

I turn to see Volenne standing in the doorway, a gentle smile on her face. She joins me at the railing, her presence as comforting as ever.

"Just thinking about everything," I reply softly. "Being back here, with the children... it's stirring up a lot of memories."

Volenne nods with understanding. "That's to be expected. This place holds so much of your past."

We stand in companionable silence for a moment, listening to the waves crash against the cliffs below.

"You know," Volenne says finally, "your father used to stand out here just like this when he couldn't sleep. Especially after..." she trails off, but I know what she means... after my mother died. After I was taken.

"I miss him," I admit quietly. "I wish he could have met Nerrisa and the kids."

Volenne places a comforting hand on my arm. "He would have loved them, Frakyss. And he would be so proud of the male you've become."

I turn to look at her, seeing the sincerity in her violet eyes. "How can you be sure? I ran away from here, from my responsibilities..."

She shakes her head firmly. "You needed time to heal, to find your own path. And look at where that path has led you. You have a beautiful family and a successful career, and you're using your gifts to help others. That's exactly what your father always wanted for you."

Her words wash over me, soothing some of the guilt and uncertainty I've carried for so long. "Thank you, Volenne," I say softly. "For everything. For taking care of this place and for welcoming us back."

She smiles, patting my arm. "This will always be your home, Frakyss. No matter how far you roam or how long you're gone. And now it can be a home for your children too."

Chapter 32 - Frakyss

The Secret Cove

As if on cue, I hear a small voice from inside. "Dad?"

I turn to see Elora standing in the doorway, rubbing her eyes sleepily. "What's wrong, little one?" I ask, crossing to her and kneeling down.

"I had a bad dream," she mumbles, leaning into me.

I scoop her up, cradling her against my chest. "It's alright," I soothe, stroking her hair. "You're safe here."

Volenne gives us a fond look. "I'll make some warm milk," she says, heading for the kitchen.

I carry Elora back to the balcony, settling into one of the comfortable chairs with her on my lap. "Do you want to talk about your dream?" I ask gently.

She shakes her head, burying her face in my chest. "Just don't let go," she whispers.

"Never," I promise, tightening my arms around her.

We sit there under the stars, the sound of the waves a soothing lullaby. Slowly, I feel Elora relax against me.

"Tell me about my grandparents," drifts up her soft voice.

I smile softly, memories flooding back. "Your grandfather, Braxin, was an incredible male. He was a historian with a passion for uncovering and preserving the stories of our people. His study was always filled with ancient texts and artifacts, and he could spend hours poring over them, piecing together the puzzle of our past.

But more than that, he was a storyteller. He had a gift for bringing history to life. When he spoke, you could almost see the ancient battles unfolding before your eyes or feel the excitement of long-ago explorers discovering new worlds.

I remember sitting at his feet as a child, wide-eyed and enthralled as he wove tales of Abrauxian heroes and legends. He had a deep, rumbling voice that seemed to resonate in your very bones, and his silver eyes would sparkle with enthusiasm as he spoke.

Your grandmother, Isda, was his perfect complement. She was an artist, with a talent for capturing the beauty of our world in her paintings. Where Braxin dealt in words and facts, Isda spoke through color and form. Their love story was legendary. They met when Braxin was researching an ancient Abrauxian art technique, and Isda was the only one who could help him understand it.

Together, they filled this house with warmth and creativity. Braxin's study might have been cluttered with books and scrolls, but Isda's studio was a riot of color and light. She died from the Grievous Plague right after I was born. I used to sit in her closed studio, marveling at her canvases that looked like windows to other worlds.

Your grandfather was particularly fascinated with the legend of Starfire and Wraith. He believed there was more truth to the story than most people realized, and he spent years trying to uncover evidence of their existence. He would take me on expeditions all over Abrauxia, exploring caves and ancient ruins, always hoping to find some clue.

But more than his work, I remember his kindness. Braxin had a way of making everyone feel important, of drawing out their stories and helping them see their own worth. He taught me that every person, every creature, has a tale to tell if we just take the time to listen.

When the Cegnu took me, your grandfather spent every waking moment searching for me, using all his connections and knowledge to try and find where I'd been taken. But as time went on, his heart broke and he died.

When I was returned to Abrauxia, his loss hit me hard. Not only was I broken, body, mind, and spirit, I felt like I'd lost my anchor and guide. That's part of why I left Romrey Island. Everywhere I looked, I saw reminders of him, of the male I looked up to.

But being back here now, with you and your sister and Isyarhi...I think I finally understand what he was trying to teach me all along. The ones we love and the people around us are the most important thing of all."

"They sound like they were amazing."

As she finishes speaking, soft footsteps announce Volenne's return. She carries a steaming mug of warm milk, the sweet aroma of vanilla wafting through the air.

"Here we are," Volenne says softly, handing Elora the mug. "An old family recipe. It always helped Master Frakyss sleep when he was little."

Elora lifts the mug to her lips. "Thank you, Volenne."

She takes small sips, her eyes already heavy with sleep. The warm milk leaves a faint mustache on her upper lip, which I gently wipe away with my thumb. As she drinks, I continue to rock her gently, humming an old Abrauxian lullaby my father used to sing to me.

The night air is cool and crisp, carrying the salt tang of the sea. In the distance, I hear the soft calls of nocturnal creatures, the melodious song of the Crikath, and the gentle rustling of wind through the silver-leafed trees that line the cliffs. Above us, the stars shine with brilliant clarity, their light seeming to pulse in time with the rhythm of the waves below.

As Elora finishes the last of the milk, her head droops against my chest, her breathing becoming slow and steady. I carefully stand, cradling her small form against me.

"I'll take her back to bed," I whisper to Volenne, who nods and takes the empty mug.

I carry Elora through the quiet halls of the estate, her warmth against my chest comforting. The rising moon's light streams through the windows, casting long shadows, turning the familiar corridors into a dreamscape of lilac and shadow.

Once I reach her room, I gently lay Elora on her bed, tucking her in. She stirs slightly, murmuring something in her sleep, but doesn't wake. I brush a strand of hair from her forehead, marveling at how peaceful she looks.

"Sleep well, little one," I whisper, placing a gentle kiss on her forehead before quietly leaving the room.

As I return to my own bed, a sense of peace settles over me. The memories that once haunted these halls now seem less painful, softened by the presence of new life and love.

The morning dawns bright and clear, Xonus painting the sky in brilliant hues of gold and lavender. I'm awakened by the excited chatter of children outside my door.

"Dad! Dad, wake up!" Elora calls, knocking sharply. "Can we go swimming today? Please?"

I chuckle, stretching as I rise from bed. "Alright, I'm coming," I call back, quickly pulling on swimming shorts before opening the door to find all three children bouncing excitedly. Their eyes are bright, hair tousled from sleep and smiles wide with anticipation.

"Can we go swimming? Please, Dad?" Elora pleads, her eyes shining. "Volenne told us about the secret cove at the bottom of the cliff!"

Lira nods eagerly, her silver skin gleaming in the morning light. "She said there are rainbow fish and glowing coral!"

"And stonebrow sunning on the rocks!" Isyarhi adds, his antennae quivering with excitement.

I laugh at their enthusiasm. "Yes, we can go swimming after breakfast. But first, let's get some food in you. I'm sure Volenne has prepared something delicious."

As if on cue, the aroma of freshly baked pastries and savory dishes wafts from the kitchen. The children cheer and race through the house, their bare feet pattering against the polished marble.

In the sun-drenched dining room, Volenne has laid out a feast fit for royalty. Golden pastries stuffed with sweet berries and savory meats, platters of exotic fruits in every color of the rainbow, and steaming mugs of rich, creamy hot chocolate.

"Good morning, young masters and mistresses," Volenne greets us with a warm smile. "I hope you're hungry."

The children waste no time diving into the spread, exclaiming over each new flavor and texture. Lira's eyes widen as she bites into a pastry and purple juice dribbles down her chin. "This is amazing!" she declares, reaching for another.

Isyarhi is methodically trying every fruit on the platter, his antennae twitching with each new taste. "I've never had anything like this before," he says in wonder.

Elora, meanwhile, is on her third mug of hot chocolate, a frothy mustache adorning her upper lip. "Can we have this every day?" she asks hopefully.

I chuckle, helping myself to a savory pastry. "Maybe not every day, but we can certainly enjoy it while we're here at Starlight Hall."

"The path to the cove is steep, so be careful," I warn as we finish breakfast. "And stay away from the Stonebrow. Their barbels can deliver a shock strong enough to stop your heart."

The kids only grin wider, their excitement barely contained. As soon as the last bite is gone, they sprint upstairs to change into swimwear. Volenne hands me a large basket of towels, lunch, and water with a warm smile. "It does my heart good to see this place filled with love and laughter again."

The descent to the beach is steep, but the teens take it with ease, Elora not far behind. The air turns cool and briny as we near the cove, the crash of waves growing louder. When we round the final bend, they all gasp.

A crescent of powdery sand spreads below, framed by marble cliffs veined with crystal. The water shifts from lavender to deep indigo, so clear we can see coral reefs swaying beneath the surface.

"It's beautiful," Lira breathes.

We set up on the sand. Isyarhi helps anchor the umbrella, and then he and Lira are off, squealing as they race into the waves. Elora wades in slowly beside me, toes curling in the cool water as rainbow fish dart around us like sparks of light.

"Look!" Isyarhi calls, pointing to a sun-warmed rock where several stonebrow bask, their turquoise and gold hides shimmering.

We spend the day swimming, collecting shells, and exploring the glowing reefs. Elora finds a hidden cave behind a curtain of seaweed. Bioluminescent coral pulses even in daylight, casting a soft glow over the sand.

Later, we picnic in the shade of the umbrella, sharing stories and snacks. The children chatter non-stop about everything they've seen.

"Can we come back tomorrow?" Elora asks, eyes shining.

I smile. "Maybe. There's still a lot of island left to explore."

As the sun dips low, the sky bleeds orange and rose. We make the slow climb home beneath blooming flowers and the soft glow of Lumivara insects swirling around us.

At the door, Volenne greets us with a knowing smile. "Dinner's ready. Rinse off, or you'll track half the cove onto my clean floors."

The kids scatter, leaving sandy footprints in their wake.

Later, scrubbed clean and glowing from the day, we gather around a feast that smells like paradise. Lira mimics the swimming patterns of fish with her hands. Isyarhi reenacts a run-in with a stonebrow, sparks crackling from his fingertips. Elora leans in close, whispering about the hidden cave and the treasures it might hold.

And for a while, the world feels simple again, full of childish wonder and light.

Just as Volenne sets down a towering confection of spun sugar and crystallized fruit, my communicator buzzes against my wrist.

Nerrisa.

I murmur a quick "Excuse me," and step through the open terrace doors into the evening breeze. Stars blink awake above the garden, and I answer the call.

"Hello, Starfire. How's the mission going?"

Her holographic image shimmers to life before me, and the concern in her eyes is immediate.

"Frakyss, we've got a situation. The Ulae'Zep just offloaded twenty-five hundred human females, fifty-four Omatu, and nine Viceus. All in stasis. They delivered them straight to the *Nostronix*."

I blink. "They transferred them to you? Why?"

She sighs, running a hand through her hair. "The commander said after the last incident, she thought it safer for someone from Earth to manage the transfer."

I nod slowly, already building a checklist in my mind.

"They're stable for now," Nerrisa continues, "but I need you to coordinate with Lord Chyrgog and Demi. Can you arrange a cruise vessel for the humans once we land on Abrauxia? The Omatu need space to build a village, and the Viceus should be handed off to Hisa. Romrey's probably best for that."

"I'll make arrangements," I say, already shifting into logistics mode. "Pearla might be a good choice to oversee the new females when they're moved to the ship. Should I reach out to her?"

"Yes. If Pearla's available, she's the one I'd want watching over them." Nerrisa nods firmly, then glances off-screen. "We're about sixteen hours out. The troqel's massive but calm. I'll release her near the palace once we arrive. After that, we'll dock the *Nostronix* at the Qirath Drift and begin moving the pods to the cruise liner."

"Everything will be ready," I promise. "The children are having a wonderful day here at the estate. I'll leave them in Volenne's care and meet you at the Qirath Drift."

She offers a small smile. "Thank you, Frakyss."

The hologram fades, and I'm left staring at the stars again grateful for the peace here, and already bracing for what's to come.

Chapter 33 - Nerrisa

For Future Reference

As we approach Abrauxia, I closely monitor the massive form of Kalyndra, filling the tank below the Nostronix. Her iridescent blue scales shimmer even in the dim light, and I sense her growing agitation as we near her new home.

"Begin atmospheric entry sequence," I order, my voice steady. "Zara, keep a close eye on the tank's temperature. We need to maintain it within one degree of optimal."

"Aye, Captain," Zara responds crisply, her scaled fingers moving over the controls.

The Nostronix shudders slightly as we breach the outer layers of Abrauxia's atmosphere. Through the viewscreen, I watch as the inky blackness of space gives way to a swirling tapestry of purples and whites, the planet's vast oceans and scattered clouds.

"Entering stratosphere," I announce. "Reducing speed to maintain temperature control."

My eyes flick between the external view and the readouts from Kalyndra's tank. The massive creature stirs, her long body undulating in the confined space.

"Tank temperature holding steady," Zara reports. "Kalyndra's vital signs are elevated but within acceptable parameters."

As we descend through layers of gossamer-thin clouds, Epree Island reveals itself. The ocean below is a mesmerizing patchwork of lilac shallows and deep amethyst depths. In the distance, I see the towering black spires of the royal palace.

"There's our target."

The Nostronix glides gracefully toward the designated spot, its massive bulk casting a shadow over the sparkling waves. As we near the surface, I can see a gathered crowd on the palace walkways.

"Prepare to open the tank," I order as we hover just above the waves. "Kalyndra, if you can hear me, we've arrived at your new home. I hope you'll be very happy here."

With a great groaning of metal and a rush of water, the tank's doors begin to open. For a moment, nothing happens. Then, with a flash of brilliant blue, Kalyndra surges down. Her massive body arcs through the air in a graceful dive before plunging into the welcoming embrace of the Abrauxian ocean.

Kalyndra breaches the surface, her vivid blue scales catching the sunlight.

"Looks like a successful delivery," I say with satisfaction. I press my communicator for King Jakvar. "One female troqel mate for King Zaphre Kragmals, chosen by the Ulae'Zep. Nerrisa Byrne, out!"

As Kalyndra disappears beneath the waves, I guide the Nostronix back up through Abrauxia's atmosphere. The ship's engines strain as we ascend, pushing against the planet's powerful gravity. The viewscreen shifts from the sparkling ocean to swirling clouds, then to the deep purple of the upper atmosphere, and finally to the star-studded blackness of space.

The massive Qirath Drift space dock comes into view, a sprawling structure of gleaming metal and pulsing energy fields. Its numerous docking arms extend like the spokes of a wheel, each capable of accommodating ships of various sizes. As we approach, I see the bustle of activity. Smaller ships zip between the struts, maintenance drones swarm over the hulls of docked vessels, and there's a constant flow of crew and passengers through the dock's many airlocks.

Adjacent to the designated slip for the Nostronix, an elegant cruise ship is docked. Glimmering bright white with elaborate silver designs on her hull, I bet she's the height of luxury inside.

"Initiating docking sequence," I announce, my hands steady on the controls. The Nostronix glides smoothly toward its designated berth, guided by the dock's tractor beams. With a series of gentle thuds and hisses, the ship's docking clamps engage, securing us firmly to the station.

As soon as we're moored, I spot a sleek ship approaching our shuttle bay. Its polished hull gleams in the starlight, and I recognize the distinctive design of Frakyss's personal transport. A smile tugs at my lips as I watch it smoothly enter the bay, the atmos shield shimmering as it allows the shuttle passage.

"Zara, you have the ship," I say, rising from my captain's chair. "I'm going to meet Frakyss and oversee the transfer of the stasis pods."

I make my way down to the shuttle bay, my heart quickening with each step. As the doors slide open, I see Frakyss stepping out of his shuttle, his tall form unmistakable even from a distance. Our eyes meet, and for a moment, the bustle of the ship fades away.

"Welcome aboard," I say as I approach him.

Frakyss pulls me into a warm embrace, his familiar scent enveloping me. "I missed you, Starfire," he murmurs against my hair.

"I missed you too," I breathe, hugging him tight.

We pull apart reluctantly, both aware of the task at hand. "How are the kids?" I ask as we make our way toward the cargo hold.

"They're having a wonderful time at the estate. Volenne is spoiling them rotten."

As we enter the cargo hold, we're greeted by the sight of thousands of stasis pods, each glowing with a soft blue light, creating an otherworldly atmosphere in the dark cavernous space.

"It's hard to believe there are so many of them," I murmur, awed by the sheer number.

Frakyss nods, his expression serious. "The humans are the salvation of my species, and hopefully, the Omatu and Viceus are for theirs."

Cargo crew members maneuver the voidlink from our cargo hatch to the elaborate space cruise ship next to us.

"Only move the humans," Frakyss calls to them. "A cargo ship will arrive to take the Omatu and Viceus to Romrey Island."

"Yes Sir," they respond as they start moving pods.

I stare at the monitors displaying the outside of the Nostronix. "That's a beautiful cruise ship."

"She's the Astral Majesty. We're lucky she hadn't been put into service yet, and Lord Chyrgog thought this would be an excellent marketing opportunity. By allowing the human females to stay on the cruise ship short-term, they will share their experiences with their new mates, their acquaintances, and the press.

He gets priceless publicity. His line of cruise ships now boasts wedding chapels for Earth-style ceremonies.

"That's a great idea, though I can think of places I'd rather get married than on a cruise ship." I laugh.

"Where would those places be?"

"Maybe on a white marble cliff overlooking the ocean on Romrey Island. Do you know of such a place?"

"I might. What catalyst would make you want to be married?"

"If the right guy asked me, I might be persuaded to say yes."

Frakyss rubs his hand down his neatly trimmed beard. "Is there a special place or way he's supposed to ask?"

"No, some women are very concerned about those things, but I'm not."

"This is good information to know for future reference." He turns and strides toward the door, leaving me staring at his broad, muscular back and swinging tail. At the last minute, he stops and turns, that familiar grin quirking one corner of his mouth. "Coming?"

"Rotten male," I mutter as I take my time catching up to him. "I should step on your tail."

"I heard that!"

"Good."

Chapter 34 - Frakyss

With This Ring, I Thee Wed

"Evruik is bringing a transport ship to move the Omatu and Viceus to Romrey Island. I've donated fifty acres for the Omatu near Starlight Hall. Kishi is already there, working with the fabricators to ready the village," I explain to Nerrisa as we fly back to the island aboard my personal transport.

The vast expanse of the amethyst ocean stretches out below us, dotted with islands of varying sizes, each a unique jewel.

"I can't believe we're bringing the Omatu and Viceus to live on Romrey," Nerrisa responds, watching the island's distinctive white marble cliffs growing larger ahead of us. "The pictures didn't do this place justice. It reminds me of the

Causeway Coast in Northern Ireland near where I was born."

Her happiness flows through our Aether connection, and it feels as if I'm seeing it for the first time. "I never thought I'd be returning here like this, let alone bringing others to make it their home."

As we approach Starlight Hall, the estate's grandeur comes into full view. The white marble mansion gleams in the sunlight, its sweeping arches and towering spires a testament to generations of Abrauxian craftsmanship. Lush gardens surround the main house, a riot of color from exotic flowers and shimmering silver-leafed trees.

We set down on the private landing pad, and as soon as the doors open, we're greeted by the children's excited shouts.

Elora and Lira race toward us, their faces beaming with joy. Not far behind is Isyarhi, with Brier seated on his shoulders and using his long antennae as reins.

"Mom! Dad! You're back!" Elora cries, launching herself into my arms. I scoop her up, marveling at how light she still feels despite her recent growth spurt.

Nerrisa embraces Lira and Isyarhi, her eyes shining with happiness. "I've missed you all," she says, planting kisses on their foreheads.

As we approach the house, I notice a flurry of activity in the distance. A group of Abrauxians are hard at work setting up the new housing structures.

"The Omatu village is coming along nicely," I observe, gesturing toward the bustling site.

Nerrisa nods, her eyes wide with wonder. "It's amazing how quickly they've made progress. And look at that view they have!"

The village is situated on a gentle slope overlooking the ocean. The acreage provides ample space for homes, communal areas, and gardens. The layout is organic, following the land's natural contours rather than imposing rigid grid patterns.

As we approach the main house, Volenne emerges, a warm smile on her face. "Welcome home, Master Frakyss. Mistress Nerrisa, I'm so pleased to finally meet you," she greets us. "I trust your journey was successful?"

"Very much so, thank you, Volenne," Nerrisa replies. "I'm pleased to finally meet you too. Frakyss has told me so much about you."

"How have things been here this afternoon, Volenne?" I ask.

"Wonderfully busy," she says with a chuckle. "The children have been exploring every nook and cranny of the estate, and Kishi has been a tremendous help in coordinating everything for the new Village. I'm pleased she left young Master Brier with us."

At the mention of Kishi's name, I remember her decision. "Ah yes, Nerrisa, I wanted to tell you. Kishi has decided to move to the Omatu village permanently. She feels it's important for Brier to grow up connected to his Omatu heritage."

Nerrisa's eyes widen in surprise. "Really? That's wonderful for her and Brier, but I'll miss having her close."

I nod, understanding her mixed feelings. "I know. But it got me thinking. What if we moved here to Starlight Hall? We could make this our permanent home and raise our family here where the children have room to run, play, grow, and learn."

Nerrisa looks at me in surprise, her eyes wide. "Are you serious? But what about our work, the shipping company?"

I smile, taking her hand in mine. "We can run the company from anywhere. And with the Omatu village nearby, we'd still be close to our friends."

As I speak, I see the idea taking root in Nerrisa's mind. Her eyes sparkle with excitement as she looks around at the grand estate, the lush gardens, and the breathtaking ocean view.

"It is beautiful here," she admits softly. "And the children seem to love it already."

I take a deep breath, my heart pounding. This feels right, more right than anything has in a long time. I squeeze Nerrisa's hand gently, then slowly lower myself to one knee.

Gasps erupt from the children and Volenne. Nerrisa's eyes widen in surprise, her free hand flying to her mouth.

"Nerrisa," I begin, my voice thick with emotion, "my Starfire. From the moment I first saw you, unconscious and vulnerable in that stasis pod, I knew my life would never be the same. You've brought light and laughter back into my world. You've given me a family, a purpose, and a love I never thought I'd find."

I reach into my pocket, pulling out a small box. Inside is a ring I had custom-made, a band of platinum inlaid with a faceted lunarite that glows from within, its colors shifting like the auroras that dance in Abrauxia's night sky.

"You told me that you might be persuaded to marry if the right guy asked," I continue, a smile tugging at my lips. "Well, Nerrisa Byrne, I'm hoping I'm the right guy. Will you do me the extraordinary honor of becoming my wife in the tradition of your people as well as mine? Will you make Starlight Hall our home, and build a life here with me and our children?"

Tears glisten in Nerrisa's eyes as she looks down at me. For a moment that feels like an eternity, she's silent. Then, a radiant smile breaks across her face.

"Yes," she whispers, then louder, "Yes! Of course, I'll marry you, Frakyss!"

Cheers erupt from our audience as I slip the ring onto Nerrisa's finger, and it fits perfectly. I stand, pulling her into my arms and kiss her deeply.

When we finally break apart, we're surrounded by excited children and a beaming Volenne.

The children, who have been listening intently, start to chatter with excitement.

"Does this mean we get to stay here forever?" Elora asks, her eyes shining.

"Can we keep exploring the secret passages?" Lira chimes in.

"And go swimming in the cove every day?" Isyarhi adds.

I chuckle at their enthusiasm. "Well, we'd have to discuss the details, but yes, that's the idea."

"Oh, this is wonderful news!" Volenne exclaims, clasping her hands together. "We must start planning the celebration at once!"

Chapter 35 - Nerrisa

Always and Forever

The wedding takes place one week later on the terrace of Starlight Hall, beneath a sky that looks too breathtaking to be real. Only our closest friends and family gather, their quiet murmurs mixing with the sound of the waves far below.

The terrace glows with a simple, wild beauty. White flower garlands drape the marble balustrades, their sweet scent drifting through the salt-heavy air. Fairy lights twinkle above, casting a golden shimmer over the stone floor. Everything feels suspended in a fragile, perfect moment.

As I step onto the terrace, the sight steals the air from my lungs. The sunset stretches in every direction, spilling purples, pinks, and golds across the sky. The ocean below glitters like molten amethyst, each ripple throwing slivers of light into the dusk.

At the end of the aisle, Frakyss waits for me. His black vest and leather trousers fit him perfectly, but it is not the clothes that hold me still. It is the way he stands, so tall and strong, with his fingers flexing slightly at his sides as if he cannot decide whether to stay still or run to me. His red eyes find mine, and the bond between us surges so fiercely that it feels like a living thing in my chest.

He lets out a slow breath, and something in the way he looks at me, wide open and unguarded, nearly breaks me. I blink hard, fighting the sting rising in my eyes, unwilling to blur this moment for even a second.

I step forward, the soft rustle of my gown whispering against the stone. The simple white fabric flows around me like water, and the beadwork scatters tiny stars across the bodice as it catches the fading light. In my hands, the bouquet of glowing Abrauxian flowers pulses gently, alive with its own quiet magic.

Each step feels both impossibly long and heartbreakingly short. The terrace, the guests, the ocean, all of it fades to a hush in the back of my mind. There is only him, standing at the end of the world, waiting for me.

And with every breath, every trembling step, I know there is nowhere else I could ever belong.

Our small group of guests watches with shining eyes as I approach. Volenne sits in the front row, her violet gaze glistening with happy tears. Beside her, Lira and Elora fidget with excitement, barely able to contain their enthusiasm.

Kishi, Isyarhi, and little Brier sit among the Omatu, their green skin shimmering softly in the fading sunlight. They have embraced their new home on Romrey Island with open hearts, and seeing them here, celebrating with us, fills me with warmth and gratitude.

Michelle Matthews and Lily Worthington, two of the human women we rescued from Echo Station, have also joined us for the occasion. Their wide eyes take in the beauty of Abrauxia. Seated near them are Evruik and Eri, smiling quietly in support.

At the head of the gathering stands Elder Xirsid, resplendent in a deep blue vest and black trousers, ready to officiate. His presence is commanding but warm, a steady anchor in this moment of joy.

As I reach Frakyss and take his hands in mine, the Elder begins to speak. His deep voice carries across the terrace with calm certainty.

"We are gathered here today to witness the union of two souls who have found each other across the vast expanse of space. Frakyss and Nerrisa, your love is a testament to the power of connection, to finding hope and joy even in the darkest circumstances. Please exchange your vows."

Frakyss draws a deep breath, his hands steady in mine, and begins.

"Nerrisa, from the moment our paths crossed, I knew my life would never be the same. You have been my light in the darkest of times, my anchor in the fiercest storms. Today, I vow to stand by your side, to support you, to cherish you, and to love you with all that I am. I promise to honor our bond, to nurture our love, and to be the partner you deserve. Together, we will face every challenge and celebrate every joy. You are my heart, my soul, and my future. I love you, now and forever."

Tears sting my eyes, but I steady my breath and find my voice thick with emotion.

"Frakyss, you are my rock, my confidant, and my greatest adventure. Today, I vow to love you unconditionally, to stand by you through every triumph and trial, and to cherish every moment we share. I promise to be your strength when you need it, to offer you comfort and joy, and to build a life with you filled with laughter, love, and endless discovery. You are my everything, and I am honored to be yours. I love you, always and forever."

As we finish, a wave of applause and cheers rises around us, the air filled with the warmth and joy of those we love most. Elder Xirsid smiles, his eyes twinkling as he steps forward with a small velvet-lined tray.

Frakyss picks up my rings first, a plain platinum band and the engagement ring crowned with a glowing lunarite stone that catches the last light of the setting sun. His fingers are steady as he slides them onto my third finger.

"With this ring, I thee wed," he says, his voice low and sure.

I pick up his ring next, a band crafted from a glowing emerald green scale, shaped with care into a smooth circle. As I slide it onto his finger, I whisper, "With this ring, I thee wed."

Elder Xirsid places a hand over ours, his voice resonating with a gravity that seems to ripple through the gathering.

"By the power vested in me by the stars and the spirits of Abrauxia, I now pronounce you husband and wife, partners in life and love. You may kiss."

Frakyss leans down, and when our lips meet, the world seems to fall away. The kiss is deep and sure, a vow of its own, sealing our promises with something far older and stronger than words.

The terrace erupts in cheers and laughter just as the sun slips below the horizon, casting a final blaze of light across the sea. A new beginning has arrived, and we step into it together.

Frakyss sweeps me into his arms as cheers fill the terrace, his deep laugh rumbling against my ear. Before he can even take a step, Lira and Elora sprint toward us, their faces alight with excitement. Elora wraps an arm around my waist and Lira grabs Frakyss's arm, nearly toppling all of us.

"You are *so* married now," Lira declares, grinning up at us.

Someone from the crowd whistles, and I hear Kishi's high voice call, "Kiss her again!"

Laughter ripples through the gathering as Frakyss leans down, brushing his forehead against mine before stealing another kiss. Around us, petals rain down, the scent of salt and flowers blending in the warm evening air. In this moment, surrounded by laughter, love, and family, it feels like the whole world is exactly where it should be.

Chapter 36 - Frakyss

Stalking a Monster

As we draw near Mars, the dusty red planet appears barren, save for a small collection of domes connected by tubes. This human outpost seems so fragile against the vast Martian landscape, a stark contrast to our advanced cloaked ship that sets down quietly nearby.

"I'm jamming their communications and video feeds," I mention as I follow her to the shuttle bay.

Nerrisa insists that ending him is not an option. She doesn't want the members of the mission to accuse each other if something happens to him. Her logic is sound, but my instincts scream otherwise.

I follow her, my eyes locked on her with a mix of nerves and admiration. As she begins to transform, the air around her seems to ripple. Her beautiful, familiar form morphs into a horrific shiny black creature. Chitinous flesh glistens under the shuttle bay's dim lights, and a long skeletal tail with a two-foot pointed end unfurls behind her.

Her hands, now ending in long claws, flex menacingly. She grins, and gelatinous saliva drips from a second smaller silver jaw that shoots out of her toothy maw.

Watching her, I feel a shiver of both fear and awe. This is the being who stands by my side, the one who shares my life and my love. And now, she is about to confront the one who harassed her and prevented her from coming to this forsaken place because she wouldn't have sex with him.

She slips through the Atmos Shield, her large reverse-jointed-hind legs allowing her to jump easily to the ground. A shiver runs down my spine. She is magnificent and terrifying.

I return to the *Vortex's* bridge and watch her on-screen as she stalks around the semi-transparent domes until she finds the one she wants. She works at a seal where the flimsy tube connects to the smaller dome, and I see damp air rise like fog into the thin atmosphere.

She continues to work at the tube until it's separated from the dome and the pressure doors at each end drop into place to prevent the loss of air. She pushes the tube a few yards away from the small structure.

Nerrisa stalks around the dome, peeking into the small circular windows on its sides. Once satisfied, she blends into the shadows and watches.

A human wearing a bulky space suit exits the airlock and stands with his gloved hands on his hips, inspecting the disconnected walkway.

Nerrisa creeps up behind him. When she's towering over him and almost touching his helmet with her long nose, her mouth draws back, and I can almost hear her hissing.

The male stumbles and turns, his head traveling upward when he sees the shiny black nightmare towering over him.

She drives her inner jaw toward his face, stopping just short of the glass visor, and he falls backward, crab-crawling to escape the terror stalking him.

He rolls over and races toward a hatch into the main building. Nerrisa reattaches the flexible tunnel to the dome and gracefully runs back into the *Vortex's* shuttle bay, disappearing from view after she crosses through the Atmos Shield.

When she returns to the bridge, she's wearing her flight suit and grinning. "Did you release the communications and camera feeds?"

"I did. And I'm monitoring their communication channels."

When I release the neural interface system, the chatter of voices fills the cockpit.

"He's finally lost it," mutters a male voice.

"We're lucky he didn't cause a catastrophic internal atmosphere failure. He needs to be restrained." Grace, the medic's voice comes through calm and clinical. She's another female I saw him harass during mission training.

"Contact Mission Control. Let them know that the mission commander, Colonel Harris, is suffering from acute hysteria and hallucinations. He is combative and creating an unsafe environment for the mission crew, and I recommend immediate removal from his command."

"You stupid fucking cunt," a voice shouts from the background. "You're the one hallucinating if you think you can remove me from my command. I'm telling you, there is an alien out there!"

"Try to remain calm, Colonel Harris. As you know, sometimes, unfortunate decisions have to be made."

The tirade in the background continues unabated.

"Just a little prick. There, you'll feel calmer soon," she murmurs, and slowly the shouting dies off.

"It's my recommendation that he be isolated in his quarters and that his interaction with the rest of the crew be limited as a precaution.

"Is that your recommendation too, Flight Engineer Baily?"

"It is. Please notify Mission Control immediately."

Epilogue - Nerrisa

The Spark of Something Greater

I still barely believe that Frakyss and I are now married. As we near the Astral Majesty cruise ship, I glance at him and smile.

Since saying our vows, my heart has been brimming with happiness and a sense of completeness. Today, we are visiting Pearla to see how she is doing with coordinating the human women's mate matchings and their integration into Abrauxian society.

The Astral Majesty is even more beautiful under the bright light of Xonus. The vessel travels just above the ocean's waves, and the entire ship is bustling with activity.

The grand dining room, where we finally spot Pearla, is filled with laughter and conversation, and the scent of various exotic dishes wafts through the air.

Pearla is busy, as we expected, but the moment she sees us, her face lights up with a warm smile, and she hurries across the room to greet us.

"Nerrisa, Frakyss! It's so good to see you," she says, enveloping me in a hug. "How are you both doing? Let's sit." She leads us to an empty table by the windows.

"We're wonderful. But how have you been? How is everything going here?"

Pearla begins to update us on her progress. Her enthusiasm is palpable, and it's clear that she takes great pride in her work. As she talks, I see the passion and dedication that drives her.

Suddenly, the door to the dining room opens, and an unfamiliar but striking figure steps in. A tall, handsome Abrauxian with an air of authority and mystery enters.

He pauses to scan the room, and when his eyes lock onto Pearla, it's as though the entire universe holds its breath. His long strides quickly bring him to our table.

Frakyss notices my reaction and grins. "Pearla, I'd like you to meet Cyrus, the Galactic Sentinel.

He's been away on a special assignment for King Jakvar for the past few years. He just returned and is interested in signing up for a match."

Cyrus's gaze never leaves Pearla. "It's an honor to meet you, Pearla," he says, his voice deep and resonant. "I've heard much about your work here."

Pearla's cheeks flush slightly, and lunarite power streaks under her skin, but she maintains her composure. "The honor is mine, Cyrus," she replies, her voice steady despite the whirlwind of emotions I can see flash in her eyes.

Frakyss and I share a knowing look before excusing ourselves from the table. "We'll leave you two to get acquainted," I say with a wink.

As we walk away, hand in hand, I'm excited for Pearla. It's clear that there's an instant connection between her and Cyrus, and I have a feeling that this is just the beginning of something incredibly special for them.

As Frakyss and I step out onto the deck, the sun burns bright overhead. I lean my head on his shoulder.

Our journey together has only just begun, but I know with all my heart that it will be filled with love, adventure, and endless possibilities.

And I sense that Pearla's own journey, intertwined with Cyrus, will be just as beautiful and profound.

Outttakes

The Ladies Room Incident

Evruik's message pings on my communicator just as I'm finishing my call with King Jakvar: **Nerrisa just landed. She's headed toward the equipment bay. Might be a good time to "accidentally" bump into her. ;)**

I don't even pretend to not take the bait. I straighten my cuffs, brush a few crumbs off my lap from the zucress Bruud offered back (traitor), and head out the side door of my office like a thief.

The hallway is quiet. I hear Nerrisa's unmistakable voice coming from around the corner, talking to Evruik about calibrating the cargo clamps. She's laughing. I stop to listen.

"Evruik, I swear if you start wearing those ridiculous reflector sunglasses inside again, I'm going to repurpose them as landing beacons."

"You're just mad because I look cooler in them than you."

"You look like a tourist who got lost at a rave."

I nearly walk around the corner and say something clever. Something casually mate-ish. Something that makes her look at *me* the way she looks at her ship.

But then she says, "I'm going to duck into the refresher before the meeting with Dyebarth. Meet me in the hangar in five."

Oh no.

I spin on my heel, not wanting to look like I was eavesdropping. The only door behind me, of course, is the ladies' refresher.

I hear Nerrisa's boots getting louder. No time. I slap my palm to the door scanner and *bolt inside.*

Where I come face to face with Eri.

Standing in front of the mirror.

Brushing her teeth.

She freezes. Foam dribbling from one side of her mouth.

I freeze. Half crouched like I'm about to perform some kind of espionage gymnastics routine.

We stare at each other in silence for exactly three seconds.

Then Eri spits dramatically into the sink and mutters, "You absolute *dumbass*, Frakyss."

I lift one finger. "I can explain."

"Nope."

"She was around the corner—"

"Still nope."

"You know I wasn't trying to sneak into the—"

"You're literally *hiding* in a women's refresher because you couldn't grow the horns to say hi to your mate in a hallway."

I sigh and lean back against the wall. "That's depressingly accurate."

Eri rinses her mouth, wipes her face, and saunters toward the door. "I'm not telling her. But if you're still in here when she walks in, I'm *definitely* watching."

She leaves.

The door *hisses* shut behind her.

Two seconds later, Nerrisa's voice drifts through the hall. "Eri, did you use mint toothpaste again? It smells like a snowstorm out here."

Panic.

I slap the panel on the ceiling and crawl into the ventilation shaft like a disgraced space possum. My knees do not thank me. Bruud, wherever you are, avenge me.

Feral Glitter Gremlin

Frakyss arrives fifteen minutes early.

He always does this, trying to look casual as if he's not incredibly eager to see me. Unfortunately for him, today's early arrival means he walks in just as the apartment hits peak morning mayhem.

I open the front door with one hand, the other holding a small pile of pink baby gifts. "You're early," I mutter.

"I brought extra hover trays," he says, then pauses, nostrils flaring. "What is that *smell*?"

Kishi dashes past behind me, hair fluffed out with steam, still in pajamas, holding a toddler-sized shoe in one hand and a spoon in the other.

"Don't ask."

From the living room comes a loud *splat*, followed by Isyarhi's voice: "That was not the trash can, Brier!"

I sigh. "We're almost ready. I promise."

Frakyss steps carefully inside, immediately slipping on something wet.

"What in all the stars?" He looks down at his boot. "Is this fish paste?"

I wince. "Brier tried to make breakfast. For the princesses."

Frakyss looks at me like I've just told him we're keeping a pet skugbat in the kitchen. "He what?"

"Used a stool to reach the counter. Opened the synth-fridge. Retrieved eight ingredients. None of them compatible."

Just then, Brier comes sprinting down the hall completely nude, trailing glitter. Actual glitter.

"Princess sparkle juice!" he declares, throwing a half-empty packet of edible shimmer powder like a tiny, chaotic confetti cannon. "For the baby queens!"

Frakyss blinks as the glitter coats his trousers.

He turns to me slowly. "You said this was going to be a *simple* trip."

I shrug and pat his chest. "You say you want to be part of my life. This *is* my life."

Brier flings himself onto Frakyss's shin like a warrior claiming his mount. "UNCLE FRAKYSS, I GLITTERED YOU."

Frakyss looks down at the child, who is now sticking to him with some unknown combination of syrup and static cling.

"I can feel the sparkle entering my soul," he says flatly.

Behind me, Kishi yells, "WHERE ARE HIS PANTS?!" and Isyarhi groans, "Why is my datapad covered in jam?!"

Frakyss meets my gaze with that deadpan Abrauxian calm. "Are we still on schedule?"

I grin. "Absolutely."

He stares at the chaos for a beat longer, then nods solemnly. "Very well. I'll prep the ship. If we're going to arrive at a royal palace with a feral glitter gremlin, we might as well be on time."

And with that, he calmly walks back out the door, Brier still attached to his leg like a tiny, sugar-dusted koala.

The Ladies' Room Incident 2.0

Somewhere between outfitting woman number five and explaining what a food synthesizer *isn't*, I realize I haven't seen Frakyss in a while.

That usually means trouble.

I tap my comm. "Frakyss, where are you?"

There's no answer.

Hmm.

Then I hear something crash. Followed by what sounds distinctly like a shriek and a *"What the HELL?!"* echoing from down the hall.

Oh no.

I rush out of the conference room and follow the sounds of chaos to the women's refresher door, which is disturbingly ajar.

Just as I'm about to push it open, Frakyss stumbles out, clutching a folded towel to his face like a shield. His horns are glittering. *Glittering.* And a trail of steaming hair product runs down one temple like an oddly fragrant battle scar.

Behind him, Michelle's voice rises in exasperation. "DID THIS SPACE VIKING JUST BUST INTO THE BATHROOM?!"

Frakyss looks stricken. "I—I thought it was the supply closet!"

"You opened a door with a pink sign that said *'LADIES ONLY: KEEP OUT UNLESS YOU'RE BRINGING WINE OR CHOCOLATE.'*"

He gestures helplessly. "In my defense, the sign was confusing."

I glance around and spot Eri slinking down the hall, looking suspiciously amused.

"Eri, *why* was he in there?"

"He asked me where the towel warmer was. I said, 'Check the pink door.' I didn't say *go in it.*"

"You *knew* that was the bathroom for the pod women," I hiss.

"Maybe."

Back in the restroom, Michelle shouts, "You owe me a new eyebrow pencil! He scared the winged eyeliner right off my face!"

Frakyss, still shell-shocked, lowers the towel. "She threw something at me. It fizzed."

"That was facial mist, *you absolute unit!*" another woman yells from within.

Eri coughs to cover a laugh. "To be fair, she has good aim."

Frakyss turns to me, glitter sparkling like betrayal on his forehead. "I don't think I'm welcome in there."

"No kidding." I drag him a few paces away, ignoring the peals of laughter echoing down the hallway. "Go back to the conference room, say something reassuring, *and don't speak unless spoken to.*"

He nods solemnly. "Understood. Should I wipe the glitter off?"

I smirk. "No. Let it be a lesson. A shiny, humbling lesson."

Back in the conference room, the women are doubled over, wiping tears of laughter from their cheeks.

"I was NOT prepared to be dive-bombed by a seven-foot underwear model with LED eyeballs while I was putting on thermal leggings!" one of them gasps.

"I was trying to help," Frakyss mutters, standing stiffly in the room like a disgraced prom king. The glitter sparkles.

The women giggle.

From the back, Lily calls out, "So, does he actually have a brother?"

I bury my face in my hands. "This is why I drink wine."

And from that day forward, the women of the Stasis Pod Squad would refer to him, always with affection, as Sparklehorn.

Also by

Lisa Clute

More Great Books from the Abrauxian Brides Series

Astrid's Abrauxian King, Book One
Naia's Abrauxian General, Book Two

Coming This Year:

Pearla's Abrauxian Sentinel
Book Four of the Abrauxian Brides Series
A former Scotland Yard investigator, one too many stellar margaritas, and suddenly Pearla is bonded to a gorgeous Galactic Sentinel. Things

are great until she learns her new husband's brother is the same jerk she once escaped. She flees to the frozen moon Roxus, hides among the yeti-like Boraleans, adopts a giant frosthound puppy, and starts building a new life. But when Cyrus is taken by Riftspawn smugglers, the pregnant and furious Pearla sets out to bring him home herself.

Demi's Abrauxian Tycoon
Book Five of the Abrauxian Brides Series
She's a brooding goth artist who trusts no one and prefers solitude to spotlight. He's a golden-skinned tycoon born to power, used to commanding worlds and winning without question. They're complete opposites with nothing in common until a crash landing in the wild mountains of North Carolina throws them together. Stranded, hunted, and furious, they're forced to rely on each other to survive. Their uneasy alliance only grows more complicated when they're rejoined by Skovul, the fierce tiger-man King with a knack for chaos and unexpected wisdom.

Phoebe's Abrauxian Assassin

Book Six of the Abrauxian Brides Series

On the storm-wracked rainforest moon of Vorrak Prime, twelve human hybrid females, engineered to kill Abrauxians, are given one final chance at redemption. Sentenced to a remote jungle compound guarded by Kael'Vorran warriors, they're under the watchful eye of First Knight Fyrdon and his self-centered Aquar'thyn mate, influencer Phoebe Ware. But these killer queens aren't interested in playing nice. As lightning splits the sky and ancient predators prowl the shadows, tempers flare, bonds ignite, and chaos brews beneath the trees. In a world where survival is earned, not given, the fiercest hearts may discover that love is the most dangerous weapon of all.

About the Author

Lisa Clute is a proud Georgia native with a PhD in microbiology, a Doctor of Veterinary Medicine, and a sneaking suspicion her cats are plotting world domination. She takes on life with humor, loud metal music, and muddy Jeep adventures. When not writing spicy sci-fi romances that make readers laugh, swoon, and question reality, Lisa dreams up wild tales where love defies gravity, dimensions, and the laws of physics—because not even space can contain it.

Made in the USA
Columbia, SC
02 May 2025